THE
GREAT
BRAIN
ROBBERY

Praise for

The Train to Impossible Places adventures

"Rollicking entertainment." The Sunday Times

"A harum-scarum fantasy adventure crammed with quirky action." The Observer

"All aboard for an unforgettable journey."
The Sunday Express

"Bursting with influences, particularly Douglas Adams and Terry Pratchett, but has a crazy, pacy charm all its own."
The Guardian

"Roller-coaster of a book." BookTrust

"Endlessly imaginative, highly inventive world-building and a plot every bit as unpredictable as the train itself."
The Bookseller

"Suspenseful rip-roaring inventive adventure."
The Independent

"All aboard for an adventure like no other." Kirkus

"A whizz-pop-bang of an adventure story that will make readers young and old want to jump on board!"
BooksForTopics

A TRAIN TO IMPOSSIBLE PLACES
Adventure

THE
GREAT
BRAIN
ROBBERY

P.G. BELL

Illustrated by Flavia Sorrentino

USBORNE

To Théo, who loves stories. I hope this one
does the trick.

This edition first published in the UK in 2020 by Usborne Publishing Ltd., Usborne House, 83-85 Saffron Hill, London EC1N 8RT, England, usborne.com

First published 2019. Text copyright © Ty Gloch Limited, 2019.

The right of P. G. Bell to be identified as the author of this work has been asserted by him in accordance with the Copyright, Designs and Patents Act, 1988.

Cover and inside illustrations by Flavia Sorrentino © Usborne Publishing Ltd., 2019

Cover type by Patrick Knowles © Usborne Publishing Ltd., 2019

The name Usborne and the devices ♀ 🎈 Trade Marks of Usborne Publishing Ltd.

This is a work of fiction. The characters, incidents, and dialogues are products of the author's imagination and are not to be construed as real. Any resemblance to actual events or persons, living or dead, is entirely coincidental.

A CIP catalogue record for this book is available from the British Library.

9781474972215 J MAMJJASOND/20 04902/2

Printed and bound in Great Britain by CPI Group (UK) Ltd, Croydon, CR0 4YY.

COUNTDOWN

Suzy sat at the kitchen table, too nervous and excited to eat. Instead, she pushed her dinner around the plate with her fork and stole a glance at the clock for what felt like the hundredth time that evening. To her surprise, it was five to seven already. Only five minutes left.

"…which is why I've decided to send an email to the school," said her mother, who was sitting beside her. She had a piece of broccoli on the end of her fork, and jabbed the air with it as she spoke. "I've never seen such behaviour. And from a teacher!"

"Hmmmph." Suzy's father nodded emphatically. He had a mouth full of chicken, and his plate was almost clean already.

"I mean, singling Suzy out like that," her mother continued. "It's no better than bullying. And I'm going to tell them so."

"Mum, please," groaned Suzy. "Just leave it."

"No, I will not leave it, Suzy," said her mother, turning the broccoli on her. "And neither should you. You have to stand up to people like that, or they'll walk all over you."

People like that in this case meant Mr Marchwood, the physics teacher at Suzy's school.

Physics was Suzy's passion, and she was never happier than when she was using it to unlock the possibilities of the world. But lately she had come to realize that the world was far stranger than she had ever dreamed of, and her schoolwork had taken a slightly more creative turn as a result. Mr Marchwood did not approve of this development and had called Suzy in for a "little chat". He had also summoned Suzy's mother, tired and impatient at the end of a long shift at the hospital. That was probably his first mistake, Suzy reflected.

"I don't understand what's happening to your work, Suzy," Mr Marchwood had said, propping his elbows on his desk. His office, squeezed into the corner of one of the school's laboratory storerooms, smelled of glue and formaldehyde, and Suzy did her best to breathe through her mouth. "It always used to be flawless, but this term it's been going completely off the rails. I'm extremely disappointed in you." He let these last words land heavily. Suzy gazed back at him, untroubled.

"But my calculations are all correct, sir," she said. "I double-checked them."

"It doesn't matter if they're correct or not," Mr Marchwood said, "if the concepts you're trying to calculate are all wrong. And by 'wrong', I mean 'impossible'.."

Suzy's mother had looked between them, clearly lost. "Excuse me, Mr Marchwood, but I'm not sure what you mean."

"I mean you can't reliably measure the velocity of a moving car if you decide to change the direction of gravity halfway through the exercise," Mr Marchwood said. "Gravity doesn't work like that."

"But what if it did?" said Suzy.

"It doesn't. It can't." Mr Marchwood was starting to look a little red in the face. "Just like you can't cut the journey time to zero by freezing time itself. It's preposterous."

"But are my answers wrong?" Suzy asked, quite calmly.

Mr Marchwood was clearly about to dismiss the question, when Suzy's mother spoke up. "Well, Mr Marchwood? It's a fair question. Are they wrong or not?"

His face reddened a little more. "Maybe not," he said.

Then, almost spitting the words, "As a matter of fact, no, the calculations themselves appear to be perfectly sound, but—"

"Then what's the problem?" said Suzy's mother. "If the answers aren't wrong, why are we here?"

"Because...because..." Mr Marchwood's face was darkening from red to purple, and fat beads of sweat had sprung up on his forehead. "Because she isn't solving the problems *properly*."

"I am, sir," said Suzy. "I'm just trying to find a better way to do it. Wouldn't it be easier not to have gravity slowing your car down? Or to get where you're going at the same time as you left?"

"No!" he spat. "I mean, yes, of course. But physics has laws! You can't just go around breaking them!"

"I'm not really breaking them, sir," said Suzy. "I'm just rearranging them a bit. It's more fun."

At that point, Mr Marchwood's right eye had started twitching, and she and her mother had finally left, with the understanding that Suzy would keep the fun out of physics in future.

Suzy looked at the clock again. Three minutes to go.

She couldn't really blame Mr Marchwood for getting angry – she knew it wasn't very nice having one's perfectly sensible view of the world overturned. After all, that was exactly what had happened to her two months ago, when she had woken in the night to find a troll building a railway through her house. The railway was a shortcut for the Impossible Postal Express – a high-speed mail train delivering packages throughout the Union of Impossible Places, a collection of fantastical realms that enjoyed only the most fleeting acquaintance with the laws of normality, as Suzy came to learn. She had been positively offended by the train's existence at first, but as she rode it from the frozen desert of the Crepusculan Wastes to the haunted depths of the Topaz Narrows and onward to the very heart of the moon, she had learned to adjust her expectations. The laws of physics weren't *wrong* – far from it, they had helped her and the train's crew escape disaster (not to mention an army of living statues) – but they weren't the neat little answer to all life's questions that she had once thought they were.

Which was why she couldn't help wishing that Mr Marchwood would show just a little bit of imagination; she was sure they would both be a lot happier for it.

"I'll send the headmistress an email as soon as we've finished dinner," Suzy's mother said, finally taking a bite of the broccoli. "Her teachers are out of control. She needs to enforce some order."

"Please, Mum," said Suzy. "You'll just annoy her."

Suzy's father swallowed his last mouthful, pushed his plate aside, and started drumming his fingertips together. Suzy recognized the gesture – it meant he was going to try and calm Mum down. On a good day, he could do it without her even realizing it had happened. On a bad day, however, he only made things worse. Suzy braced herself.

"I think the most important thing to remember," said her father, "is how Suzy feels about all this." He turned his long, pale face towards her. "Suzy? How do you feel about all this?"

"I'm fine, Dad. Really."

Two minutes left!

He nodded, wanting to show that he was listening and understood. "And you'd tell us if anything at school was weighing on your mind?"

"You know I would," she said, happy that she hadn't had to lie. The thing that was weighing on her mind had nothing to do with school.

"Of course it's on her mind," said her mother. "Can't you see how distracted she's been lately? Look, she's hardly eaten a thing." She glared accusingly at Suzy's plate, as if the food was somehow complicit in the situation. Suzy speared a bit of chicken with her fork and set about eating it, but her mind was on the time, and she hardly tasted anything.

Because today, after two months of waiting and hoping, she was going back to the Union of Impossible Places. And according to the gold-edged invitation she had hidden away in her bedroom, she was to be "ready for collection" at seven o'clock sharp. She had no idea who was going to collect her, or how they were going to do it, but she couldn't wait to find out.

One minute!

She was so excited that her hands were shaking, and she set her fork down again. Luckily, her mother was too distracted to notice.

"Physics has always been Suzy's best subject," she went on. "So why have her grades been slipping these past couple of months? None of her other subjects are affected. I refuse to believe it's a coincidence."

Her father continued to drum his fingertips together. "Maybe she's looking for a creative outlet." He turned back to Suzy. "Is that it, darling? Do you feel restricted at school?"

"Hmmm?" said Suzy, not really listening. "Yeah, sure. Probably."

Thirty seconds...

"There you are, you see?" said her father. "I told you we shouldn't have let her give up the violin."

"The neighbours moved to Gdansk to get away from

7

that violin," her mother snapped. "And anyway, that was when she was six. She's eleven now."

Ten, nine, eight...

Suzy's mother skewered another piece of broccoli. "No, Calum," she said. "I know it might sound crazy, but there's something funny going on. I can feel it."

Suzy's father opened his mouth to reply, but all that came out was a tremendous yawn. Without another word, he slumped forward onto the table, fast asleep. Suzy and her mother both gasped in shock, but while Suzy jumped to her feet, her mother swayed in her chair. Her fork slipped from her hand, and Suzy just had time to pull her plate out of the way before she, too, toppled forward onto the table. Within seconds, both Suzy's parents were snoring loudly.

"Wow," said Suzy. "That was fast."

"D'you like it?" came a gruff voice from behind her. "We upgraded the sleepin' spells. Got a bit more kick to 'em now."

Suzy turned as a small brown knobbly creature ambled into the kitchen from the hall. It had bat-like ears, an enormous nose, and was wearing grubby overalls. It stopped in front of Suzy and peered up at her. "Were you always this tall, or 'ave you grown?" it said.

Suzy burst into a huge grin and threw her arms around

the creature. "Fletch!" she said, picking him up and squeezing him. "I missed you."

"Gerroff," he muttered, but made no move to dislodge her. She finally set him back on his feet. "Are all humans this touchy-feely?"

"Only when we're very pleased to see someone," she said.

"Bah!" Fletch exclaimed. "Makes me glad I'm a troll." He sniffed. "You ready?"

"Almost," she said. "I just need to get changed. I couldn't do it while Mum and Dad were awake. They would have asked too many questions."

"Hurry up then," said Fletch. "We can't afford to be late."

She took a few steps to the door, but a twinge of guilt made her hesitate.

"What you doin'?" said Fletch as she hurried back to the table.

"Just saying goodbye," said Suzy, bending to plant a quick kiss on first her mother's and then her father's forehead. "I know they'll be fine, but it doesn't really seem fair to leave them like this."

"Well, I'm not taking 'em with us," said Fletch, helping himself to a chicken drumstick from her mother's plate. "I'll wake 'em up as soon as we get back. Now get on with you. It's not every day we get invited to a royal reception.

9

We don't want to keep His Majesty waitin'.""

That was enough to put the smile back on Suzy's face, and she dashed out of the kitchen.

Her rucksack was packed and ready, and hidden under her bed. She pulled it out and hurriedly double-checked the contents. She had a water bottle, a notebook and pen, and a small first-aid kit. But, most importantly, she had a large book bound in dark-red leather.

Its cover was scarred and pitted, with several deep slashes running across it, but the title, embossed in gold, was still legible: *The Knowledge: An Instructional Handbook for Impossible Postal Operatives*. She pulled it out and flipped it open to the handwritten dedication on the title page:

> Dear Suzy,
>
> No one ever became a Postie without a copy of *The Knowledge* in hand, so I've sent you mine. Take its words to heart and they won't let you down. It's also thick enough to use as a shield against angry Thrippian bowmen (in case you were wondering about the state of the cover). See you soon!

Sincerely,
Wilmot

As always, Suzy smiled at the words. Like Fletch, Wilmot was a troll. He was also her boss – the Postmaster of the Impossible Postal Express – and her best friend, and she had missed him more than anyone else these past two months. The book, like all her correspondence with the Impossible Places, had magically appeared on the doorstep one morning, probably via a remote spell of some sort. She knew it couldn't have been delivered by hand, as the Express was out of action. But all that was about to change…

She flipped through the book until she found her invitation, kept flat between the central pages. It was printed on thick, cream-coloured paper, and in elaborate, looping handwriting it read:

His Trolltanic Majesty,
King Amylum III,
ruler of all Troll Territory,
cordially invites you to rejoin
The Impossible Postal Express
at platform one hundred of Grinding Halt Station.

Formal dress required

She replaced both the invitation and the book in her bag and hurried to her wardrobe, throwing the doors wide.

It was stuffed full of winter coats, old sweaters and shoes, but she reached through them, feeling for the secret hanger she had suspended from a nail right at the back. She found it, and pulled out a uniform of smart red felt and glimmering gold brocade. She paused to pick a bit of fluff off the sleeve of its long coat and run her thumb over the lettering of the badge pinned to its lapel:

The Impossible Postal Express
Deputy Postal Operative

She changed quickly and took a moment to soak up the feeling of finally being in her official postal uniform. It felt very good indeed – the uniform consisted of black trousers with gold piping down the seams, a white shirt with a red waistcoat, and a red greatcoat that fell to her knees. The coat had the same gold piping as the trousers, large circular gold buttons embossed with the Impossible Postal Service crest, and satisfyingly large pockets. There was also a red cap with a black peak and, last of all, black boots. After a moment's thought, she left the boots in the wardrobe and instead pulled on her trainers, which were bright red, and so at least matched the jacket. They were more comfortable than the boots, and on her last visit to the Impossible Places she had done a lot of running, mostly for her life, so she thought they might be a good idea.

It certainly beats pyjamas and slippers, she thought, looking in the mirror.

Suzy had barely laced up her shoes when there was a knock on the door, and Fletch let himself in without waiting to be asked.

"Ready to go and be a postie?" he said.

Suzy shouldered her rucksack and gave him an enormous grin. "Absolutely," she said.

Suzy could feel the excitement running through her as she followed Fletch downstairs and along the hall...to the cupboard under the stairs.

"Here we go," he said.

"What, in there?" she asked, surprised. The cupboard was small and crammed full of cleaning equipment and spiders. At least, it *had* been – because when Fletch opened the door, she saw a dark and cavernous space, as big as her school assembly hall. It was lit by a lamp standing on an old-fashioned pump cart – a simple rectangular platform on wheels, powered by a large see-saw handle mounted in the middle – which in turn stood on a pair of tracks that ran to the dark opening of a tunnel mouth ahead of them.

"I made a few adjustments," said Fletch, starting towards the pump cart. "You know how it is."

As an interdimensional engineer for the troll railways, it was Fletch's job to lay new tracks as they were needed. Sometimes that meant squeezing them, and the trains they carried, into spaces that were never designed to take them. In those cases, a little stretching of the local dimensions was called for.

This was all possible thanks to fuzzics, the strange collision of science and magic that lay at the heart of most troll technology.

"At least you didn't take over the whole hallway this time," she said, climbing up onto the pump cart with him.

"Yeah, well," he said, "I'm being discreet." He released the brake and the cart began rolling towards the tunnel mouth. "Next stop, Trollville," he said, giving her a wink.

Suzy trembled with excitement from her cap to her trainers. After two months, she was finally heading back to the Union of Impossible Places. The Express, and her friends, were waiting.

GRINDING HALT

Cold wind howled through the darkness of the tunnel, pulling at Suzy's hair and coaxing tears from her eyes.

It was hard work powering the pump cart. Suzy and Fletch stood at opposite ends of the small rectangular vehicle, facing each other over the see-saw-like handle mounted in the middle. Suzy was riding backwards, but kept looking over her shoulder to see where they were going.

"C'mon," Fletch called over the howl of the tunnel. "Put a bit of effort into it!"

"I am!" Suzy shouted back.

Whenever Fletch pulled down on his side of the pump, her side rose up, and she had to lift both feet off the floor and apply all her weight to force it back down again. It was tough going, but she had the sense that she and Fletch were slipping through reality at incalculable speeds, and she couldn't help the joyous tingle that ran down her spine and made the hairs on her arms stand up.

The tunnel was a sort of wormhole, she knew – a shortcut through the fabric of reality, and part of a complex network connecting all corners of the Union of Impossible Places. There were thousands of scientists across the world who had spent years trying to figure out if such things were even possible, and here Suzy was with one in her understairs cupboard. The thought made her laugh out loud.

"Save your breath for pumping," Fletch said, a lopsided smile hiding just under the surface of his habitual grimace. "We're nearly there!"

They rocketed out of the tunnel and straight into the jumble of dirty yellow industrial buildings that comprised the upper layer of Trollville. The troll capital wasn't just a city – it was an enormous bridge, spanning the fathomless depths of a rocky gorge. The upper surface of the bridge, known as the Overside, was home to all the civic and industrial quarters on which the trolls had made their reputation – chimneys smoked, cranes performed stately pirouettes, and dozens of trains shuttled back and forth along the expanse of tracks that ran like a steel river through the middle of town.

Suzy was overjoyed to see it again. She had only had a brief taste of the city's lively, unpredictable atmosphere on her last visit, but she had missed it ever since. She wondered if she would have a chance to visit the Underside – the residential quarter where Wilmot lived, suspended beneath the bridge with nothing but the dizzying drop into the gorge below it.

Fletch shut his eyes and drew in a long draught of air through his prodigious nostrils. "Ah, sniff that!" he said, his nose hairs twitching. "No smell like it in the Union. One of these days I'll bottle it, you see if I don't."

Suzy sniffed. The air of Trollville smelled like smoke and engine oil, with a faint aftertaste of bananas. It wasn't unpleasant, but she couldn't imagine anyone but the trolls wanting to smell it wherever they went. Then she wondered what her own world must smell like to Fletch – cooking oil, fresh laundry and her mum's jasmine perfume, probably – and decided it probably wasn't such a strange idea, after all. Home was always good to have around.

All thoughts of home soon fell away though, as the track the pump cart was following peeled away from the others and plunged deeper into the city, winding through the streets at ground level and forcing them to lower their speed. This was a part of Trollville that Suzy had never seen before; grand townhouses reared up on either side, their brickwork scrubbed and shining, and bunting hung between their balconies. The streets were busy with trolls all dressed in their finest clothes, but the crowds parted to let the pump cart roll through. Suzy saw parasols and ludicrously tall stovepipe hats, a few of which seemed to have been fashioned from actual stovepipes. Long tables had been set out on the cobbles and were being piled high with food. Buskers congregated on every street corner, armed with instruments that looked like reclaimed scrap, pouring out their music in a cheerful collision of toots, whistles and clanks. It looked like the biggest street party she had ever seen.

"Wow," said Suzy. "I had no idea the celebrations were going to be this big."

"Didn't you?" Fletch looked surprised. "The Express is the most famous train in Troll Territory, my girl, and it's not every day it gets a new lease of life. The king's declared a city-wide holiday. Everyone's goin' all out."

Perhaps that explained why so many heads were

turning to follow her in her postal uniform, Suzy thought. It felt a little odd to be the centre of so much attention, but at least everyone looked pleased to see them. She raised one hand from the pump and waved at the crowd. Many of them waved back enthusiastically.

"Less wavin', more pumpin'," Fletch grumbled.

Suzy returned both hands to the pump. "How far is it to the reception?" she asked. "My arms are getting tired."

"See for yerself," said Fletch, and pointed past her.

Suzy turned to look in the direction they were heading. Their track, along with a host of others emerging from nearby streets and cuttings, was veering towards an enormous spherical building of greenish glass and wrought iron. It was easily two hundred metres tall, and had several broad openings up and down its sides from which tracks issued, snaking away across the city on tall viaducts.

"It's incredible!" she said.

"It's Grindin' Halt," Fletch replied. "The biggest station in Trollville."

Suzy marvelled at it as they left the townhouses behind them and approached the sphere. Now that they were closer, she could see the station's different levels through the glass, stacked one on top of the other, like the layers of a gigantic wedding cake.

And they were *moving*.

Suzy forgot all about pumping and simply stared in astonishment as one of the levels halfway up the sphere began revolving like an enormous turntable. It was loaded with trains, all facing out towards the glass, and when the right one was lined up with the nearest opening, the rotation stopped. A moment later, the train was fired out of the station like a bullet from a gun, and went screaming away along one of the viaducts. In just a few seconds, it had vanished into the distance.

"Wow!" said Suzy, laughing.

"Keep your eyes in your head and your hands on the pump," said Fletch. "I'm not doin' this all by myself."

There was a moment of darkness as the cart entered the sphere through an opening at its base.

It was like gliding into a massive machine, and Suzy

21

almost let go of the pump again to cover her ears. The air was hot, and filled with a chorus of hisses and whistles from the trains that stood panting at platforms all around them. The platforms and tracks all radiated outward from the centre of the sphere, where a huge iron column, twice the width of Suzy's house, held up the levels above. The cart coasted towards it, through an opening in its base and into a wide circular chamber, where Fletch applied the brake so suddenly that, had she not been holding the pump handle, Suzy would probably have been thrown off. She fished a strand of hair out of her face and glared at him.

"Royal reception, is it?" a voice called.

Suzy looked around. A young female troll in a green-and-white station uniform stood against the chamber wall, a small megaphone to her lips. A large control panel covered with flashing buttons was fixed to the wall beside her.

"How did you guess?" said Fletch.

"The postal uniform's a dead giveaway," said the troll. She mounted a small stepladder that stood in front of the panel, until she could reach the uppermost button. The chamber door slid shut and, with a juddering and grinding of gears, the three of them began to rise.

The troll hurried back down the ladder and folded

it away. "Yeah, I've been ferrying people up there all afternoon," she said. "Looks dead fancy."

The elevator finally jolted to a stop. "Top floor," the troll announced. "Platform ninety-two. Short-stay parking. Enjoy the bash." She tipped her hat as they pumped the cart out through the doors.

"Cor," said Fletch, looking around in admiration. "There's some pretty flash wheels up 'ere. Look!" The platforms were shorter here at the top of the sphere, which meant there was little room for the lengthy passenger trains that had crowded the lower level. Instead, a collection of small locomotives stood buffer to buffer at the platforms. Most of them didn't even have carriages behind them, and Suzy guessed they were the rail-faring equivalent of luxury sports cars. They were painted in rich reds and golds, and sprouted all manner of elaborate exhaust pipes, flywheels and, in one puzzling case, wings.

"A Mark Three Puffing Devil!" said Fletch, who didn't seem to know where to look first. "And a Telford Dragster Classic! Blimey."

The pump cart came to a final stop, nuzzling the buffers of a tiny open-topped locomotive that looked like a steam-powered chariot.

Before either of them could step down onto the platform, a middle-aged troll in a gold frock coat and white powdered wig appeared, and greeted them with a curt nod. A royal courtier, Suzy guessed. For some reason, the tip of his nose was flat and shiny, like worn stone.

"Are you Deputy Postal Operative Suzy Smith?" he said.

"I am," said Suzy with a flush of pride.

"And are you Interdimensional Engineer Fletch?"

"Yup," said Fletch.

The courtier looked between them both. "If I may see your invitations, please?"

Suzy shrugged her rucksack off and retrieved her invitation from inside it. Fletch, meanwhile, dipped into one of the pockets of his overalls and produced a badly crumpled and slightly oil-stained scrap of card that was just about recognizable. "It's well-travelled," Fletch said. "Same as me."

The courtier took both invitations, although he held Fletch's between finger and thumb and at arm's length. After a moment's consideration, he said, "The invitation specifies formal dress, sir. And I'm afraid your current attire is a little..." He pursed his lips. "Basic."

Suzy could hardly believe what she had heard, and flushed with angry embarrassment on Fletch's behalf. To her surprise though, he just laughed.

"I'd like to see you knock 'oles through reality in

those glad rags," he said. "But as it 'appens, I've brought me suit."

He unzipped his overalls and stepped out of them. Suzy stared. He was wearing a pin-striped suit, once black, but now soft grey and shiny with age. The elbows had been patched and one of the shoulders had been repaired with blue thread. Nevertheless, he looked smarter than she had ever seen him before.

"Will this do?" he asked, giving a little twirl. "I wear it to everything. Weddings, funerals. Court hearings."

The courtier looked him up and down and huffed. "That will be adequate. Now, if you would both care to follow me, His Majesty and his esteemed guests await the pleasure of your company at the reception on platform one hundred." Without waiting for an answer, he turned on his heels and strode away, his flattened nose in the air.

"I can't believe how rude he was to you!" Suzy hissed as she and Fletch fell into step behind him.

"Not worth makin' a fuss over," Fletch whispered back. "The thing to remember about snobs is they're always terrified you're better than them in some way. And most of the time they're right."

Suzy felt her anger cool a little as she pondered this, though she sincerely hoped the king would be nicer than his courtiers.

They followed the courtier along the platform and up a flight of steps onto a footbridge that ran in a ring around the entire level. The bridge was busy with other guests, all finely dressed and heading in the same direction.

"Make way!" the courtier cried. "Make way for His Majesty's personal guests!"

Suzy smiled apologetically at the people who whispered and stared as she passed. Most of them were trolls, although there were other species present as well. Suzy saw a trio of people who looked like cats, complete with whiskers and tails; a tall blue flamingo-like creature in a fabulously elaborate hat; and a flock of fairies with jet-black wings, hovering in place like hummingbirds. People must have come from all five corners of reality to be here, she pondered. It added a tinge of nerves to her excitement.

The crowd thickened as they went, finally gathering into an untidy knot at the top of the stairs leading to platform one hundred.

"What is the meaning of this?" said the courtier, fighting his way through. Suzy tucked her elbows in and followed close on his heels, with Fletch behind her. "You're blocking the thoroughfare!" the courtier continued. "Guards? Why are all these people waiting?"

They emerged from the throng to find two troll guards

in polished armour and gold wellington boots blocking access to the stairs. They were armed with long tubes of dented brass, flared at one end, which looked alarmingly like rocket launchers. She hoped they were simply ceremonial.

They certainly didn't seem to be intimidating the small human figure in the pearlescent white suit who stood facing the guards. Suzy couldn't see his face, but his folded arms and stiff back suggested he was angry.

"Sorry, sir," said one of them. "We'll be able to let people through once we've persuaded this young gentleman to be on his way." He nodded with weary patience to the figure, who huffed in frustration.

"I'm not going anywhere until you double-check the guest list!" he said. "Don't you know who I am?"

Suzy blinked in surprise. *She* certainly knew who he was – she recognized the slightly nasal whine of his voice from her last visit to the Union, when it had been speaking to her from the confines of a snow globe. This was only the second time she had seen him in his true human form. "Frederick?" she said. He whirled round to face her. It was Frederick alright – he was pale, with a pinched face and a mop of dirty blond hair.

"Suzy!" he said. "You're here! You can tell them."

"Tell them what?" she said.

27

"To let me in, of course," he said. "There seems to have been some mix-up with my invitation."

"Is this true?" the courtier asked the guard who had spoken.

"The young gentleman doesn't *have* an invitation, sir," said the guard.

"And that's the mix-up," said Frederick. "Clearly it must have been lost in the post or something."

"They were sent directly via remote spell," said the courtier. "I saw to the deliveries myself."

Frederick flushed, though whether through anger or embarrassment, Suzy couldn't tell. "But I *must* have been invited. I'm the Chief Librarian of the Ivory Tower!"

Many of the people around them gave a low hiss of displeasure at these words. Frederick's face fell, and Suzy caught a flicker of disquiet in his eyes. She felt similarly nervous – what was happening here? She knew Frederick could be annoying, but he was a good person at heart. He had helped her save the Union.

"Then I don't know why you expected an invitation at all," said the courtier. "Now stop blocking the way, or I'll have the guards escort you out." The guards took half a step forward, ready to act, and that's when Suzy made a decision.

"Let him through," she said.

Frederick looked shocked, although not as shocked as the courtier.

"That is absolutely out of the question!"

"Why?" she said. "I'm sure the king won't mind if I bring a guest with me."

A look of barely restrained horror crossed the courtier's face. "You can't do that! It's against protocol!" He seized her arm and tried to pull her towards the stairs. "Now come along!"

"No." Suzy wrenched her arm free. "I'm not going anywhere without Frederick."

A scandalized whisper rippled through the onlookers.

"With the greatest possible respect, miss," said the courtier, fighting to keep his voice under control, "I must insist that you leave this boy behind and follow me."

"What happens if I don't?" Suzy folded her arms and hoped that her nervousness didn't show. Would she get in trouble with the king? All she knew was that Frederick needed her help, and that was enough to make her stand her ground.

"If you don't...? But you must!" The courtier flapped his hands in mounting distress. "His Majesty can't inaugurate the new Express without every member of the crew present!"

Suzy felt a touch of confidence return. "Then it looks

like a lot of people are going to be very disappointed," she said. And just to reassure herself, she took Frederick's arm and linked it through hers. *There*, she thought. *Now we're inseparable.*

Frederick gawked at her with a mixture of shock and admiration. The courtier, meanwhile, ground his teeth.

"Perhaps…" he began.

"Yes?" said Suzy. "Perhaps what?"

"Perhaps on this occasion," he said, "it might just be possible to arrange access for the young man. As your plus-one."

Suzy felt Frederick stand a little straighter, and she gave the courtier her warmest smile. "Thank you," she said. "That would be fantastic." She ignored the mutters of disapproval from the crowd.

"About blinkin' time," said Fletch. "Can we get a move on?"

"Very well," said the courtier, through clenched teeth. He nodded to the guards, who snapped to attention and stood aside. Then he moved to the top of the stairs and cleared his throat. "My lords, ladies and gentlemen," he announced. "Pray welcome our honoured guests, Senior Interdimensional Engineer Fletch, and Deputy Postal Operative Suzy Smith." And then, under his breath, "Plus guest." He bowed so low that his nose scraped the ground.

So that's why it's flat, Suzy thought. Then, together with Fletch and Frederick, and with a renewed feeling of excitement that made the hairs on the back of her neck prickle, she stepped past the courtier to get her first look at the royal reception.

3

A ROYAL DISASTER

latform one hundred looked spectacular. Its entire
length had been covered with a thick red carpet,
and the guests – hundreds of them, glittering like
stained glass in their fine outfits and jewellery – mingled
between enormous vases filled with bouquets of exotic
flowers, some of which released brightly-glowing puffs of
pollen that drifted on the air like fairy lights. Troll waiters
in white jackets cruised through the crowd on motorized
roller skates, distributing drinks and nibbles. A string
quartet played. It was every bit as wonderful as Suzy had
imagined, but she hardly noticed because her eyes were
drawn to the track beside the platform, where the Express
was waiting.

At least, she assumed it was the Express – it was

certainly a train of some sort, but it had been covered over with a vast sheet of white silk. She frowned as she tried to trace the familiar outline of the Express through it, and failed.

When she had first encountered it, the Express had consisted of a large locomotive called the *Belle de Loin*, which pulled a tender full of nuclear-fusion bananas, a submarine-like Hazardous Environment Carriage, and a sorting car that acted as a post office on wheels. Very little of the train had survived her last adventure however, and the shape beneath the sheet looked...different.

"How many changes did they make during the repairs?" she whispered to Fletch as they descended the stairs.

He looked at her sideways. "Lots."

Suzy bit her lip. She had known all along that the Express wouldn't be exactly as she had known it – there hadn't been much of it left after the crash – but she was beginning to suspect she was in for a shock.

"Thanks for getting me in," said Frederick as they reached the foot of the stairs. "What you did back there was brilliant."

"Don't mention it," Suzy said, disentangling herself from his arm. "I can't believe they didn't send you an invitation."

Frederick snorted but couldn't hide the blush of

embarrassment that was creeping up his neck. "Obviously some sort of admin error."

"But you came anyway," she said. "I'm glad."

"You didn't think I'd miss the big relaunch after all we went through together on the old Express, do you?" he said airily. "Besides, I still feel slightly responsible for everything that happened."

Suzy had to bite the inside of her cheek to keep from blurting out something she might regret. *Slightly* responsible? When she first met him, Frederick had been the most wanted person in the whole Union. He had uncovered a secret plot by Lord Meridian, the heartless ruler of the Ivory Tower – storehouse of the Union's knowledge – to blackmail the leaders of the Impossible Places so he could control them from behind the scenes. Frederick had neglected to mention any of this to Suzy at the time, of course. Instead, he had pretended to be a prince, cast out of his kingdom by a usurping uncle. She had found it easy enough to believe him – he was trapped in the form of a frog inside a novelty snow globe thanks to a powerful curse, and his parents, hoping to exchange him for some ready cash, had sent him in the mail to the fearsome sorceress Lady Crepuscula, which was how he and Suzy had crossed paths – he had been her very first delivery. Frederick had pleaded with Suzy not to hand him over, and choosing to temporarily ignore her duties as a postie, she had smuggled him to safety. Or so she had thought.

Instead, the following hours had been a blur of fear and danger, ending in the calamitous crash at the Ivory Tower that had ruined the Express. Lord Meridian had been overthrown by his sister, Lady Crepuscula, who had restored Frederick to his true form, and on balance, things had ended well.

But Frederick was *definitely* responsible.

"I dunno about you two," said Fletch, "but I'm starvin'. Is there any grub at this shindig?"

"That looks like a buffet over there," said Suzy, pointing to a row of tables on the far side of the platform.

"Smashin'," he said. "I'll see you both in a bit." He scurried away, rubbing his hands together in anticipation.

"Did he just come for the food?" asked Frederick, watching him go.

"It wouldn't surprise me," said Suzy. "Come on. Wilmot and the rest of the crew must be here somewhere."

They set off into the crowd, which parted around them. At first, Suzy thought the guests were being helpful, but she quickly realized that they were just stepping back to get a better look at her. Monocles were screwed into place and opera glasses raised, until she began to feel like a specimen under a microscope.

Progress was slow. Suzy had to stop every few seconds to return a greeting or acknowledge a compliment, and while she was grateful for the appreciation, it all felt a bit overwhelming: she was in a crowd of strangers, and every single one of them knew who she was.

Frederick clearly had no such reservations, however, and strolled alongside her as though the entire reception had been organized in his honour. He waved and smiled with an easy confidence, even though he was mostly getting looks of polite bafflement in return.

They made their way to the centre of the platform, where everyone seemed to be gathered around to watch something, although Suzy couldn't make out what it was through the throng. Then she heard a familiar voice.

"So there we were, through the tunnel but out of control. The brakes were gone. Most of the cab too, for that matter, and there was the end of the line, dead ahead. Beyond it lay the Ivory Tower. Our destination was in sight, but it promised to be the end of us. We were a runaway train!"

There was a smattering of *oooohs* from the audience. Suzy squeezed through the press of bodies until she could see the troll who was speaking. It was Stonker, the driver of the Express, resplendent in his blue-and-silver uniform. He was leaning against one of the enormous vases, clearly basking in the attention of his audience.

"I've been in some scrapes in my time, of course," he said, twisting the tip of his huge handlebar moustache around a finger as he peered into the mists of time. "But none like this. I knew it was going to take some jolly quick thinking to pull us out of it in one piece."

"So what did you do?" someone asked.

"Do? Why, I…"

Stonker trailed off as a huge figure loomed up beside him and nudged him with a paw as big as his head. The whole crowd shuffled back a step. Suzy couldn't blame them for being intimidated; Ursel, the Express's firewoman, struck an imposing figure. She was a brown bear, and stood easily two metres tall on her hind legs, as she was doing now. She wore spotless denim overalls, and her fur, much to Suzy's surprise, was a rich chestnut colour. That shouldn't have been surprising for a brown bear of course, but during Suzy's first visit to the Union, Ursel's fur had been bright yellow – a side effect of handling the fusion bananas that powered the Express.

Now she raised her great head and sniffed the air.

"Hello," said Stonker. "Caught wind of something, have you?"

Ursel's snout twitched. She cocked her head to one side. Then, with one bound, she leaped across the space to the watching crowd, which scattered before her. All except Suzy.

"Growlf!" said Ursel, scooping Suzy up into a hug that lifted her feet clear off the floor.

"I missed you too!" said Suzy, wrapping her arms as far around Ursel's frame as she could manage and burying her face in the soft fur of the bear's neck.

"Suzy Smith! As I live and breathe!" Stonker strolled over as Ursel set Suzy down. "How the devil are you, my girl?"

"I'm fine, thanks," said Suzy, trying to keep her balance as he clapped her on the shoulder. "It's good to see you again."

"Likewise!" He stepped back to admire her uniform. "Look at you. Every inch the true postie."

"Thank you," said Suzy.

"Certainly better than that old dressing gown of yours."

Frederick, who had been hovering behind Suzy throughout this exchange, cleared his throat.

"And who's this?" said Stonker.

"You remember Frederick," said Suzy.

"Good heavens," said Stonker. "The snow globe?"

Frederick grimaced. "Yes," he said. "That was me."

Stonker gave him the same slap on the shoulder he had given Suzy. "I've never socialized with one of our deliveries before, but it's good to have you here. How's life at the Ivory Tower?"

Those members of the crowd within earshot exchanged startled looks and began muttering darkly among themselves. Suzy couldn't hear what they were saying, but most of them were glowering at Frederick, who drew himself up to his full height and pressed his lips into an impassive line.

"It's fine, thank you," he said, looking Stonker in the eye but speaking loud enough for the crowd to hear. "As you know, we're under new management and now offer a comprehensive public-facing service." Then he peeled his lips back into a fixed grin.

"Right," said Stonker, taking a discreet step back. "Jolly good."

When Frederick's grin didn't waver, Suzy stepped up beside him. "Are you alright?" she whispered.

"Of course I am," he said. He wouldn't look at her, but seemed to be reading the faces of the crowd.

"I don't believe you."

"Would I lie to you?" he said and, before she could answer, added, "Where's Wilmot?"

"The Postmaster?" said Stonker. "He's supposed to be here, but we've not seen him yet. Can you smell him anywhere, Ursel?"

"Grrrunf," said Ursel. "Rrrrowlf."

"She says he's definitely somewhere nearby," said Stonker. "But he's hard to pinpoint in the crowd."

Their audience was cautiously regrouping, although they gave both Ursel and Frederick a wide berth.

"Mr Stonker?" said a skinny troll in a bowler hat. "Please don't leave us in suspense any longer. What happens next in your story?"

"Yes," said an elderly clockwork lady beside him. "How did you stop the Express from crashing?"

Stonker thrust his chest out. "I didn't, madam!" he said. "We smashed straight off the end of the tracks and into the Ivory Tower."

The crowd gasped.

"The Express was ruined," said Stonker, "but she had brought us safely to our destination. The stronghold of Lord Meridian himself! And the rest, as you know, is history." He swept his cap off his head and bowed as the crowd applauded. A few bold individuals came forward with autograph books. Stonker pulled a fountain pen from an inside pocket and, with a satisfied smile, allowed himself to be surrounded.

"How come he gets all the glory?" said Frederick. "We were there too."

"I don't care about glory," said Suzy. "I just want to be a postie."

"Runk." Ursel nodded in agreement.

"And a fine ambition that is too," said a voice.

Happiness swelled in Suzy as she saw a particularly wizened old troll tottering to the front of the crowd with the help of a cane. He wore a faded old postie's uniform with several medals pinned to the chest, and half his bald scalp was fashioned from reflective chrome. "Back for more, eh?" he said, smacking his gums at her. "I was hoping you would be."

"Mr Trellis!" Suzy took his hand and squeezed it gently. "I didn't know you'd be here."

"Oh, we're all here," said Mr Trellis, indicating a group of elderly trolls shuffling up behind him and elbowing the other guests aside. They, along with Mr Trellis, were several members of the Old Guard – retired posties with millennia of experience between them. They normally spent their days in a quiet rest home in the city's Underside, but here they all were, in ancient and ill-fitting uniforms. They crowded round, blinking at Suzy through thick spectacles and turning ear trumpets in her direction.

"Who's this?" said one.

"That's not the same girl as last time, is it? She looks taller."

"Has she seen my pudding? I put it down somewhere."

"You see?" said Mr Trellis. "We're all here, even if

we're not all there, so to speak. We're here to see you and the crew off on your next adventure. It does a soul good to see the new generation in action." He rubbed his thumb over his medals. "I just wish I could come with you."

"So do I," said Suzy. "Although I'm hoping for a bit less of an adventure than last time. I'd like to see the Union without running for my life."

"Oh, every time's an adventure," said Mr Trellis. "Did I ever tell you about the time I fought off a swarm of razor-wing butterflies in the tree city of Cornus?"

There was a collective groan from the rest of the Old Guard. "Not this one again," someone muttered.

"I've always wanted to visit Cornus," said Frederick eagerly.

"Well!" said Mr Trellis with a gummy smile. "Let me tell you all about it."

Suzy saw her chance. "Excuse me," she said, and slipped away into the crowd to find Wilmot.

Suzy pushed her way through the mingling guests until she reached the very end of the platform, but there was still no sign of Wilmot. Where could he be? She was gazing out at the rooftops of the Overside through the glass panels of the station wall, and wondering if she should try searching again, when she sensed someone standing behind her.

"Could I interest you in some refreshment, miss?" It was one of the white-suited troll waiters, carrying a silver tray piled high with small dark-brown pies. "They're fresh."

Suzy started, embarrassed at being caught off guard. "No, thank you," she said, avoiding the waiter's eyes. "I just need to find my friends."

"I can help you with that, miss." He looked at her expectantly, a big smile on his face, and it was only then that Suzy realized who he was.

"Wilmot?"

"Hello, Suzy!" He grinned. "What are you doing all the way back here?"

"Looking for you!" she said. "Why are you dressed as a waiter?"

"Oh, this?" He looked down at himself as though he had forgotten what he was wearing. "The Express has been out of action for so long, I decided to get a part-time job to keep myself busy. Mum really wanted me to go back to school, but there's a waiting list. So here I am!"

"But why are you working as a waiter at your own reception?" Suzy asked. "Shouldn't you be in your Postmaster's uniform?"

"Oh, that." Wilmot looked a little sheepish. "I may have inadvertently double-booked myself."

"Then you need to go and tell someone," said Suzy. "You can't miss the inauguration because you're serving pork pies."

"Actually, they're Don't Ask pies," he said. "Would you like one?"

Suzy squinted at them. "What's in them?" she said.

"Don't ask."

She wrinkled her nose. "Thanks, but I've already eaten."

A loud rasping buzz rang out, quelling the hubbub of the party. At the other end of the platform, the royal guards had taken up positions on the footbridge stairs and raised their rocket launchers onto their shoulders. For a horrifying instant, Suzy thought they were going to open fire, but then they put their lips to a curly brass tube sticking out of the side of each launcher and blew. The buzzing noise rang out of the end of the weapons – which weren't weapons at all, she realized. They were instruments. Just not particularly tuneful ones.

"What are those things?" she asked.

"Kazookas," said Wilmot. Then, with a note of excitement, "It's starting!"

The courtier from earlier appeared at the top of the steps.

"My lords, ladies and gentlemen," he proclaimed through a small megaphone, "His Trolltanic Majesty, ruler of all Troll Territory, King Amylum the Third."

The guards gave another blast on their kazookas, and the courtier stepped aside.

Suzy rose up on tiptoes, waiting for the king to appear at the top of the stairs. Instead, something small and round came zooming through the air over the walkway, trailing smoke and sparks in its wake. It moved too quickly for Suzy to make out many details, but she got a flash of pearly teeth set in a manic grin, and a burst of laughter as the thing shot by overhead. It looped the loop above the crowd, eliciting a chorus of *oohs* and *aahs*. Then everyone ducked as it swooped low above their

45

heads before touching down at the foot of the stairs in a halo of smoke.

"Thank you, Trollville!" said a voice from inside the smoke. It cleared to reveal the king, down on one knee, head bowed, and his arms extended in triumph.

He was short and round as a ball, dressed in a silver-sequined jumpsuit and matching crash helmet. White lace frothed at his cuffs and collar, and a jet pack that looked like it had been fashioned from an antique radiator and several French horns was strapped to his back. His skin was bubble-gum pink, accentuated by a black beauty mark in the shape of a heart on one cheek.

The crowd burst into applause as he got to his feet and removed his crash helmet, revealing a perfectly bald scalp. The courtier hurried to his side and presented him with a wig of jet-black hair, teased into a quiff so enormous that Suzy wondered if it hadn't been done with magic. A tiny crown sat atop the quiff, like a surfer riding the crest of a tsunami.

"You all came to see me!" said the king, settling the wig into place before blowing flamboyant kisses to the crowd. His voice was surprisingly deep and resonant for his size. "I'm humbled, ladies and gentlemen. Humbled!" This display continued as the courtier took him gently by the elbow and led him towards a low stage that had been set up in front of the Express.

"Wow," said Suzy. "That's not the sort of entrance I expected."

"Me neither," said Wilmot. "He usually messes up the landing. He had to conduct his last event from the back of an ambulance."

An entourage appeared at the top of the stairs and followed in the king's wake. Suzy recognized Gertrude Grunt, Wilmot's mother, former Postmistress General and current matron of the Old Guard's rest home, resplendent in a set of Impossible Postal Service dress robes. Beside her was a stocky troll with purplish-blue skin in identical robes, festooned with medals.

"That's Mr Prott, the current Postmaster General," whispered Wilmot. "They say he once franked five thousand letters in a single hour. By hand!"

An assortment of minor dignitaries and hangers-on then followed.

"Would the crew of the Express please take their places so the ceremony may begin," the courtier called.

"Quick!" said Suzy. "Where's your Postmaster's uniform?"

"I stowed it under one of the buffet tables," said Wilmot. "But are you sure I—"

"Yes!" she said, pushing him in that direction. "Now go!"

She watched, nervous, as the procession made its way through the crowd to the stage, where a row of folding chairs had been set up. King Amylum, meanwhile, watched as his courtier produced a bicycle pump and connected it to a crumpled ball of sparkly golden plastic that sat in the middle of the stage. He began pumping and, with much huffing and wheezing, the ball slowly expanded into the form of a bulbous armchair. Suzy remembered her dad spending the best part of a week lounging in something similar in a swimming pool on holiday once. She checked and wasn't surprised to see a cup holder moulded into the armrest.

With a dreadful squeaking of plastic, the king settled himself into the chair.

"Ready!" Wilmot reappeared at her side, now dressed in his Postmaster's uniform. It was very much like her own, but much older, more ornate, and several sizes too big. He peered over the collar as though he had taken cover behind it. He was still holding the tray of pies.

"You're not bringing that, are you?" she asked.

"Yes," he said. "Technically, my shift doesn't finish for another hour. This way, I can do both jobs at once."

"Fine," she said. "But hurry up. The others are almost there." Taking him by the hand, she dived into the crowd. They emerged a moment later just behind Ursel, Stonker and Fletch, who were making their way up onto the stage.

"Ah, there you are, Postmaster," said Stonker, glancing over his shoulder. "I thought we'd lost you."

"I'm here alright, Mr Stonker," said Wilmot. "Don't Ask pie?"

Stonker looked at him askance. "Maybe later."

The king's entourage took their seats along the back of the stage, and Wilmot exchanged an excited smile with his mother as he and the rest of the Express crew took up positions beside the throne: Ursel and Stonker on the king's right, and Wilmot and Suzy on his left. Suzy smiled and nodded to Gertrude as well, but got a hard stare in return. She swallowed her embarrassment and turned away. She couldn't blame Gertrude for being angry with her – Wilmot had put his own life at risk to protect Suzy on their last adventure, and for a while they had all been convinced that he had died in the attempt. It looked as though Gertrude wasn't quite ready to forgive her yet.

"Who are these people, Grotnip?" said the king. He regarded the crew with bemusement.

The courtier bowed again, his nose scraping the stage. "The crew of the Impossible Postal Express, Your Majesty. The reception is in their honour, if you recall. You're inaugurating their new train in preparation for its first delivery."

"Am I?" The king seemed genuinely amazed. "I thought I was opening something. I'm usually opening something." He looked up at the sphere. "Does this place need opening?"

"Grinding Halt has been open for two hundred years already, Your Majesty."

The king took this information on board. "So, no giant scissors required."

"None, Your Majesty."

"Pity," he said. "I always enjoy the giant scissors. I wonder who makes them."

"Giants, Your Majesty. Now if you would care to concentrate on the matter at hand…"

"Grotters?"

For the briefest of seconds, Suzy saw the corner of Grotnip's mouth twitch and his nostrils flare. But when he spoke again, he was as calm as ever. "Yes, Your Majesty?"

"I think I'm developing a starboard list." Sure enough, the king was slowly sinking into the depths of the seat, and Suzy could hear the slow hiss of escaping air. "Get pumping, man!"

Grotnip snatched up the bicycle pump, which was still attached to the valve on the side of the throne, and recommenced pumping.

The crowd waited in respectful silence, while Suzy

watched the two of them in dismay. *Am I the only one who thinks this is weird?* she wondered.

Before she could pursue the thought any further, platform one hundred started to tremble underfoot. The sensation ran through Suzy's body, making her soles tingle. The crowd must have felt it too, as a little wave of excited chatter broke out. "What was that?" Suzy asked. Wilmot pointed at the glass wall of the sphere. It was moving. Or rather, the level on which they were standing was moving – rotating clockwise until the end of platform one hundred lined up with an opening in the dome. A banner reading BON VOYAGE! had been hung above it. With a screech and a clank, the rotation stopped.

"Your Majesty," said Grotnip, panting with the effort of keeping the throne inflated. "Everything is ready, and the Express is scheduled to leave in just a few minutes. You may start the inauguration." He wiped his brow with his sleeve. "And perhaps you'd prefer to stand?"

Suzy felt the hairs on her arms rise at his words. She had spent weeks imagining what her first official delivery as a Postie was going to be like – the places she would see and the people she would meet – and now here she was, just moments away from it all.

"Alright, Grotters," said the king. "Just tell me what these good people want to hear, and I'll say it."

Grotnip gave an exasperated gasp. "It's just as we rehearsed it, Your Majesty. You simply have to congratulate the crew on their bravery and continued service, followed by the words 'We bestow our royal blessing on this fine troll train.' Then the Express will be unveiled and your part in this evening's proceedings will be over."

"And then can I get out there and meet people?" said the king. "I don't want to keep my fans waiting."

"If you so wish, Your Majesty," said Grotnip, who was starting to sound rather short of breath. "But those words are very important. 'We bestow our royal blessing on this fine troll train.' The inauguration won't be complete without it. It's tradition."

"Blessing…train…adoring crowds," said the king. "No problem."

He sprang out of the throne and strode to the front of the stage, while Grotnip discarded the pump with obvious relief.

"Good evening, Trollville!" said the king, stretching his arms wide as though he could embrace them all. "Are you having a good time?"

He got a smattering of polite nods and murmurs in response.

"Of course you are!" he declared. "And we're going to have such a great evening together, but first we've got to launch this train. So let's get it out on the rails and then get on with the party!"

There was a bigger, more heartfelt round of applause in response to this.

Suzy's excitement was building to such an intensity that she could feel her whole body shaking. She balled her hands into fists but it didn't help. She was so focused on thoughts of what might be to come, that she barely even noticed people in the audience shaking as well, and swaying on their feet. A few of them turned to each other with worried expressions.

But then the king started swaying too, and Suzy was suddenly trembling so badly she had to steady herself against Wilmot. Because *she* wasn't trembling at all, she realized – Grinding Halt was.

"We bestow our royal blessing—" the king began, but then platform one hundred gave a ferocious jolt and he was thrown to the floor, along with half the audience.

The stage bucked like a mule beneath Suzy, throwing her to the ground. She landed hard and reached for something to hold on to as the floor shuddered beneath her. She found Wilmot's hand and held it fast.

Tables overturned. Glasses shattered. People screamed.

"What's happening?" shouted Wilmot as his Don't Ask pies scattered across the stage.

Suzy tried to answer but couldn't make herself heard over the rumbling growl that now filled the air. It pulsed in time with the tremors that ran through the floor, and made her teeth rattle. She cupped her free hand to her mouth and bellowed, "Earthquake!"

AFTERSHOCK

Suzy tightened her grip on Wilmot's hand as the juddering floor threatened to pull them both in opposite directions. She clenched her teeth to stop them rattling together. All she could hear was the groaning of strained metal and the screams of the crowd as platform one hundred tilted and yawed like a ship in rough seas.

"Guards!" Grotnip shouted over the turmoil. "Look to the king! Women and children last! Get His Majesty to safety!"

The guards did their best, but couldn't stay on their feet and were sent flailing off the stage. Suzy felt her hold on Wilmot slipping and cried out in panic. Then she was smothered by a flurry of brown fur as Ursel rolled over her, and she found herself held tight in a bear hug, along with Stonker, Fletch and Wilmot.

"Well done, that bear!" said Stonker.

Outside the protective circle of Ursel's arms, the earthquake reached a roaring crescendo. The glass panels overhead cracked with a noise like thunder. Then, in an instant, it was over.

Silence fell, broken here and there by the tinkle of falling glass.

Ursel released her hold, and Suzy rolled free.

"Is everyone alright?" she said.

The rest of the crew climbed unsteadily to their feet.

"All shipshape here," replied Stonker, although the ends of his moustache were badly frayed.

"Grunk," confirmed Ursel, dusting herself down.

"Same here," said Wilmot, retrieving his cap from the floor. He joined Suzy as she looked out across platform one hundred. People were picking themselves up, nursing bruises and scrapes, but none of them appeared to be seriously hurt. She was relieved to see Frederick, his suit now slightly crumpled, pushing his way through the crowd towards them with the Old Guard in tow.

"Wow!" he said, jumping up onto the stage. "That scared the life out of me! I didn't know Trollville was in an earthquake zone."

"It isn't!" said Wilmot, looking more worried than Suzy had at first realized. "There's never been an earthquake in Trollville before. Ever!"

She found his concern contagious. She had never experienced an earthquake before either, and now that the immediate danger had passed she could feel the sense of shock setting in. A chill stole through her body, and she hugged herself to make it stop.

Gertrude hurried over, and conducted a quick but thorough inspection of first Wilmot, and then the Old Guard. "Are any of you hurt?" she asked.

"It'll take more than a shaky floor to see any of us off," said Mr Trellis. "It's a bit like that time I was caught in a landslide in the Whispering Mountains. I'd been delivering a postcard to the Grand Vizier, when—"

Before he could continue there was a roar of rockets, and the king rose above the stage, powered by his jet pack. His wig had slipped and now stuck out sideways.

"I'm getting out of here!" he shouted. "Everyone follow me to safety!" Grotnip and the guards raced towards him, but he hovered just out of reach.

"We can't follow you like that, Your Majesty," said Grotnip, trying to jump and grab the king's boots. "Now please come back down and let's all leave the building in a sensible fashion."

His words were enough to put Suzy's shock on hold. "Wait," she said. "What about the Express?"

"What about it?" said Grotnip. "We can't go ahead with the relaunch now. This is a crisis situation!"

Suzy looked from Grotnip to the shrouded form of the Express. Her thoughts were cloudy and scattered, but she had the terrible feeling that everything she had spent the last two months hoping for was being snatched away. "We can't stop now," she said, a second before one of the huge glass panels fell from the roof and struck one of the neighbouring platforms with a mighty crash.

"I'm issuing a royal decree," the king announced. "Everybody run for your lives!"

"Wait!" tried Suzy, but the crowd had taken the king at his word and were already stampeding towards the exits.

"Make sure everyone gets a signed photo, Grotters!" said the king as he rocketed towards the hole in the station roof. "And remember: no refunds!" He shot out into the open air and zoomed away across the city, leaving a spiralling trail of smoke behind him.

What little colour was in Grotnip's face drained away. "Quickly!" he said to the guards. "Contact the palace. Call the police. Organize a search. We have to get him back!"

He and the guards joined the undignified rush for the stairs.

"What should we do?" shouted Frederick.

"We're safe 'ere as long as the roof holds," said Fletch, appearing beside them. "Better than gettin' trampled." He spoke with his mouth full, and held up a plate heaped with Don't Ask pies.

It took several minutes for the crowd to disperse, leaving a swathe of trampled flowers and overturned tables in their wake. Suzy regarded the devastation sadly. "Now what?" she asked.

"I need to get back to the rest home immediately and make sure nobody's hurt," said Gertrude. "Mr Trellis? Wilmot? With me, please."

"Oh no!" said Wilmot, leaping to her side. "I hope everyone's alright." He turned to the others. "Are you coming?"

"Absolutely," said Stonker. "The crew of the Express is at your disposal, Mrs Grunt."

Fletch tipped the contents of his plate into his pockets. "There'll be some patchin' up to do at the rest 'ome, I expect. Best I tag along an' all."

"Thank you," said Gertrude. "We'll leave immediately."

The crew and the Old Guard followed her from the stage, although Suzy gave a last, mournful look back at the Express. That's when she realized that Frederick wasn't following them. "Aren't you coming?" she asked.

"Can I?" he asked. "It's just, I haven't been invited." Then under his breath he added, "Again."

"Hrunf," said Ursel.

"Yes, I wouldn't recommend staying here either," said Stonker. "There's no telling how unstable the building is now."

"And it's not as if you can get back to the Ivory Tower any time soon," said Fletch.

"But there's a direct train from Trollville every hour," said Frederick. "And I've already bought a return ticket."

Fletch laughed. "No one'll be runnin' trains out of town after that little kerfuffle, my lad."

"You mean I'm stuck here?" said Frederick.

"At least until the engineerin' teams check the lines are stable."

"Wait," said Suzy. "That means I can't get home either!"

Fletch shrugged. "So? You weren't plannin' to head back until tomorrow mornin' anyway, were you?"

She felt the shock stealing back into her body, making her palms prickle. "Yes, but what if it takes longer than that to get the trains running again? I've got school tomorrow! My parents have got work. And I just left them there asleep!"

"I'm afraid there's nothing we can do about it right

now," said Gertrude, who had paused halfway up the steps to the footbridge. "You're welcome to join us, Frederick, but I must insist that we all get a move on."

Even from this distance, Suzy could see the concern etched on Gertrude's face and she felt a pang of remorse. Her friends' home had just been rocked to its foundations. The rest of the Old Guard might be in danger. Her own concerns seemed trivial in comparison.

Nevertheless, she couldn't help but feel a deep sense of sorrow as she mounted the stairs and left platform one hundred, and the Express, behind her.

Reaching the rest home was not an easy task. Grinding Halt was already swamped with anxious tourists trying to find a way out of the city, and it was all the station staff could do to keep them under control.

"Please listen to me!" shouted a nervous-looking porter from the top of a pile of suitcases. "There's nothing we can do to help right now!" His words were met with a chorus of boos and jeers. "All train services have been cancelled until further notice. Grinding Halt is closed. Please disperse!"

"Where are we supposed to go?" someone shouted

back. The porter had no answer, and the shouting of the crowd grew angrier. The noise and the press of bodies made Suzy feel scared, and she linked hands with Wilmot and Frederick as they struggled down one flight of emergency stairs after another, finally arriving at a row of passenger elevators on the ground floor concourse. A sign above the doors read *Underside*, but another porter, weary and streaked with dust, was turning people away.

"They're all out of order because of the quake," she said. "I'm really sorry. If you're trying to reach the Underside, you'll have to take the stairs." She pointed to a nearby line of trolls that snaked back and forth three times across the full length of the concourse. It wasn't even moving.

"We'll never get there at this rate," said Gertrude. "Are there no buses available?"

"Not from Grinding Halt, ma'am," said the porter. "Half the signalling network is down. But you might be lucky and find one outside somewhere."

Gertrude set her mouth in a determined line. "Then that is what we shall do. Are you able to walk a little further, Mr Trellis?"

"Don't worry about me," said Mr Trellis. "My kneecaps are made from titanium, remember?" He rapped his cane against his artificial leg, which made a hollow ringing sound. "They'll outlast the rest of me."

They stepped outside Grinding Halt to find the city in chaos. Traffic was at a standstill, as the strange assortment of home-made vehicles that the trolls drove lay abandoned and overturned. Water arced from broken pipelines beneath the roads, and every building Suzy could see was marred by a web of ugly cracks. Trolls stumbled through the wreckage, looking confused and scared.

Suzy could scarcely believe what she was seeing. *It's even worse than I realized*, she thought.

"We should try the Underside station on Meteor Street," said Wilmot. "That's the closest."

"Good thinking, Postmaster," said Stonker. "And stick close together. We don't want to lose anyone."

"Agreed," said Suzy.

They picked their way through the streets, passing a troll police officer striding over the chaos on telescopic stilts, his helmet topped with a flashing blue light.

"Please remain calm," he called through a megaphone. "The situation is under control."

"I dunno who he thinks he's foolin'," muttered Fletch.

They reached the Underside station, where they were met with another lengthy line. It seemed to be moving, however, and they soon discovered that, in addition to the stairs, one of the station's six elevators was still working.

It was another half an hour before they finally boarded.

To Suzy's surprise, the lift had seats, complete with over-the-shoulder harnesses like those on a roller coaster. Ursel was far too large to squeeze into them, and simply had to stand with her forepaws braced against the ceiling. Suzy soon discovered why the harnesses were necessary – when they were all strapped in, the lift was fired like a cannonball down through the city's superstructure, and when she finally staggered out into the winding streets of the Underside, she felt as though she'd left her stomach behind.

"Are you alright?" Wilmot asked, as she put her hands on her knees and tried to regain her breath.

"I'll be fine," she said, feeling doubly glad that she hadn't accepted his offer of Don't Ask pies. "I just need a moment."

"I'm afraid we don't have a moment," said Gertrude. "Quickly, please."

Suzy couldn't blame her for being anxious – the most likely part of the city to suffer the worst effects of the quake was surely the Underside. It hung upside down beneath the arch of the bridge that formed the city, its roofs and spires and weather vanes all pointing down into the bottomless depths of the canyon below. She was only mildly surprised to discover that the lift had flipped upside down at some point on its journey, so that when she

64

stepped outside the doors she was, from the Underside's perspective, the right way up.

This was all thanks to Negotiable Gravity – an unfathomable mixture of troll technology and magic, which redirected gravity in whichever direction the trolls found most convenient. And for reasons Suzy still couldn't understand, hanging by the soles of their feet over a perilous drop was their idea of convenience. Personally, she just found it gave her vertigo to look up – or was it down? – and see the pit yawning overhead, so made a point of keeping her eyes on the pavement.

Even so, there was no way she could avoid seeing the damage that surrounded her. The street lamps flickered uncertainly, and most of the houses they passed sported broken windows and missing roof slates. A clean-up was already in full effect though, and every front door stood open, the occupants turning out onto the streets with brooms and dustbins. The trolls might have been caught by surprise, but they clearly weren't about to sit idle. It lifted Suzy's spirits a little to see it.

Night was falling by the time they finally reached the Valley View Rest Home. It was a large, elegant building, even though its curtains now flapped like ragged sails out of the empty window frames and a crack ran up the building's facade from top to bottom.

Please don't collapse, Suzy thought as they stepped inside.

On her last visit, the rest home had been an oasis of calm and ordered business. Now, it was a frenzy of activity. The nurses hurried back and forth, carrying mops and brooms, hammers and saws. The wood panelling of the lobby was cracked, the portraits had fallen off the walls, and the black-and-white tiled floor was littered with debris and grime.

Wilmot's Aunt Dorothy – Gertrude's sister – appeared, pushing a wheelbarrow full of broken crockery. She dropped it when she saw the crew and hurried over. She was small and plump, and dressed in her usual nurse's uniform. Her skin, normally the same amber shade as Gertrude's, was white with plaster dust. "Oh, thank heavens!" she exclaimed, throwing her arms around Gertrude. "I was worried something had happened to you all."

"We're in one piece, thank you," said Gertrude. "But what about the rest of the Old Guard?"

"All fine, barring a few scrapes and bruises," said Dorothy. "Though it gave us quite a fright, I can tell you." She pulled a handkerchief from the pocket of her apron and mopped her brow with it, but as it was even dirtier than she was, all it did was leave a greasy stain on her skin.

"I've got the Old Guard settled down in the lounge while the rest of us do emergency repairs."

Gertrude looked around the lobby. "How bad is it?"

"Pretty bad," said Dorothy. "The power keeps going out, half the plaster's come off the ceilings and we've got leaks all over the place."

Fletch sniffed. "I can 'ave a look at the pipes, if you fancy."

"Yes please," said Gertrude. "And can someone help to keep an eye on the Old Guard? I don't want them wandering."

"Leave them to me," said Mr Trellis, starting towards the door marked *Residents' Lounge*. "I'll soon whip them into shape."

"Thank you, Mr Trellis." As soon as he had gone, Gertrude turned to Stonker and Ursel. "Would you two mind supervising his supervision? It tends to get a little rowdy."

"It would be our pleasure," said Stonker, with a knowing smile. Ursel grunted in confirmation, and they set off together.

"Right," said Gertrude, rolling up her sleeves. "Let's get to work. What needs doing?"

"We're starting at the bottom and working our way up," said Dorothy. "I've got as far as the kitchen, but I've not even looked upstairs yet."

"Oh no!" said Wilmot. "My room!" He bolted for the stairs.

"I'll help," said Suzy, chasing after him.

"And me!" said Frederick.

The three of them thundered upstairs to the landing, around a corner and down a long carpeted hallway lined with doors. "These are the Old Guard's rooms," Wilmot explained, as he dodged around several nurses who were repairing cracks in the wall with lengths of tape. At the far end of the hall was another, narrower flight of stairs, without a carpet, and the three friends clattered up them. They emerged into a short, plain passage with just two doors leading off it. The light bulb overhead flickered. "This is where Mum and Aunty Dorothy live," said Wilmot, panting.

"What about you?" said Frederick. "Don't tell me you share with your mum!"

"Of course not," said Wilmot. "I'm upstairs again."

"What stairs?" said Suzy.

There was a click as Wilmot flicked a switch on the wall, and a square panel in the ceiling slid open. With a rattle and a clunk, a flight of steps unfolded from inside the opening, extending like a concertina until the bottom step came to rest on the floor.

"These stairs," Wilmot replied. "Come on up!"

He raced up the stairs in a few seconds flat and disappeared through the opening. A little hesitantly, Suzy followed him.

She emerged through the opening, only to bump her head on what appeared to be the underside of a table. Annoyed, she crawled forward on all fours, trying to find a way out from underneath it. But there was none. There was just more table in every direction. She was lost in a small forest of table legs. "Wilmot?" she called.

"Over here," came the reply. She looked and saw Wilmot's legs a short distance away. He must have been standing up, because she couldn't see his top half. She scrambled over and found him standing in a square hole cut in the table. He shuffled to one side to give her space to join him. "Come up and look," he said.

She stood and found herself looking down on a miniature landscape of rolling purple fields, stretching away towards a small village on top of a hill. Beyond that she saw a frozen landscape of icy mountains and volcanoes, and further away still was a walled desert city surrounded by palm trees. It was a whole world in diorama, criss-crossed with dozens of railway lines. Because the table wasn't a table at all – it was a model railway. Suzy had been crawling beneath it, and the "table legs" had been the wooden beams supporting the entire structure. They were in the rest home's attic, close underneath the sloping roof tiles, some of which were now missing.

"What do you think?" said Wilmot, giving her a hopeful smile.

Suzy said the first thing that came into her head. "It's huge." The diorama stretched from one end of the room to the other, weaving around the roof beams and the few items of furniture that had been squeezed into the last available spaces, including Wilmot's bed.

"My dad started it years ago," said Wilmot, righting a copse of trees that had fallen in the earthquake. "I've been working on it since he…" He paused and his eyes dropped to the floor. "Well. Ever since. It's taken me ages, but it's nearly finished." He pointed to the desert, which mostly consisted of layers of chicken wire and papier mâché, half-painted.

Suzy looked at the diorama again with fresh understanding, and placed a comforting hand on his. "I think it's brilliant," she said.

"Hey, nice place!" said Frederick, popping up from another hole in the middle of the arctic region. "Oh, wow! Is this bit based on the Trans-Petrekov line?"

"Yes," said Wilmot, with a sudden grin. "It's even got working cryovolcanoes. They erupt ice. Watch!" He reached underneath the layout and flicked a switch. There

70

was a spark of energy, a loud bang, and one of the model volcanoes rocketed straight up in the air and struck the ceiling, where it exploded in a shower of papier mâché. They all ducked, and Wilmot's face fell. "Perhaps it was damaged in the quake," he said.

Suzy picked a fragment of papier mâché out of her hair. "Is this really the first earthquake Trollville's ever had?" she said.

"Yes," said Wilmot. "And not just the first in Trollville. It's the first in all of Troll Territory, ever!"

"But that can't be right," she replied. "Everywhere gets earthquakes sometimes, even if they're only minor ones. I don't know what it's like here, but the surface of my world is made up of things called tectonic plates. They're like huge rocky platforms that are always moving, although very slowly. Sometimes they grind together and cause earthquakes. It's natural."

"Is your world one of those spherical ones?" said Wilmot. "Because I've heard they have a few design flaws like that. Troll Territory was engineered differently."

She gave him a blank look in response. "Engineered?"

"Yes." He shrugged. "According to the legends, we trolls never used to have a homeland of our own, so our ancestors decided to make one eons ago. They gathered raw materials from all across reality, taking spare parts

71

that other Impossible Places didn't want, and bolted them all together to form Troll Territory. It doesn't have any moving parts. It's completely stable."

"Until today," put in Frederick. Suzy scowled at him.

"How could they build a whole world though?" she asked. The idea was so huge that her mind was struggling to keep hold of it. "The technology you'd need to do that would be absolutely incredible."

"Oh, it was," said Wilmot. "According to the stories, our ancestors built huge powerful machines that walked like giants and burrowed like moles. They say they could pick up whole mountains, and dig beds for rivers and oceans. No one's ever seen technology like it since."

Suzy frowned. "So is any of it true?"

"Nobody knows," said Wilmot. "You know what legends are like. But it's exciting to think about, isn't it?"

Frederick leaned his elbows on the painted surface of an ice floe. "If it *is* true, do you think it could have something to do with the earthquake?"

"I've no idea," said Wilmot. "Ancient engineering isn't really my strong point. I prefer to build my worlds on a smaller scale." He picked up a model locomotive that had been lying on its side and set it back on the rails.

"Can we give it a test run?" asked Frederick.

Wilmot smiled. "I was hoping you'd ask."

He was reaching for the controls when the whole building groaned around them. There was a juddering, banging sound from inside the walls, and Suzy gripped the table as the floorboards trembled beneath her. "It's another earthquake!" she said.

Then the dull *whump!* of an explosion sounded from somewhere deep inside the house, and the other noises stopped abruptly. In the ensuing silence, Suzy heard raised voices and running feet downstairs.

"That wasn't an earthquake," said Wilmot. "Something else has happened!" He vanished beneath the layout, like a mole into its hole.

Suzy gave the model railway a last look, and then followed him.

SPARE PARTS

Suzy, Wilmot and Frederick raced downstairs to the rest home's lobby and straight into several centimetres of water. It sprayed from the cracks in the walls and fountained up between the floor tiles.

"What happened?" asked Suzy. "We heard an explosion."

"It's the plumbing!" cried Dorothy, who was splashing around in circles, distributing umbrellas to the nurses. "Where's Fletch? He was supposed to be fixing it!"

With a lot of sloshing and muttered curses, Fletch appeared from a side door. He was dripping wet from head to foot.

"It wasn't me!" he said. "It's the central heatin' boiler down in the basement. The circulator pump's blown. Everythin's backin' up."

Gertrude emerged from the residents' lounge, with Stonker, Ursel and the Old Guard in tow. "Can't you shut off the water supply at the mains?" she said.

"Tried that," said Fletch, a steady trickle of water dripping from the tip of his nose. "It must 'ave been damaged by the quake, because it ain't workin'."

"Then what are we going to do?" said Gertrude. "The water's going to do more damage than the earthquake if we let it carry on like this."

Fletch wiped his dripping nose on his sleeve. "You got a spare pump?"

"No," said Gertrude.

Fletch considered this for a second, while the water lapped around his ankles. "I can probably lash one together, if I can find the parts."

"Then please find them quickly," said Gertrude, her patience clearly at breaking point. "Dorothy? Help me move the Old Guard up to their rooms, please. We can't have them standing around in cold water."

Dorothy set about herding the Old Guard towards the stairs, with Stonker's help. Fletch, meanwhile gave a perfunctory salute and kicked his way through the flood towards the front door. "Fancy comin', Ursel?" he called. "You know your way around a pump."

"Hrrrnk," said Ursel, and lumbered after him.

"And what should we do?" asked Suzy, squeezing against the bannister to give the Old Guard room to get past.

Fletch sucked his breath in through his teeth, then motioned for her to follow. "The more eyes we've got lookin', the quicker we get the job done," he said. Suzy exchanged a determined look with Wilmot and Frederick, and the three of them hurried after Fletch.

Suzy's trainers squelched uncomfortably as she and the others followed Fletch out onto the street. It was fully dark now, but the trolls' clean-up efforts continued undaunted – where the street lamps had failed, they worked by torchlight.

"Where are we supposed to find parts for a pump?" Suzy asked. "It's night-time and there's been an earthquake. I don't think any of the shops are going to be open."

"This is Trollville," Fletch replied, setting off at a brisk trot. "There's always parts goin' beggin' if you know where to look for 'em."

Ursel made a gruff chuckling sound in her throat.

They hurried along for a few minutes, dodging the

growing heaps of fallen masonry that the trolls were piling in the middle of the road, and stepping warily over jagged cracks that yawned open between the cobbles. Fletch led them down one street after another, seemingly at random, until they finally reached a broad crossroads. On the corner opposite them stood what looked like an enormous lean-to shed. Suzy wasn't sure if it had suffered in the quake, but the whole building seemed to be leaning in every direction at once. Its large rolling doors stood open and light spilled out from inside. A sign above the gates read: *T. Lane – Machine Parts Exchanged.*

"Totters will sort us out," said Fletch, joining the steady flow of trolls trooping into the building. Most of them were streaked with grime and dust from the repair work, and Suzy noticed that each of them was carrying some sort of appliance or bit of machinery. Some of these were as simple as light switches and toasters, while others she couldn't even begin to identify.

As they filed in, each troll presented their contraption to a small female troll sitting on a stool just inside the doors. She was as purple and wrinkled as a prune, but her bottle-green eyes were sharp and lively. She peered over a clipboard at each component, scribbled down a quick note with a stub of pencil on a string, and nodded to a large skip beside her. As each new arrival tossed their offering in, she tore a raffle ticket from one of three rolls on a toilet-roll holder on the wall beside her, and handed it over.

"Blue items only," she told the portly young troll in front of Suzy and the others, and handed him a blue ticket. The other ticket rolls were red and yellow, Suzy noticed. The young troll shuffled off, looking disappointed.

"Alright there, Totters?" said Fletch, stepping forward.

She looked him over, no doubt weighing the decision of whether or not to comment on his soaking wet suit. "Fletch," she said at last. "Empty-handed again, I see."

He gave her an easy smile. "I would have brought somethin' but it's been a busy evenin'."

"You're telling me," said Totters. "Lots of people needing parts in a hurry. Speaking of which, what can I do you for?"

"I'm lookin' for a class two triple-valve heat pump. It's pretty urgent, so I brought some helpers with me." He nodded at Suzy and the others. "Everyone? This here is Totters, the owner. There's not a spare part in all of Troll Territory she can't lay her hands on."

Totters cast a disinterested eye over the group before consulting her clipboard. She pursed her lips. "I don't reckon as I've got a triple-valve in stock right now," she said. "But you're welcome to scavenge for parts and make your own." She pulled a handful of tickets from the rolls beside her. "I can do you one red, two yellow and two blue," she said, passing them to Fletch. "That should be enough for whatever you need."

"I dunno what this city would do without you, Tots," said Fletch, palming his tickets. "Just put it on my tab."

Totters made a noise halfway between a laugh and a cough. "It's a good job I like you," she said. "But I've been looking for a Cosmo Venturan power adaptor, if you're in that neck of the woods any time soon."

Fletch winked. "I'll bring you half a dozen."

"Get on with you." Totters favoured him with a smile and waved them all through.

Suzy looked around. They were in an indoor scrapyard, piled high with old mechanical detritus. Much of it seemed to be railway-related – signal poles stood like a copse of trees in one corner, while an assortment of wheels, sleepers and rails were stacked against the walls. In amongst it all were rows of shelves and a series of large industrial bins, all painted either red, yellow or blue. All were loaded with scrap, and forty or so trolls were jostling for space as they hurriedly inspected their contents.

"So what parts are we looking for?" asked Suzy, raising her voice over the babble and clatter.

Fletch pressed a blue ticket into her hand. "Check

every blue bin and shelf," he said. "See if you can't find me a nice length of pipe."

"No problem," she said. "I'll meet you back here in five minutes."

All the shelves and bins she could see were surrounded by a scrum of trolls, so she headed deeper into the building, down aisles of colour-coded shelves and past the hulk of an old troll steam locomotive, which dominated the centre of the scrapyard. The further she went, the quieter things became, until the commotion of the crowd faded to a background hum.

She found herself wondering just how long she was going to have to stay in Trollville. While she had been looking forward to seeing the city again, she hadn't expected to end up trapped here. It was bad enough not being able to head out aboard the Express, but she couldn't go home either. Would the trains be running tomorrow? Or the next day? What would she tell her parents when Fletch finally broke the sleeping spell and woke them up? They might have been asleep for days by then!

She was still turning the question over in her mind when she realized she wasn't alone. She had rounded the rear corner of the old locomotive into the dingy back end of the scrapyard. Some way ahead of her, through the pools of shadow, was a troll sorting through a yellow bin.

He wore a heavy black donkey jacket, fingerless gloves and baggy trousers. His skin was a stony grey, and there was a look of intense concentration on his face. If he noticed her at all, he didn't react.

"There's got to be *something* here that fits!" she heard him mutter.

Something about him made her pause. She had the uncanny impression that she had seen him somewhere before. She searched her memory, trying to imagine how they could possibly have met. Had he been at Grinding Halt? It seemed unlikely.

Before she could get any closer, something large dropped out of the air and landed behind the troll with barely a sound. It was a figure, tall and broad-shouldered, shrouded in a cape and hood of midnight blue. It reared up over the troll, and Suzy was about to call out a warning when the hooded figure spoke.

"What are you doing here, you fool?" The voice was deep, and as thick and smooth as honey. The grey troll whirled around in terror.

"Boss!" he said, pressing his back to the bin. Meanwhile Suzy shrank back behind the cover of the old locomotive, but poked her head out to keep the two figures in sight.

"I-I'm still looking for parts to fix the drill," the troll stammered. "I just need some copper piping."

"And have you found any?"

The troll swallowed audibly. "No."

The hooded figure reached out and caught the troll by the lapels of his coat, lifting him bodily off the ground. Suzy stared in horror at the figure's hand – its skin was thick and scaly, and the fingers ended in long black curving talons. She couldn't guess what sort of face lay within the shadow of the hood, but the troll shut his eyes and turned away from it, too scared to look.

"I hired you to do a job," the figure snarled. "You're supposed to be the best in the business."

"And I am, I swear!" said the troll, his feet kicking uselessly in mid-air. Suzy noticed, for the first time, that his boots were encrusted with some sort of glittering yellow powder. "How many safes and bank vaults have I broken into for you? Loads! I've never failed you!"

"You failed me tonight," said the figure. "This is the biggest heist of our careers, and not only did your drill fail to break open the vault, it set off an earthquake that almost killed us."

They caused the earthquake? Suzy couldn't help but gasp. It was a tiny sound, but the cloaked figure dropped the troll immediately, and turned to scan the shadows. A pair of huge round golden eyes stared out from inside the hood. They seemed to glow with an inner fire, except for the pupils, which were large and black as night. A hunter's eyes. Suzy drew her head back before they could pinpoint her, and waited for the sound of the figure's footsteps to approach her hiding place. But there was just a moment's silence before he spoke again.

"We've wasted enough time. I want the drill repaired and the vault split wide open by dawn. Understood?"

"I understand, boss, it's just…"

"Just what?"

The troll seemed to be considering his next words very carefully. "It's this whole job, boss. I don't like it."

A long, slow hiss of displeasure emerged from the hood, and Suzy felt a renewed prickle of fear on the troll's behalf. She inched her head out from behind the locomotive again, and saw the figure circling the troll. She got another glimpse of those large, lamp-like eyes. The troll avoided looking at them.

"I don't like being stuck down there so far under the ground," the troll said. "Those caves weren't meant for the likes of you and me. And I reckon the ancient trolls left the vault down there because they didn't want anyone to mess with it."

"Of course they didn't want anyone to mess with it, you clod!" his boss replied. "All their riches are locked inside it. Diamonds as big as boulders. Enough gold to buy the Ivory Tower! You seemed happy enough to take the job when I promised you a share."

The troll shuffled uncomfortably. "I know. But that was before the earthquake."

"Then make sure it doesn't happen again."

"But that's just it, boss, I can't! As soon as the drill touched the vault, the quake started. And the more power we used, the worse it got. It was like the vault was fighting back."

"Are you saying you can't open it?"

"I'm saying if the drill's motor hadn't blown when it did, we'd have brought the whole cave down on ourselves. You can see for yourself what the quake did to Trollville."

"Trollville doesn't matter," his boss replied, prompting a flash of anger in Suzy. "If the vault wants to put up a fight, we'll just hit back harder."

"But, boss! If we start drilling again, the whole city could collapse!"

"Let it. By the time we're finished, you'll be rich enough to build your own city and rule it as king. Who will be left to stop you?"

"Me!" shouted Suzy, and immediately clamped her mouth shut. The word had escaped her before she had even realized she was going to speak, and now both the hooded figure and the troll were looking around in surprise.

She stepped into view, her blood coursing like ice water in her veins. She squeezed her hands into fists, determined not to show any fear.

"A spy!" said the hooded figure.

"No," Suzy replied. "Just a Postie in the right place at the right time."

"I don't believe you." Except for his eyes, the figure's face remained hidden by the shadows of the hood. "You're working for that meddling Cloudwright, aren't you?"

"The meddling who?" said Suzy.

"I should have known he wouldn't have the courage to reclaim his property for himself, but I'm surprised he sent a girl to do it."

Suzy stiffened at the insult. "I have no idea what you're talking about," she said, sharply. "But I'm not going to let you destroy Trollville."

"No?" The hooded figure sounded amused. "Look me in the eyes and say that." He fixed her with a hard stare, and Suzy met it unflinchingly.

Then, little by little, she realized she really wasn't afraid any more. A strange calm had overtaken her, as though the smouldering coals of his eyes were warming her whole body, making her feel safe and reassured. She had nothing to fear. All she had to do was keep looking. Keep looking into those eyes…

"That's it," said the figure, raising his hands. His talons were as sharp as knives, but Suzy hardly noticed. They couldn't hurt her – she was too comfortable.

"Boss?" Suzy heard the troll's voice as if from very far away. "Boss, stop it! Let's just get out of here."

Slowly and calmly, with his hands outstretched, the hooded figure advanced.

"Suzy!"

It was Wilmot's voice, and Suzy blinked at the sound of it. In an instant, the spell on her mind was broken. She saw the grasping hands reaching for her and threw herself sideways. The figure's talons closed on empty air, and he hissed with frustration.

"Just stay still and let me kill you!" he said, raising his hand to strike.

There was a bellowing roar, and he froze. Suzy scrambled clear and saw that Ursel, Wilmot, Frederick and Fletch were racing down the aisle towards her. She almost laughed with relief at the sight of them.

"Leave her alone!" shouted Frederick.

The grey-skinned troll had run for cover behind his boss. "What do we do now?" he cried.

Ursel reared onto her hind legs and roared again,

so loud that Suzy had to cover her ears.

"Back to the caves!" the figure cried. He turned and grabbed the troll under the arms. Then, with a whoosh and a snap, his cloak split open down the back and two enormous feathered wings emerged. Their span was so large that they swept bits of scrap off nearby shelves, and their feathers were golden-brown tipped with silver. Suzy just had time to ponder how beautiful they were before the figure sprang into the air, still carrying the troll. Ursel reared onto her hind legs and tried to grab the trailing end of his cloak, but he was already out of reach.

"I'll remember your faces," the figure spat. "And I'll make sure you all regret this!"

"Frowlf!" Ursel growled.

"Language!" said Wilmot.

With another beat of his wings, the figure rocketed straight up and through an open skylight in the roof, the troll dangling from his arms. Then they were gone.

"Are you hurt?" said Wilmot, racing to Suzy's side and helping her up.

"Just a bit shaken," she said. "Thanks for the rescue."

"Just in the nick of time too, by the looks of it," said Fletch, looking warily at the skylight. "We found the parts we needed and came looking for you."

Other trolls came running now, drawn by the noise.

Soon, a small crowd surrounded them.

"Who were those two reprobates anyway?" asked Fletch. "And what were they up to?"

That was when the true scale of everything she had overheard struck Suzy. Her legs felt suddenly weak, so she sat down and stared blankly at the spot from which the troll and his boss had lifted off. The troll had left a pair of gritty yellow boot-prints behind. They sparkled slightly.

"What is it?" said Wilmot, dropping to his knees beside her. "What's wrong?"

"Trollville's in really big trouble," she said. "There's going to be another earthquake."

"What?" said Frederick. "How can you know that?"

"I'll explain everything," she replied. "But first we've got to warn people."

6

BACK IN BUSINESS

Suzy returned to the rest home with the others, where she reported her story to an increasingly worried-looking Gertrude and Dorothy. They sat halfway up the stairs, keeping their feet dry, while the Old Guard gathered with waterproofs and umbrellas on the landing, and listened in respectful silence.

"And you say they plan to start the drilling again before dawn?" asked Gertrude.

"Yes, as long as they can repair their drill," said Suzy. "And they only need a few bits of pipe for that."

"Then we have to assume that they'll manage it," Gertrude said. "That means we're all in danger."

"We have to stop them," said Suzy. "I know they're in a cave somewhere nearby. They said it was made by the ancient trolls."

"But nobody knows where those caves are hidden," said Stonker, his brows knitted together. "Or if they're even real."

"They're real alright," said Suzy. "And the two I overheard have found a way in."

"This is all well an' good," said Fletch. "But while you're all chinwaggin', I've got a boiler to fix." He picked up a canvas sack filled with the parts they had brought back from Totters' junkyard, and splashed away towards the basement with it.

"I don't know what to do," said Suzy.

There was a moment of silence while everyone thought.

"I've got it!" burst out Dorothy. "We'll talk to Kevin."

"Who's Kevin?" asked Frederick.

"He's my cousin-in-law's niece's husband," she replied. "I used to babysit him when he was little. But he's all grown up now and joined the police. He still knows to listen to his Aunty Dorothy though. Just you wait and see."

Trollville's central police station proved to be a big squat box of a building in the heart of the Overside. Kevin, by contrast, was a pale and skinny troll, almost lost from view behind the assortment of old-fashioned rotary phones, piles of paperwork and abandoned mugs of tea that covered the station's reception desk. He was holding a phone receiver to each ear, and a third in the crook of one elbow, while valiantly trying to take notes with a pen gripped between his teeth.

"Hello, Kevin," said Dorothy, slapping her hand down on the desk. "We need a word, my dear."

Kevin looked at her with an expression of dawning horror, and spat the pen out. "Aunt Dorothy!" he said. "You haven't got another parking ticket, have you?"

"It's bigger than that," said Dorothy, manoeuvring Suzy to stand at the desk beside her. "There's a crime in progress, and this young lady needs to speak to someone important about it. The higher up the chain, the better."

"No can do," said Kevin. "I mean, there's nobody here except me. Everyone's out helping with the clean-up or trying to catch the king."

"The king?" said Suzy.

Kevin nodded as best he could without dropping the phones. "He took off from Grinding Halt on a jet pack and hasn't come back down yet. We're tracking him as best we can."

"Then she'll just have to speak to you," said Dorothy. "It's urgent."

"So is everything else," said Kevin. "I've got the palace, the mayor's office and the Chief Superintendent on the line."

Dorothy leaned over the desk and brought her finger down on the phones, one after the other, cutting off the calls. "There. Problem solved."

Kevin dropped the receivers and made a small, strangled noise in his throat. "That's probably an arrestable offence!"

"You can call them back in a minute and tell them everything Suzy has to say," said Dorothy. "You'll thank me later."

Kevin looked around the group, realized that this was an argument he wasn't going to win, and sighed deeply. "Tell me all about it," he said, readying his notebook.

It only took Suzy a few minutes to relate what had happened to her at Totters' place. Kevin didn't comment, although his brow furrowed as the story went on. When she had finished, he leafed back through his notes and sucked on the end of his pen.

"So, just to clarify," he said, "you overheard a male troll and another male person of indeterminate species discussing how they triggered today's earthquake by attempting to drill into a vault full of treasure, buried somewhere underground." He gave her a quizzical look. "Is that about right?"

"Yes," said Suzy, trying to ignore just how ridiculous it all sounded. "They said they were in a cave made by the ancient trolls, and they're going to start the drilling again. You have to stop them before they destroy Trollville!"

Kevin circled a few words in his notepad. "You also say the person who attacked you mentioned a Cloudwright," he said. "Do you have any idea what he could have been talking about?"

"No," said Suzy. "I don't even know what a Cloudwright is."

"That's easy," said Frederick, behind her. "A Cloudwright is a type of sorcerer. They use clouds in their magic."

Kevin added this to his notes. "And you don't know what this Cloudwright has to do with anything?"

Suzy shook her head. She was beginning to feel slightly foolish. "No."

Kevin puffed out his cheeks and closed his notebook. "I honestly don't know what to do with this. The allegations are very serious, but unless we know who we're looking for and where to find them, I don't think there's much the police can do to help."

"But we know they must be *somewhere* underneath Trollville," said Suzy.

Wilmot perked up. "What if they found a way in

through the Uncanny Valley?" he asked.

"Unlikely," said Kevin.

Suzy shook her head. "Sorry, but what's the Uncanny Valley?"

"It's the valley beneath Trollville," said Wilmot. "Nobody knows how deep it is. It's uncharted."

"Which is precisely the problem," said Kevin. "It would take months to search the Valley properly, even if we had the trolls available to do it. And until the clean-up is completed and the king is safely back in the palace, I'm afraid I'm all you've got."

Suzy felt a sickly twist in her stomach. "But we're all in danger!"

"Uuunf," said Ursel. "Rrrrolf, grunf."

"Ursel's right," said Stonker. "If we can't stop the drilling, then we've no choice but to evacuate the city. Immediately."

Kevin's mouth dropped open. "I don't have the authority to do something like that!"

"Then who does?" asked Suzy. She heard the main doors of the station swing open behind her, and Kevin pointed over her shoulder.

"He might."

She turned to see a familiar figure hurrying towards them. "Grotnip!"

The king's courtier slowed as he saw them. "I assume you're all here to volunteer for the search?" he said.

"No," said Suzy. "We need your help. Trollville—"

He waved her into silence. "Then it will have to wait," he said, pushing his way to the desk. "Sergeant, what's the latest?"

"Search teams reported the king heading in a south-westerly direction over Meteor Street a few minutes ago," said Kevin. "But this young Postie here has—"

"Splendid," said Grotnip. "I estimate that he'll be out of fuel in around fifteen minutes. Where would that put him?"

Kevin unrolled a map of the city across the desk and plotted a rough trajectory with his finger. "Assuming he doesn't change his current heading, he should come down somewhere near Gaswork Gardens. Shall I redirect some officers there?"

"Yes," said Grotnip. "And tell them to have some sandwiches ready. His Majesty is always more difficult to handle when he's hungry."

"Very good, sir."

While Kevin reached for the phones, Grotnip turned back to Suzy. "Now, what was it you wanted?"

"There's going to be another earthquake," she said.

"How can you possibly know that?"

"Because I just confronted the people who caused the last one," she said. "We need to evacuate Trollville, tonight, before anyone gets hurt."

"Evacuate?" Grotnip looked incredulous. "What rampant buffoonery is this? How would we move everyone in a single night? The trains are still out of action. Besides, where would they all go? Have you considered food and shelter?"

"Surely it would be better to worry about that once everyone's out of danger?" said Wilmot.

"Indeed," said Stonker. "Can you give the order or not?"

"No," said Grotnip flatly. "Such an order would have to come from the Council of Elders or His Majesty himself."

"Fine," Suzy shot back. "We'll talk to the Council of Elders then."

"Um…" Wilmot raised a hand. "I'm afraid there isn't one at the moment. They all resigned in disgrace when people learned that Lord Meridian had been controlling them. We haven't nominated any new candidates yet."

"So it's just the king?" said Suzy.

"And he won't be persuaded to issue such a decree without some solid evidence," said Grotnip.

"Unless you tell him to," said Dorothy. "Oh, now don't

look at me like that, Mr Grotnip. Half of Troll Territory knows His Majesty couldn't tie his shoelaces without you giving him instructions."

"Madam!" Grotnip flared his nostrils in consternation. "I would never dream of unduly influencing His Majesty's decisions. I merely offer him advice when needed. Which happens to be frequently."

"Then please give him *my* advice," said Suzy, "and tell him to clear the city. He'll save a lot of lives."

"I can't advise His Majesty to take such a radical step on the say-so of a Postie," said Grotnip. "And a deputy, *human* postie at that."

Suzy flushed with embarrassment and anger, but before she could say a word, Wilmot stepped forward and gave Grotnip a hard look.

"Mr Grotnip. Deputy Postal Operative Smith is a valued member of my staff and, as such, has my total support. This city and its people are in danger. We need to act."

Suzy resisted the urge to hug Wilmot as she watched conflicting expressions of annoyance and doubt chase each other across Grotnip's face.

"You don't understand my position," he said. "If we evacuate and avert disaster, His Majesty will be rightly hailed as a hero. But if the decision turns out to be needless

– if we force millions of people out of their homes for no good reason…" He trailed off.

"You're afraid of embarrassing him?" said Suzy, feeling her anger rise.

"It's my job to protect His Majesty from his own mistakes," said Grotnip. "And I work very hard to keep them to a minimum." He regained some of his former confidence and looked Suzy in the eye. "If you can present me with compelling evidence that we are in danger, I will ensure that His Majesty acts on it. Until then, Trollville will soldier bravely on, as it always has."

"But that's crazy!" said Suzy.

"It is my final word on the subject," said Grotnip. "Strong and stable leadership, for a strong and stable city. Good day to you all." He turned on his heel and strode out.

"What a disagreeable fool," said Stonker.

Suzy watched the door swing shut behind Grotnip and felt a cold weight of dread settle in her stomach. "He walked away," she said. "The city's in danger, and he just walked away! How could he?"

"It's not your fault, my dear," said Dorothy. "I expect he'll change his mind once the ground gives way underneath him. But before that happens, we need to do what little we can and help Gertrude and the others evacuate."

"And we've still got to find some way of getting you home," said Wilmot.

"No!" Suzy protested. The idea of going home and leaving Trollville to its fate stuck in her chest like a knife. What did Wilmot expect her to do? Just carry on going to school, doing her homework and pretending everything was normal while she waited for news? And what if the news never came? What if the worst happened and the city was destroyed before her friends could get to safety? She would never see them, or the Impossible Places, again.

"I won't let this happen," she said. "We need to do something!"

"I quite agree," said Stonker. "But what do you suggest?"

"Grotnip wants evidence," said Suzy. "So we need to find him some. And quickly."

"But how are we supposed to do that?" said Frederick. "You heard what Kevin said. A search could take ages."

Suzy teased at the edges of the question with her mind, looking for a way into it. At last, she found one.

"What about the Cloudwright?" she said. "The creature with the wings talked about having taken something from a Cloudwright. He thought I was there to help get it back."

"You think the Cloudwright might be looking for those two as well?" said Wilmot.

Suzy shrugged. "Maybe. And if he is, perhaps we can

work together to find them."

"That's not a bad idea," said Frederick. "There aren't many Cloudwrights out there, and as far as I know they all work in the same place."

"Where's that?" said Suzy.

"A place called Cloud Forge."

"Of course!" Wilmot brightened. "I've made a few deliveries there in the past."

And just like that, the plan clicked into place in Suzy's mind. "How about making another one?" she said.

"What do you mean?" said Wilmot.

A slow grin spread over Suzy's face. "Let's take the Express to Cloud Forge."

"Now hang on a moment, young lady," said Stonker, drawing himself up. "We can't just go haring off into the night. Not in Trollville's hour of need."

"But Trollville needs us to do this," she said. "We might be its only hope of stopping the next earthquake. Nobody else is going to do anything."

"Hey!" Kevin, who finally seemed to have abandoned any hope of returning to the phones, looked hurt. "I'm doing my best."

"But even if you can find the Cloudwright," said Frederick, ignoring him, "what makes you think he'll tell you anything?"

"Because people should always be pleased to see their Postie," said Suzy. "There's a whole chapter about it in *The Knowledge*." She shut her eyes and dredged up the passage from her memory. "*A good Postal Operative is not only courteous and efficient but embodies the ideals of honesty, courage and trust. A dependable figure who is always to be welcomed.*" She opened her eyes again. "And then there's three pages about what to do if you're invited in for tea. Basically, never take the last biscuit."

"Oh, spot-on!" said Wilmot. He and Suzy grinned at each other.

"So wait a minute," said Frederick. "Your big plan to save the city is just to chat to people until one of them tells you something useful?"

"You'd be surprised how hard it is to stop them sometimes," said Wilmot. "I think it's a good plan."

Suzy positively glowed with pride.

"But you can't take the Express anywhere," said Kevin, who was looking increasingly exasperated. "All the rail lines out of the city are closed, remember?"

That brought the conversation to an abrupt halt – until Dorothy leaned over the reception desk and picked up one of the phone receivers. "You said you were talking to the mayor's office? Perhaps you could ask him to reopen just one line. Temporarily."

Kevin's face went a pale green. "I'm really not supposed to do things like that."

"We'd only need it open for ten minutes," said Stonker.

"And you'd be the hero who helped save Trollville when no one else was willing," added Dorothy, waggling her eyebrows. "I'd tell your mum as much. She'd be ever so proud."

Kevin's pallor receded, and a blush of pink appeared in his cheeks. "I'll do my best," he said.

"Good man!" said Stonker, clapping Kevin on the shoulder. "I suppose that means we'd better get a move on." He rubbed his hands together in anticipation.

"Great!" said Frederick. "Lead the way."

Stonker looked at him with surprise. "You're coming with us?"

"Yes," said Frederick. "You'll need my help if you're going to Cloud Forge. It's a very exclusive place."

"Meaning what?" said Suzy.

"It's just that they're used to dealing with very important people, that's all," he said. "You know – people like me. Imagine how thrilled they'll be when the Chief Librarian of the Ivory Tower arrives. I could really help." He gave them such a hopeful smile that Suzy found it hard to be quite as annoyed with him as she wanted to be.

"What do the rest of you think?" she asked.

"We certainly need all the help we can get," said Wilmot. "But—"

"Excellent!" said Frederick. "I promise you won't regret it."

Wilmot nodded, but vaguely, and did his best to avoid the hard stares that Stonker and Ursel were levelling at him.

"Then why are we all still standing here?" said Suzy. "Let's go!"

Platform one hundred was just as they had left it, except that the moon was now riding high above the city, its light slanting in through the broken glass panels to spotlight the shrouded form of the Express.

"Still sleeping soundly," said Stonker. "What do you say we wake the old girl up?"

Suzy felt a twinge of nervous anticipation in her stomach as Stonker crossed to the tassel that still hung down from the beam overhead.

"I was so looking forward to getting the seal of royal approval," said Wilmot.

"Rowlf," said Ursel. "Hrrrrrunf."

"Ursel's right," said Stonker. "There'll be plenty of time for dedications and parties later. Right now, it's time to get to work." He cleared his throat. "Ladies and gentlemen, the Impossible Postal Express." Then he pulled on the tassel, and the sheet was drawn away.

The Express had changed. It took Suzy a moment to process it, but as soon as she did, all her apprehension vanished.

Standing at the head of the train was the *Belle de Loin*, the mighty locomotive that pulled the Express. The trolls had worked their usual engineering magic – perhaps literally – and the mismatched boiler was just as she remembered it, with the addition of a fresh coat of dark green paint. Most of the driving wheels had been replaced, although they still didn't quite match, and the new chimney looked even more wonky than the old one.

But that wasn't all. The red-brick cottage that had served as the driver's cab was gone, replaced by a grander, more formidable structure that looked like a miniature Tudor mansion, complete with stained wooden beams and white plaster. Three storeys high, and top-heavy, it leaned at a slightly drunken angle, as though it was on the verge of collapsing.

Suzy hurried up to it, taking in every new detail. "It's incredible," she exclaimed. "I love it!"

A new tender was coupled to the rear of the cab, identical to the old one except for a coat of green paint to match the boiler and, behind that, the welcome sight of the sorting carriage, its red paint now restored and shining.

Finally, at the end of the train, was something brand-new. Suzy had to look twice to make sure she wasn't imagining it: a small beige caravan, barely six metres long, of the sort she had once stayed in on a wet camping trip in north Wales.

"What's that?" she said.

"That's our new Hazardous Environment Carriage," said Wilmot. "Good, isn't it?"

"Um, maybe," she said. The last H.E.C. had looked like a submarine on wheels.

"It's a bit small," said Frederick.

"Compact," Wilmot corrected him. "It's got all the latest features."

"Chop-chop, everyone," said Stonker. "Let's get started."

They all followed him up the ladder to the metal gangway that ran along the side of the *Belle*'s boiler to the cab's front door. It was made of old warped wood, painted black, and a large brass knocker jutted out from it, shaped like a troll's face with a ring through its nose. Stonker pulled a key from his pocket, unlocked the door and held it open for them.

A smell of warm bread and wood polish escaped, and Suzy paused on the threshold to fill her lungs with it. *Now this is what home smells like*, she decided.

She took care to wipe her feet on the mat, and stepped inside.

She found herself in what must once have been the kitchen of the old house: thick wooden beams supported the ceiling; copper pots and pans hung from the walls; a sink stood beneath one window, fed by an old-fashioned water pump; and a cast-iron stove occupied the fireplace in the front wall.

"It's all so different," said Suzy, still taking it in.

"She's better than ever," Stonker confirmed. "We've got a new twin-injection banana boiler. If you thought the *Belle* was fast before, she'll really knock your socks off now – quite literally. It's a fault with the new magical overlay: incompatible with socks above a certain speed, for some reason. We're still working out the bugs. And then, of course, there's this." He patted the badly cracked mantelpiece of white marble above the fireplace. "We salvaged the hearth from the wreck at the Ivory Tower. That's why she's still the *Belle de Loin*, despite all the changes; she's got the same heart."

Suzy smiled and rested her own hand on the mantelpiece alongside Stonker's. "I'm glad," she said.

Stonker nodded his approval. "Ursel and I need a few minutes to get the boiler up to full steam," he said. "If you have to prepare anything for the journey, I suggest you do it now. Time is against us." He turned to the *Belle*'s controls – a twisting mass of pipes and dials that covered the rest of the cab's front wall – and began making adjustments.

"Come on, Postal Operative Smith," said Wilmot. "To the sorting carriage!"

"Yes, Postmaster," Suzy chimed. A thrill ran through her. This was what she had been studying so hard for all those weeks – she was finally going to be a Postie again, and this time she wouldn't make any mistakes. She couldn't afford to. The fate of Trollville depended on it.

"What should I do?" said Frederick.

"Be a good chap and make sure the track is clear of debris," said Stonker. "And then we'd all better hope that young Kevin was able to get the line open."

Frederick hurried back outside. Ursel, meanwhile, was pulling bunches of bananas out of a metal hatch in the rear wall of the cab. Sparks of blue energy fizzed and crackled across her paws as she carried them to the stove and tossed them in. These were fusion bananas, the strange power source that fuelled the *Belle*'s magical boiler. They were potent but unstable, and Suzy was quite happy to leave them in Ursel's care while she followed Wilmot to the cab's rear door.

He beamed at her and, with a flourish, pulled it open. But before he could react, an avalanche of mail spilled out of the doorway and knocked him flat on his back. "Oh," he said. "I forgot about the mess."

Suzy waded through the piles of letters and parcels, and helped him to his feet. "What's all this post doing here?" she said. The door should have led outside, to the gap between the locomotive and the tender. Instead, she found herself looking at the interior of the sorting carriage.

"Where's the tender gone?" she said, bewildered.

"It's still there," said Wilmot. "But we don't need to go scrambling over it to get from one bit of the train to another any more – the refurbishment team cut out the space between the doors. We've now got instant access from the cab to the sorting carriage, and from the sorting carriage to the H.E.C."

"That's definitely an improvement," said Suzy, who remembered only too clearly her precarious trip across the fusion bananas piled high on the old tender. Although getting into the sorting carriage now wasn't a markedly different experience, as she and Wilmot had to scramble up the shifting pile of mail on all fours just to reach the doorway. "Why is there so much of it?" she asked as they

110

half-climbed, half-swam through the mess into the sorting carriage beyond.

"We've been delivering as much as we can by remote spell and carrier griffin, but there's still a bit of a backlog," he said. "It's amazing how quickly it all builds up, isn't it?"

Once inside, Suzy was astonished at the change. The sorting carriage was Wilmot's pride and joy – a mobile post office, where mail was sorted and readied for delivery. It had been cosy and neat during her last visit, but now it looked like an untidy storeroom. The shelves and pigeonholes overflowed with mail, bundles of letters were stacked like bricks from floor to ceiling everywhere she looked, and Wilmot's desk was almost lost beneath an untidy pile of packages, rolls of brown paper, and bundles of loose string as big as tumbleweeds.

"We're bound to find something for Cloud Forge in all this," she said.

"Oh!" Wilmot exclaimed. "Before we do, I've got something for you."

He fought his way over to his desk and, to Suzy's surprise, disappeared underneath it. She heard him rummaging around for a few seconds, before he popped back up. He was holding something big in his hands.

"It's as much a part of a Postie's uniform as the badge, really," he said, picking his way through the chaos to

111

her side. "And you can't do the job properly without it." He held the object out to her – it was a large leather satchel, fastened with a brass buckle in the shape of the Impossible Postal Service crest.

"A delivery satchel!" she cried, feeling a wonderful swirl of pride and excitement as she secured the strap over her shoulder. "Thank you!"

"You're very welcome," he said, blushing with pride. "Let me show you how to use it."

"No need," she said. "There are two compartments inside. One for post to be delivered, and one for collections." She unfastened the buckle and lifted the flap to demonstrate. "Plus there's a lockable secret pocket inside the lining, for the secure storage of valuables."

"That's right," said Wilmot, looking at her with renewed pride. "I can see my copy of *The Knowledge* has been useful."

"So useful!" said Suzy. She finally had someone to talk to about her months of careful study, and it all came spilling out. "I've read the whole book three times through, cover to cover. I filled a spare exercise book with revision notes. I've even given myself tests."

"I used to do that!" he said, grinning. "Let's try one now. Where will we find the post for Cloud Forge? The postcode starts with CF."

Suzy closed her eyes and searched her memory. "*In the regulation layout of a sorting carriage,*" she recited, "*postcodes are arranged in alphabetical order, clockwise, when viewed from the Postmaster's desk.*" She opened her eyes and looked around the carriage with new understanding. "So if I stand here…" She waded through the post to stand behind Wilmot's desk. "Any postcode starting with *C* should be on…" She looked around again. "…that set of shelves over there."

"Excellent work," said Wilmot.

After a brief search, during which she dislodged another avalanche of mail, she found what she was looking for.

"Got some!" she said, holding aloft a small bundle of envelopes. "And they're nearly all addressed to Cloudwrights."

"Excellent work," said Wilmot. "Let's just hope that one of them is the person we're looking for."

He was interrupted by a shudder that ran through the carriage and made its old boards groan. Suzy felt her stomach trying to crawl up her throat as more letters rained down around them.

"Another earthquake!" she cried.

But the tremor died away as quickly as it had started, and Stonker's voice reached them from the cab.

"Don't worry, that was just the *Belle* clearing her

throat," he called. "It means we're up to full steam. Everyone in position, please."

"Come on," said Wilmot. "I need to talk to Mr Stonker before we leave." They scrabbled back up the mounds of mail, through the door and tumbled into the cab just as Frederick re-entered through the front.

"The track's clear," he announced. "And the signal just turned green."

"Excellent," said Stonker. "Kevin came through for us. Strap in, everyone. We're off!"

"Wait!" said Wilmot.

Stonker paused with his hand on the controls. "What is it, Postmaster? We're all ready to go."

"But I'm not," said Wilmot. "Because I'm not coming."

They all stared at him in shock.

"What?" said Suzy. "But you have to!"

"I can't." His expression was apologetic, but his voice was firm. "Someone has to stay behind to operate the station's dispatch controls, or the Express won't be able to go anywhere."

"Good grief!" said Stonker. "I hadn't thought of that." His brow furrowed. "We'll just have to find someone else to operate them. We can't leave you behind."

"There isn't time," said Wilmot. "The line will only be open for a few minutes."

"But what about me?" said Suzy. "I can't do this without you."

He smiled at her. "Actually, I think you can. You've come a long way in just two months, Suzy. I wouldn't leave the Express if I didn't think the post was in good hands."

Suzy blushed. She wanted to feel proud, but she mostly felt upset and disappointed. And very, very nervous. "Thanks," she mumbled.

Stonker put his hand out. "It won't be the same without you, Postmaster."

"Thank you," said Wilmot, shaking Stonker's hand. He did the same with Frederick and accepted a bear hug from Ursel, before turning to Suzy. "You'll do brilliantly," he told her.

His calm assurance made her suck in a breath and stick her chest out. If he could be brave, so could she. "I'll do my best to make you proud," she said.

He smiled. "I already am," he said, and slipped out through the front door.

"Grownf," said Ursel.

"Yes, indeed," said Stonker. "A fine lad. Just like his dad." He brushed away what might have been the beginnings of a tear.

A moment later, there was a loud crackling sound

from outside the cab. It was followed by a whine of feedback, as platform one hundred's PA system sprang into life.

"Hello?" Wilmot's voice boomed through the speakers, loud and distorted. "It's me again. I'm at the dispatch controls. Let me know when you're ready to launch."

"Better hold onto something, everyone," said Stonker with a manic glint in his eye. "This is going to have quite a kick to it."

Ursel spread her arms wide, and Suzy and Frederick ran to her, letting her enfold them both. Suzy had a clear view through the cab's front window to the opening in the glass wall ahead. Moonlight glinted off the tracks of the viaduct that wound away across the rooftops outside. She gripped Ursel's arm and tensed her body.

Stonker released the brake lever and opened the *Belle*'s whistle. The piercing shriek echoed around Grinding Halt.

"Good luck, all of you," came Wilmot's voice. Then the Express blasted forward, and Suzy was thrown back into the soft fur of Ursel's chest. They were moving at an incredible speed – Suzy felt as though a gigantic hand was pressing her flat into Ursel, and the Overside raced past in a blur. Fear and excitement bubbled up inside her, and she wasn't sure whether to laugh or scream. *I really missed this*, she thought. Within a minute, they had plunged into a tunnel, leaving Trollville behind.

Stonker clung to the controls, leaning against the G-forces like a man walking into a gale. "It's nice to be back in business!" he cried over the scream of the wheels. "Next stop, Cloud Forge!"

Suzy smiled back. Beneath her excitement though, she was still in shock at Wilmot's decision to stay behind. She felt vulnerable without him by her side, and she began to worry that all her studying wouldn't be enough.

But no. She had proved herself this far, and Wilmot was trusting her to do the job. This was no time for insecurities. Not when everyone in Trollville was depending on her.

7

PLAN B

The worst of the flooding had receded by the time Wilmot returned to the rest home. The nurses still bustled back and forth, but now carried suitcases bursting at the seams with clothes and piled them by the front door. Fletch stood in a puddle in the middle of the lobby, drying inside his ears with an old rag. His eyes widened at the sight of Wilmot.

"What're you doin' back?" he said. "Yer Aunt Dorothy said you were leavin' on the Express."

"The others did," said Wilmot. "I came back to help."

Fletch grunted. "Yer mum's already got everythin' organized. The best thing you and I can do is keep out of the way. We'll be headin' for the hills soon."

"But what about the rest of the city?" Wilmot asked. "We've got to warn people!"

"Yer aunt's phonin' everyone she can think of and tellin' 'em to spread the word," said Fletch. "But I don't know how much good it's goin' to do. Some of the phone lines are still down, and I don't reckon people are goin' to be too keen to pack up and run in the middle of the night without someone official breathin' down their necks about it."

Wilmot regarded the growing pile of luggage by the door and felt his spirits sink. Fletch was right – even if Aunt Dorothy could persuade a few hundred people to leave the city, they would be abandoning more than a million others to whatever fate awaited them. Everything depended on Suzy and the crew finding the Cloudwright. But what if they couldn't?

There has to be something else we can do, he thought. *We need a Plan B.*

"Fletch," he said. "The troll that Suzy met in the scrapyard…Suzy forgot to mention it at the police station, but she told us his boots were covered in yellow dust. And he left those footprints behind. Do you remember?"

"What of it?" said Fletch. "He must have been steppin' in all sorts of stuff in that scrapyard. We all were."

"Yes, but none of us ended up with yellow dust on us,"

Wilmot said. "Which means the troll must have picked it up before he went looking for his bit of pipe."

Fletch considered this for a few seconds. "Sounds logical. But where?"

"I don't know," said Wilmot. "But if we can figure that out, we might get a clue about where he'd been before we met him."

Understanding dawned in Fletch's eyes. "And you reckon that'll tell you how to find this cavern of theirs."

"Maybe," said Wilmot. "It's worth a try, don't you think? If we can find the cavern, and the drill, there might not be any need to evacuate Trollville at all. We can just send the police down to arrest everybody."

Fletch puffed his cheeks out. "It's not much to go on. How many places in Trollville can you find yellow dust?"

"I don't know," said Wilmot. "But I know some trolls who might."

The carpet of the residents' lounge was still soaking wet, and squelched heavily underfoot as Wilmot and Fletch entered. The Old Guard were all here, dressed and in their outdoor coats, waiting for the word to leave. They brightened at the sight of Wilmot.

"Hello, Postmaster!"

"Quite a kerfuffle we're having, isn't it?"

"Are you all packed?"

Wilmot returned the greetings, then cleared his throat. "Do any of you know where I could find yellow dust near Trollville? Not like normal dust – it's heavier, and it glitters."

The Old Guard turned to one another. There was a lot of whispering and nodding.

"Like rock dust?" said Mr Rumpo, a troll with a lopsided face and half an ear missing.

"Maybe," said Wilmot. "Do you know where it comes from?"

Mr Rumpo turned back to the others, and they went into a huddle. There was some more murmured conversation, and more nodding. At last, the Old Guard all turned to face him.

"It sounds like lapis luteus," said Mrs Falgercarb. "Quite a rare type of stone. In fact, I've only ever seen it in one place in Trollville. The old Hobb's End mine, down on the south-east side."

"The Hobb's End mine?" said Wilmot. "I've never heard of it."

There was a chorus of "oooooh"s and "aaaaah"s from the Old Guard.

121

"It's a very sorry tale," said Mr Trellis, stepping forward. "My mother used to sit me on her knee and tell it to me." He cleared his throat, and the others gathered around him. "Years ago, when our grandparents were building Trollville, they dug a mine into the face of the Uncanny Valley. They mined all the best stone, and used it to build the city we know today." He gestured with his cane at the room surrounding them. "But one day something went wrong. They dug too deep, there was some sort of disaster, and a whole tunnel fell in. A lot of good trolls were lost that day." The Old Guard nodded in solemn agreement. "The survivors refused to go back. They claimed the whole mine was cursed. Some even said they'd tunnelled into something weird and unnatural that was best left buried. So they sealed off the mine, and Hobb's End has been sitting there ever since. Abandoned."

"We used to dare each other to knock on the gates of the old mine workings when we were children," said Mr Rumpo.

"I remember!" said Mrs Falgercarb. "They used to say that if you knocked three times, the ghosts of the old miners would knock back."

Wilmot repressed a slight shudder. "And what about the dust? This lapis luteus?"

"It's debris from the mine," said Mr Trellis. "Scrap.

Too soft to build with. The houses around Hobb's End used to be covered in it. That's why nobody lives there any more."

Wilmot's brain fizzed with all this new information. An abandoned mine on an abandoned street. A disaster deep underground. He exchanged a glance with Fletch.

"I hope you're not thinkin' what I think you're thinkin'," Fletch said.

Wilmot gave a small shrug. "It certainly sounds like it could be the place, don't you think?"

"The place for what?" asked Mr Trellis, shuffling over. "What's on your mind, Postmaster?"

"It's nothing really," said Wilmot. He was conscious of the rest of the Old Guard clustering around, doing their best to eavesdrop. "But if I wanted to go and have a quick look at Hobb's End, how would I get there from here?"

Fletch winced. "You can't go lookin' for it now. Your mum'll go bonkers!"

"I'm just going to take a quick look for signs of anything suspicious," said Wilmot. "I'll come straight back. Mum will hardly know I've gone."

Mr Trellis smacked his lips and chuckled. "On the trail of those n'er-do-wells who assaulted poor Suzy, I'll be bound." He gave Wilmot an exaggerated wink. "Did I ever tell you about the time I tracked down a gang of mail thieves in the custard mills of Splott?"

"Yes," said Wilmot. "Often. Now please, Mr Trellis, I'm running out of time."

Mr Trellis winked again. "Just head to the most south-easterly corner of the Underside," he said. "Where the city meets the rock face. You can't miss it."

"Thank you," said Wilmot. "I'll be back before you know it."

"Don't fear, Postmaster. Fletch and I will cover for you."

Fletch scowled. "I don't fancy gettin' on the wrong side of your mum," he said.

"You won't have to," said Wilmot, backing towards the door. "Tell her it's a scouting mission. What could go wrong?"

THE NAVIGATION ROOM

By the time the Express emerged from the tunnel, Suzy was already at the cab window, anxious to see what awaited her. Blazing sunlight streamed in, forcing her to shield her eyes, and it was a moment before she could blink away the glare and look out. And down.

The Express was racing along a railway line cut into the side of a narrow mountain ravine. Its steep slopes were clad in dense tropical foliage and fell away to a ribbon of surging white water below.

Blade-like peaks of dark grey rock pierced the jungle beyond; wisps of cloud clung to their tips, waterfalls spilled down their sides, and rainbows arced from one peak to another, like ghostly bridges. It was beautiful.

It was also sweltering, and a thick muggy heat began to squeeze its way into the cab from outside. The sun had clearly been up for hours here.

Suzy still wasn't entirely sure how time worked in the Union – each Impossible Place seemed to keep different hours, so it could be early morning in one while it was late afternoon in another – which was why she had made sure to bring her watch from home. No matter what time it was in Trollville, or Cloud Forge, or anywhere else, her watch kept ticking away the seconds at the same steady pace, so she could tell exactly how much time had passed at home. Right now, the watch told her it was almost midnight there, and she felt a little thrill of excitement. She was never normally up so late. She pictured her street: the rows of identical houses with their darkened windows, a hundred sleeping souls waiting for their alarm clocks to start a new day of work, school and routine. And here she was, riding with her friends into a magical land, half a reality away, under the light of a different sun. It was hard not to feel a touch of satisfaction at the thought, despite her nagging worries. She was supposed to be at school in the morning, and her parents had work. What would happen if she didn't make it back in time? It seemed a silly thing to worry about when the fate of a whole city was at stake, but Suzy had never deliberately missed school before. It felt strange.

She wished she had Wilmot here to talk to.

"We've not made bad time for our opening run," said Stonker, checking his pocket watch. "The old girl's still warming up. She'll only get faster." He gave Ursel a congratulatory clap on the shoulder.

"Grunk." She clapped him back, almost knocking him over.

"Hey!" Frederick had joined Suzy at the window and was pointing at the sky. "Look at that!"

Suzy looked, and saw a single large cloud hanging in the sky above one of the nearby peaks. Even from this distance, she could tell that it wasn't a normal cloud – it boiled and seethed, releasing forks of lightning in all directions. And deep inside it, silhouetted by the lightning, something moved. Suzy couldn't make it out, but it looked large and alive.

"Oh, wow!" said Frederick. "Is that what I think it is?"

"I have no idea," said Suzy.

"Have you got any binoculars in that satchel?" He was hopping from foot to foot with excitement now.

"Of course not," she said.

Ursel loped past with another pawful of bananas. "Grrurl hrrrrnf," she said, and gestured towards the ceiling with her snout.

"Good point," said Stonker. "Why don't you pop upstairs to the navigation room and take a quick look?"

"We have a navigation room?" said Suzy.

Stonker smiled. "It's new." He pointed to a narrow wooden door in the corner beside the sink. "Straight up the stairs and the first door on your left. But don't be long – we're almost there."

"Come on!" Frederick had already taken off at a run, and Suzy hurried to keep up with him.

A narrow spiral staircase lay behind the door, and they clattered up it to a small landing, where they found another door marked with a compass symbol. Frederick threw it open and tumbled inside, Suzy close at his heels.

"Wow," they both said in unison.

The navigation room took up the whole of the cab's first floor. A long row of windows, made of little diamond panes with old wobbly glass in them, wrapped around the front and side walls, giving a panoramic view of the valley outside. The rear wall, meanwhile, was lined from floor to ceiling with hundreds of pigeonholes, each containing a tightly wound canvas scroll, their ends capped and labelled.

"Are these maps?" asked Suzy.

"Of course," said Frederick. "We've got something like it in the geography section of the Ivory Tower – only ours is much bigger, of course. You unroll them and read them on this." He thumped the heavy wooden table that sat in the middle of the room. It had brass clips at all four corners, presumably to hold the maps flat.

Suzy stepped around it and looked out of the window. The *Belle*'s boiler and chimney were in front of them, the rock face rushed past immediately to their right, and to the left she could see across the ravine to the bizarre storm cloud.

An antique telescope stood on a tripod in front of the windows, and Suzy let Frederick manoeuvre it into position, while she took up one of several pairs of binoculars that rested on the window sill and trained them on the cloud.

They were almost parallel with it now, and she realized just how big it was. Gold-and-pink lightning reached down to scorch the tip of the peak beneath it, and again she saw the dark shape writhing in its centre. She caught her breath in shock. She couldn't be certain, but it looked like there was more than one shape in the cloud. She got the impression of long, snakelike bodies coiling and rolling together.

"This is incredible!" said Frederick, his eye to the telescope. "They're fighting!"

"What are?" she said.

Before he could answer, the cloud emitted a dazzling flash, followed by a clap of thunder loud enough to make the windows rattle. Suzy fought to keep the binoculars in focus as the cloud broke open and something emerged.

"Dragons!" said Frederick.

Suzy's mouth dropped open. The dragon looked like one of the paper ones her class had made for the Chinese New Year celebrations in school. Its head was broad and square, surrounded by a mane of golden fur, but its body was long and serpentine. It had no wings but seemed to swim through the air, the azure scales of its body winking in the light. It opened its mouth and belched a cloud of steam and lightning, accompanied by a low roll of thunder. It rose into the sky above the ravine, pawing at the air with its birdlike claws.

A few seconds later, a second dragon emerged from the cloud. Its scales were red and its mane bright green, and it had clearly come off worse in the fight. Blood ran from several wounds in its side, and it limped away through the sky before finally dropping out of sight behind one of the nearby peaks.

"Dragons are real!" said Suzy, as much to herself as to Frederick.

"Of course they are," said Frederick. "But they're rare. And these are thunder dragons, which are rarer still."

Suzy focused on the spot where the red dragon had vanished, and felt a surge of concern. "You mean they're endangered? Shouldn't we do something to help that red one? It looked hurt."

"It would fry us before we got close," said Frederick. "And they're always fighting. They're very territorial. Besides, if they didn't fight, we wouldn't be here."

She lowered the binoculars and gave him a questioning look. "What do you mean?"

"I mean that any minute now we should see…aha! Here they come!" He pointed, and Suzy saw that a flock of brightly coloured objects had appeared in the air, some way off over the jungle. They couldn't be birds – they were too big and oddly shaped. She trained the binoculars on them.

"They're flying machines!" she said. There were about twenty of them, of all different types and designs. Some were little more than hang-gliders, while others reminded Suzy of the sort of contraptions Leonardo da Vinci had designed: pedal-powered craft with flapping canvas wings and corkscrew propellers. She saw a miniature dirigible, an old-fashioned biplane, and even someone with a jet pack like King Amylum's. And they were all heading towards the cloud in which the dragons had been fighting. "Who are they?"

"The Cloudwrights," said Frederick. "Look at them go!"

"Those are the people we're here to see?" She watched the fleet of craft with renewed interest. One of those pilots might hold the key to stopping the drill and saving Trollville.

Sensing the approaching fleet, the blue dragon twisted in the air, bringing its great shaggy head around to face them. Its maw opened, and Suzy shut her eyes, not wanting to see the destruction that would surely follow. The flash of lightning from the creature's mouth was so bright that she saw it through her eyelids.

But at a cheer from Frederick, she looked again and saw that the aircraft had all scattered like birds, wheeling and banking as the dragon spat a second bolt of lightning after them, and a third. The shots came close, but the aircraft danced clear. The dragon roared in frustration.

Then the craft were past it, making straight for the cloud, which was already beginning to dissipate, going ragged at the edges. In quick succession, they dived into its heart from all directions, bursting in and out of it in a flurry of banking turns.

"What are they doing?" asked Suzy.

"Collecting the spellcloud," said Frederick, his eye still to the telescope. "The dragons make it when they fight. It's the main ingredient in the Cloudwrights' magic."

The dragon roared again and swung back towards the cloud, but then the Express rounded a bend in the ravine, and the vista was swept from their sight.

Suzy gave a strangled cry of frustration. "Will they be alright?"

"I don't know," said Frederick. "It's a dangerous business."

This did absolutely nothing to allay her fears. Their investigations wouldn't get very far if the person they were looking for had just been incinerated by a dragon.

Ahead of them, the valley widened before splitting

into two and flowing around a conical hill that rose, shaggy and green with vegetation, from the surging waters. The hill was crowned with a star-shaped fortress, its tangerine-coloured walls glinting in the sun. Peaked roofs of blue and gold tiles poked up above the parapet.

"That's beautiful!" Suzy exclaimed. "Is it Cloud Forge?"

"Yes," said Frederick, who looked equally captivated. "I can't wait to see inside it!"

The Express slowed to an easy pace as a small station came into view up ahead. It was built into the side of the ravine and had the same blue roof and thick orange walls as Cloud Forge itself.

"Come on," said Suzy. "This is our stop."

She raced him down the stairs, double-checking the contents of her satchel as she went. The bundle of letters was secure and ready for delivery. Now all she needed was the Cloudwrights themselves. Surely one of them had the information that could help her save Trollville?

"Here we are," Stonker announced, bringing the train to a halt at the platform. "We'll park up in a short-stay siding and wait for you."

Ursel concurred with a nod. The fur of her paws was already starting to take on a yellowish tint, Suzy noticed. She tried to give them both a brave smile as she and Frederick stepped out onto the gangway, but her mind was itching again. Something felt wrong.

Maybe it was Wilmot's absence, or maybe it was the cloying heat that smothered her as she climbed down to the platform. Judging by the look on his face, Frederick was feeling it too. After a moment's thought, it finally came to her.

"Where are my socks?" she said, stopping to pull the hem of her trousers up. Her ankles were bare.

"Mine have gone too," said Frederick.

"I did warn you," said Stonker, leaning out of the cab door. "We're not sure where they disappear to, but we've started carrying an emergency supply. Here." He produced two balled-up pairs of long woollen socks and tossed them down. "I'll make some adjustments to the controls while you're gone and see if I can fix it."

They found a bench and pulled the new socks on, while a small crowd of waiting passengers gathered to admire the Express. As with the royal reception in Trollville, they seemed to have been drawn from across the Impossible Places.

I wish Wilmot was here to see this, Suzy thought.

Essex **Library** Services

Vange Library
Renewals/Enquiries. 0345 603 7628
Visit us online: libraries.essex.gov.uk

Customer ID: **********3552

Items that you have borrowed

Title The great brain robbery
ID   30130219299178
Due: 12 February 2022

Total items 1
Account balance £0.00
Borrowed: 3
Overdue: 0
Hold requests: 0
Ready for collection: 0
22/01/2022 11.34

Items that you already have on loan

Title: Cat's cookbook
ID: 30130301600242
Due: 12 February 2022

Title: You are my happiness
ID: 30130301599030
Due: 12 February 2022

Thank you for using Essex Libraries

I wonder if he's made it out of Trollville yet?

Their laces tied, she and Frederick headed for the exit, where a simple rope bridge connected the station to Cloud Forge.

"Nice to see you out on the rails again!" a giant stick insect called after them.

"Thank you," she replied. "Come rain, shine or meteor shower, the Impossible Postal Express will deliver!" The crowd rewarded her with some polite applause, and she left the station with a spring in her step. *I've been waiting months to say that*, she thought.

CRASH LANDING

The rope bridge connecting the station to Cloud Forge was strung high above the foaming torrent at the bottom of the valley. Suzy looked down through the slats and watched a couple of bright red birds sail past beneath her. *It's a good thing I'm not scared of heights,* she thought. Nevertheless, she found she was gripping the sides of the bridge so hard that the rope burned her palms.

Frederick clearly had no such reservations and was bounding ahead, pausing every few seconds to turn back and chivvy her along.

Cloud Forge loomed ahead of them, two arms of its star-shaped fortifications spread wide as if in welcome. From this close, Suzy realized that the walls were clad from top to bottom in glazed tiles, each with an intricate pattern of geometric shapes picked out in orange and umber and white. Some sort of cloister ran along the battlements – a series of open-fronted archways beneath a sloping roof.

Suzy was halfway across the bridge when she chanced to look back along the valley in the direction from which the Express had come, and saw dark shapes moving against the sun. She squinted, fearful that it might be a dragon, but the shapes were too small and numerous. "Frederick!" she cried. "It's them! The Cloudwrights are back!"

The aircraft came wheeling up the valley, looping and rolling in triumph. There was no urgency to their flight any more, no dragon in pursuit, and as far as Suzy could tell, every one of them had made it back safely.

"This is perfect!" called Frederick as the craft began circling Cloud Forge. "We can be there when they arrive."

He took off at a run and disappeared through the open gateway that stood at the far end of the bridge, but Suzy lingered, watching one craft after another peel off from the great wheeling flock and alight neatly inside the archways above the walls.

They're hangars! she thought.

She had taken a few steps along the bridge in pursuit

of Frederick when a high-pitched whine reached her from further down the valley. She looked and saw that not all the aircraft had returned safely after all – a hang-glider with a propeller mounted on top was still struggling homeward. The whine came from its engine, which trailed smoke, and Suzy could see a scorched hole in the fabric wing. She stopped and watched in horrified fascination as the hang-glider dropped and climbed, stalled and shook, fighting hard for every few metres of altitude it could manage.

She was so fascinated, it took her a moment to realize that the hang-glider was heading straight for her. "Look out!" she cried, waving her arms in warning.

The pilot, just visible as a yellow crash helmet and a pair of goggles, didn't seem to notice. They were too busy fighting to maintain control. As they drew closer, Suzy saw a large glass jar hanging from a strap beneath the pilot's body. Then the hang-glider was upon her, and she threw herself flat, pressing her face against the wooden slats of the bridge.

She felt the rush of air tug at her hair and clothes as the hang-glider whistled overhead. Then something heavy struck the bridge, making it rock alarmingly from side to side. Suzy gripped the slats and screwed her eyes shut, not wanting to look down. Had the hang-glider struck the bridge? Was the whole thing going to collapse?

After a few seconds, the rocking subsided, and she realized the whine of the hang-glider's engine had risen in pitch. She looked up and saw it climbing rapidly, in an uncontrolled spin, up and over the walls of Cloud Forge. The engine coughed and died; the hang-glider hung suspended for an instant, pointing at the zenith. Then gravity took over, and it plunged out of sight into the heart of the fortress.

Suzy heard the dull crunch of the impact, and then the shouting and screaming began. A cloud of dust billowed out of the open gates.

Suzy got to her feet, shaken but relieved to be unharmed. She was about to make for the gates when something bumped against her heel, and she looked down to see the jar that the hang-glider pilot had been carrying. It must have come loose, or perhaps been jettisoned, as the hang-glider had passed overhead.

She picked the jar up. It was heavy, about half a metre tall and sealed with a large cork. She held it up to the sun and examined the white mist that swirled inside it. Colourful sparks of energy danced through it like fireflies, and she realized she had seen this before.

Spellcloud.

Tucking the jar under her arm and fighting to keep her

balance, she ran along the bridge towards the gates. Somewhere inside the fortress was the Cloudwright who might hold the key to saving Trollville. She just had to find them.

The heart of Cloud Forge was a large oval courtyard, three storeys tall and ringed with brightly painted shopfronts. Suzy found it in chaos.

It was full of people and creatures in clothes as fine as any she had seen at the royal reception. Some of them ran in a headlong panic, shouting for attention and crashing into one another, while others huddled nervously together, staring in helpless confusion at the wreck of the hang-glider, which lay like a broken kite on the flagstones. Suzy could barely bring herself to look at it – it had clearly been a bad crash.

A second, smaller crowd surrounded it, already hard at work on freeing the pilot. They wore an odd assortment of work clothes, from aprons to hairnets and even, in one case, a welding mask. The shop staff, Suzy guessed. She saw Frederick among them, and hurried over.

"Is the pilot alright?" she asked.

"I don't know," he replied. His cheeks were flushed

from running and the effort of helping to roll the still-smoking engine to one side.

"Cirrus! Cirrus, can you hear me?" A young human man with a trio of tape measures draped around his shoulders was down on his hands and knees, trying to wriggle underneath the ragged canvas sail.

The engine was rolled away, and the staff finally succeeded in lifting the broken sail. A woman sprang to her feet from beneath it. She was tall, with dark skin and an athletic build. She wore muted yellow flying leathers and matching crash helmet, which she removed to reveal a closely cropped fuzz of tight curls. She pulled her goggles up onto her forehead and looked around.

"Cirrus!" said the young man. "Are you hurt?"

"Never mind me," Cirrus said firmly. "What about my catch?" She pushed through the crowd, heading for the gate.

"Excuse me," said Suzy, stepping into her path. "Do you mean this?" She held up the jar of spellcloud.

Cirrus stopped and her whole face lit up in a delighted smile, revealing perfect, gleaming teeth. "I do!" she said, and bent at the waist until her eyes were level with Suzy's. "Thank you." She accepted the jar and turned it over in her hands, checking it closely. "I'm sorry I buzzed you on the bridge."

"Buzzed me?" said Suzy, who felt both energized and intimidated by this woman.

"The near miss," said Cirrus. "My engine was giving out, so I had to ditch my catch if I was ever going to be light enough to make it back." Satisfied that the jar was intact, she gave it a kiss and straightened. "I didn't really think it would make it in one piece."

"I'm amazed *you* made it in one piece," said Frederick, appearing at her side. "That was quite a crash."

They all regarded the ruined hang-glider. "Yeah, I think I'm going to need a new rig," said Cirrus. Then she brightened and slapped the side of the jar. "And thanks to this, I'll be able to upgrade."

"So this stuff is spellcloud?" said Suzy.

"Grade A and dragon-fresh," said Cirrus. "Thanks for not stealing it."

Suzy's mouth dropped open in shock. "I would never do that!" she said.

Cirrus gave an apologetic smile. "Don't take it personally," she said. "But this stuff's very valuable."

Suzy pulled herself up to her full height and did her best to look dignified. "You can always trust a Postie."

"This is why *I'm* in charge of public relations," said the young man with the tape measures, who inserted himself into the middle of the group. He had a look of studied

144

patience on his face, although there was no disguising the warmth in his eyes when he looked at Cirrus.

"Oh, hello, Jasper," said Cirrus. "You two? This is Jasper, my apprentice and seamster. He fixes things."

"Except hang-gliders," said Jasper flatly. "Although given the number she gets through, perhaps it's time I started."

"It was worth it though, Jasp," said Cirrus, holding the jar aloft like a trophy. "Look! Ten full quarts of the good stuff. Right from the heart of the cloud!"

Jasper's deadpan expression slipped a little, allowing a faint smile through. "I must admit, that is impressive."

"What exactly do you do with it?" asked Suzy, her curiosity getting the better of her.

"Earn a living," said Cirrus. "I really owe you one."

Suzy knew it was probably just an offhand comment, but she jumped on it before Cirrus could turn to leave. "Actually, there *is* something you might be able to do for us," she said.

Cirrus paused. "Sure. Fire away."

"We're looking for a Cloudwright," said Suzy. "But we don't have a name. Maybe you could help us track him down?" She did her best to look hopeful.

"No problem." Cirrus beamed. "I know everyone worth knowing. Follow me."

She set off across the courtyard with a confident stride, and the crowd parted around her like water. "Thanks for your help, everyone," she said as she went. "Can someone clear the mess up?"

Jasper sighed. "That's my cue," he said. "If you'll both excuse me?" He hurried off, leaving Suzy and Frederick to follow in Cirrus's wake.

"Good thinking," Frederick whispered.

"Thanks," Suzy replied. "If Cirrus can point us to the Cloudwright we need, we could be back in Trollville in no time. And besides, I've got to give her this." She pulled a letter from her satchel. It was addressed to:

Cirrus Tramontane – Haute Couture
Cloud Forge

It matched the sign above the shop that Cirrus led them to.

"This is me," she said, kicking the door open and marching inside without pause. The shop was small and packed with neatly ordered shelves of fabric in more textures and colours than Suzy could have imagined possible. A couple of dressmaker's dummies loitered in one corner behind a small workbench, one of them with four arms, but the centrepiece of the room was a large wooden frame strung with threads of silver fabric like piano wires. "Do you like my loom?" said Cirrus. "I made it myself."

"Your what?" said Suzy.

"Her loom," Frederick cut in. "For weaving fabric."

"That's right," said Cirrus, setting the jar down on the workbench. "I'm making a ball gown from spider silk at the moment." She plucked one of the threads on the loom and it sang with a warm, clear note. Suzy thought she saw a glimmer of rainbow colours where it vibrated.

"Now tell me," said Cirrus. "Who are you looking for and why?"

Suzy thought for a moment. She liked Cirrus and didn't want to lie to her, but there wasn't really time to recount the whole story of what was happening in Trollville either. "We're looking for a male Cloudwright," she said at last. "We don't know who he is, but we think he's trying to trace some stolen property that's made its way to Trollville, and we might be able to help." She exchanged a look with Frederick, who gave her a little nod of encouragement.

"Really?" Cirrus looked worried. "Nobody's reported any thefts. Everyone in Cloud Forge would have heard about it. What was taken?"

Suzy opened her mouth before realizing she didn't know how to answer.

147

"We'd prefer to keep that confidential until we've traced the owner," said Frederick, coming to her rescue. "Although we do have descriptions of the thieves."

"That's right!" said Suzy. "One is a troll with grey skin, and the other is...well, he's tall, with clawed hands, brown feathered wings and large orange eyes that sort of glow."

Cirrus frowned. "They don't sound familiar, but I've got a terrible memory for faces. What were they wearing?"

"The troll just wore old work clothes, I think," said Suzy. "But the other one, the one with the wings, had a dark blue cloak and hood."

Cirrus's eyebrows crept up her forehead. "Full length?"

Suzy nodded.

"What sort of material?"

"I don't know," said Suzy. "But it looked light. Maybe... maybe silk?"

"And it had two slits down the back so he could open his wings," added Frederick.

Cirrus's eyes lit up. "Now that *does* sound familiar. Give me a second and I'll check my customer records." She bounded to a nearby shelf, fetched down a heavy ledger, and began leafing through it.

A buzz of nervous anticipation crept through Suzy's veins. She could feel it fizzing like the jar of spellcloud on

148

the workbench. While Cirrus continued to pore over her ledger, Suzy leaned in towards Frederick and whispered, "I still don't understand what she uses the spellcloud for. Why is it so important?"

"Because it's raw magical energy," he whispered back. "Locked away in droplets of water vapour." He prodded the jar on the desk, prompting a little storm of electric crackles inside it. "Do you know how condensation works?"

Suzy rolled her eyes. "Of course. You cool a vapour down and it turns into a liquid. Like steam on a windowpane."

"Exactly. Well the Cloudwrights do the same thing with the spellcloud. It's easier to work with as a liquid, and it keeps its magical charge."

"I soak my threads in it before I start weaving," said Cirrus, without looking up from her ledger.

"So the clothes you make are magical?" said Suzy.

"A little," said Cirrus. "I tailor the magic to the customer's needs, the same as the clothes. Aha!" She jabbed a finger down at an entry in the ledger. "I knew that cloak you described sounded familiar. It's one of mine."

"You made it for him?" said Frederick.

"That's right," Cirrus replied. "Moonspun silk, midnight blue. Practically weightless, flows like water, with almost no air resistance. I own a few pieces myself."

Perfect if you spend a lot of time flying, thought Suzy. "So he came here? The creature with the wings?"

"Yes," said Cirrus. "I think I remember him now. He wasn't very friendly."

"That's an understatement," said Suzy. "So what happened? Did he say anything?"

"Not really." Cirrus stared hard at the entry in the ledger, willing the memories to resurface. "He placed his order by remote spell one evening about two months ago and turned up the next day to collect. I had to stay up half the night to get it finished in time."

"Did he give you his name?" asked Frederick.

Cirrus consulted the ledger. "Mr Brown," she said, then wrinkled her nose. "Now that I look at it again, and assuming he's your thief, I guess that's probably not his real name."

Suzy agreed, and felt the crackle of anticipation die away. "He was already covering his tracks," she said. "I don't suppose he gave you an address? Or any way of tracking him down?"

"Sorry," said Cirrus, shaking her head.

Despondency settled over Suzy like a shroud. Her plan was falling apart. How could she hope to save Trollville now?

"Wait!" Cirrus snapped the ledger shut. "I've just remembered something else. When Mr Brown, or whatever he's really called, collected the cloak, he left without taking his receipt so I had to chase after him."

"And?" said Frederick.

"And I caught up with him just as he was disappearing into Cloudwright Rayleigh's workshop across the courtyard. So maybe Rayleigh can tell you more."

Suzy felt a renewed surge of hope and delved into her satchel. She pulled out a dog-eared letter and held it aloft with a grin. "One delivery for Calvus Rayleigh. You said he's across the courtyard?"

"That's right," said Cirrus, before a doubtful look crossed her face. "You remember I said I know everyone worth knowing around here?"

"Yes," said Suzy.

"Well I don't know Rayleigh. I don't think anyone in Cloud Forge really does."

"Why not?" said Frederick.

Cirrus pursed her lips. "Let's just say he doesn't play well with others. Most of us have learned to avoid him."

"A Postie never shrinks from her duty," said Suzy. "Which reminds me..." She handed Cirrus her own letter. "Sorry it's late," she said. "But deliveries should be more regular now that the Express is back in action."

Cirrus received the letter as though it was a Christmas

present. "I love getting letters!" she said, tearing the envelope open and pulling out a folded sheet of yellow notepaper crammed with spidery handwriting.

"Anything good?" asked Frederick, as she lowered her nose to the page.

"From my parents in Propellendorf," said Cirrus. "We don't see each other as much as we'd like." Her smile grew as she read on, until she was positively beaming. "That's made my day," she said, folding the letter back into the envelope. "Thank you."

Suzy felt her spirits lift. This, at last, was what being a Postie felt like. "All part of the service," she said. "And thanks for your help. Now if you'll excuse us, Cloudwright Rayleigh's delivery is overdue."

They found the entrance to Rayleigh's workshop tucked just inside the courtyard's main gates. Unlike the other establishments, there was no shop window and no sign – just a wooden door, once painted black but now faded and peeling. A tarnished plaque screwed to it read:

C. Rayleigh
Artisan

"This isn't exactly what I'd expect for a Cloudwright," said Frederick, giving the door a look of mild disdain. "What's he doing in a place like this?"

"And what would 'Mr Brown' want with an artisan?" Suzy wondered aloud. "Let's find out." She knocked. Then, when nobody answered, she knocked again. "Hello?" she called, cupping her hands around her mouth and pressing them to the door. "Cloudwright Rayleigh?"

"I wouldn't expect an answer if I were you." They turned at the sound of Jasper's voice. He had successfully dismantled the frame of the hang-glider and was cutting up the canvas sail with a large pair of tailor's scissors.

"Why not?" asked Suzy. "Isn't he in?"

"Who knows?" said Jasper. "He disappears for days sometimes, and he didn't go aloft with the other Cloudwrights earlier. But he might just be refusing to answer the door."

"Why?" asked Frederick, suddenly alert. "Is he hiding something?"

"Not really," said Jasper, cutting another strip of sail free. "He just doesn't like people very much. And between you and me, the feeling tends to be mutual." He gave them a conspiratorial wink.

"But I need to see him," said Suzy. "It's really important!"

"Sorry," said Jasper, with a helpless shrug. "You can always hang around and see if he shows up. But I wouldn't hold your breath." He bundled the freshly cut strips of sail together. "I'd better go and hand these old offcuts to Cirrus. I'm sure she'll want to turn them into something fabulous." He got that warm look in his eyes again. "Best of luck, you two." He smiled and hurried away.

Suzy watched him leave and felt the pieces of her plan coming undone again. "Now what?" she said. "We can't just sit here waiting for Cloudwright Rayleigh. Trollville's running out of time!"

"Maybe we could ask around," suggested Frederick. "One of the other Cloudwrights might know where he is."

It wasn't much to go on, but Suzy knew she had little choice. "Fine," she muttered. "I suppose I've got to deliver the rest of these letters anyway. I'll ask the recipients what they know about Rayleigh." She pulled the bundle of envelopes from her satchel and leafed through them. "I don't have letters for every Cloudwright though, so you'll have to visit the others. Pretend you're a customer and see what you can find out."

"No problem," said Frederick. "Let me see the addresses so I know who not to visit."

As he checked the letters, Suzy took another look around the courtyard. Jasper had left the broken hang-glider frame in a neat heap, and the rest of the shop staff had returned to their own work. Even the customers had calmed down, and were browsing the shop windows as though nothing had happened.

"Got it," said Frederick, returning the letters. "I'll meet you back here when we're done." He hurried away in the direction of the Spellcloud Ice Cream Parlour.

"He'd better not spend all afternoon in there," Suzy muttered to herself. Then she straightened her cap, polished her badge with her sleeve, and set out in search of answers.

10

TROLL HUNT

Wilmot's footsteps echoed along the pitted pavement of Hobb's End. Broken, empty houses loomed over him on either side, full of darkness. The windows and doors were missing. The street was, as Mr Trellis had promised, long abandoned.

I'm amazed I've never heard of this place before, Wilmot thought. *But then I suppose it's not exactly on any postal routes.*

The street came to a dead end, terminating in the sheer rock face of the valley's side, in which a gigantic pair of iron gates had been set. They were chained and padlocked. This had to be the entrance to the old mine workings. A warning sign fixed to the gates declared:

DANGER!
BE SOMEWHERE ELSE!

"Now what?" Wilmot wondered aloud. His words echoed strangely down the street, and he glanced around, feeling exposed. For a second, he thought he saw a dark shape lurking beneath one of the dead street lights, but as he looked, it faded into the surrounding shadows. "Hello?" he called. Nobody answered. Nothing stirred. He drew his uniform coat a little tighter around himself.

"A little light should help," he said to himself, and pulled his Impossible Postal Service standard-issue clockwork torch from his pocket. He wound the key that stuck out of the bottom, switched the torch on, and began a proper inspection of the gates. They were pitted with rust and very large – big enough to accommodate trucks and wagons. *Or drilling equipment*, he mused. But could they really hide the entrance to the long-lost caverns of the ancient trolls? And if they did, how was he going to get past them? The padlock holding them closed was large and solid. *I wish I had Suzy here to help me*, he thought. He missed her. Ever since their last adventure together, he had been looking forward to working with her again. It felt strange not to be out on the rails together now. But he was letting his doubts get the better of him, he realized.

Suzy had a job to do, and so did he
– if they couldn't locate the drill
before the renegade troll was able to
repair it, then Trollville was doomed.

He was still wondering what to do when he heard a faint sound behind him. He whirled around and was just in time to see a dark figure disappear into a pool of deep shadows halfway down the street. He stiffened with fear.

"I know you're there!" he called. He pointed his torch at the doorway where the figure had disappeared, but its light was too weak to reach it.

"Show yourself." And then, because he had always been taught that people responded well to good manners, he added, "Please?"

For a moment, nothing happened. Then, very slowly, the figure shuffled towards him, leaning on a cane. The shadow of the houses lay long across the street, so it wasn't until the figure was almost within reach that Wilmot could make out his features.

"Mr Trellis?"

"Hello, lad," said the elderly troll. "Sorry. I didn't mean to scare you."

Wilmot was too surprised to speak, which Mr Trellis seemed to take as a sign of acceptance. He ambled

up to the gate and tapped it with his cane. "I see you've found it then."

"Er, yes," said Wilmot. "But what are *you* doing here? You're supposed to be at the rest home. Mum will be evacuating everyone soon!"

"Oh, that," said Mr Trellis. "I figure if she won't miss you for a little bit, she won't miss an old coot like me either. Have you found a way in yet?"

"No."

Mr Trellis laughed. "Thought not. This gate's older than I am, and it's not going to give way anytime soon." He raised his hand in a sweeping gesture meant to take in the whole gate, but he overreached himself, and Wilmot had to dart forward and grab him before he toppled over backward.

"Mr Trellis, you really shouldn't be here. I should take you back. If the people who caused the earthquake really are in there, I don't want you running into them."

"Scoundrels!" shouted Mr Trellis, shaking his fist at the place. "Let me have a look at that padlock."

He elbowed Wilmot aside and shuffled over, eyeing the lock at close range. "This looks simple enough," he said, and produced a small penknife from his coat pocket. "These were standard issue in my day." He set about unfolding a variety of different tools from the side of the penknife. "Nail file," he said. "Magnifying glass. Geiger counter. Thing for getting stones out of a centaur's hooves... Aha! Here it is." He unfolded a small, narrow blade. "Letter opener!" He slid the tip into the lock and, very delicately, manoeuvred it until Wilmot heard a *click*. "Good for opening things besides letters," said Mr Trellis.

The padlock sprang open and dropped to the ground with a thud. Slowly, with a painful, protracted creak, the huge gates swung open and a cloud of thick yellow dust billowed out, making them both choke.

"Wow!" said Wilmot, between coughs. "You did it!" As the cloud dispersed, he wound his torch again and pointed it into the darkened void of the entrance. Roughly hewn blocks of yellow stone were stacked in towering pyramids to the left and right. Some of the blocks were three times Wilmot's height. "There's enough stone here to build a whole city!" His voice was swallowed by the huge space, and it was several seconds before the echo reached his ears.

"This is the masons' yard, where they used to cut the stone into bricks," said Mr Trellis. "The mine shafts must be further in."

Wilmot tightened his grip on the torch. "I have to go and check," he said. "The king won't order an evacuation unless I find proof to back up Suzy's story."

161

"I'm right by your side, Postmaster," said Mr Trellis. "Let's go and find those scallywags." He didn't wait for Wilmot, but shuffled over the threshold. "Tally ho!"

"Wait for me!" said Wilmot.

The masons' yard was like another world. The air was colder in here, and the darkness seemed to suck the light straight out of the torch. Wilmot angled the beam upward, but the stacks of stone were so tall that their summits were lost in shadow.

A clattering sound drew their attention to one of the stacks up ahead, and the torchlight picked out deep fractures in the blocks at its base. A small avalanche of gravel rattled down its side, dislodging larger chunks that crashed to the ground and split open.

"It must have been damaged in the earthquake," Wilmot whispered. "We'd better be careful."

They waited for the avalanche to end, then inched past the stack in silence, giving it as wide a berth as possible.

At last they reached the immense wall of bare rock that marked the end of the masons' yard. A row of twenty large cargo elevators ran along it. All of them were rusted, shuttered and dark. Except one.

"This one's been repaired recently," said Wilmot, hurrying up to it. The metal doors gleamed in the torchlight, and the call button set into the wall beside it glowed red. "That settles it. This *has* to be how the troll and his boss got into the caverns. They're connected to the mine!" He felt a giddy mixture of pride and relief. He had done it – he had found the proof he needed to convince Grotnip and the king to act. "We need to get the authorities down here right away," he said. "They'll take care of everything. We won't even need to evacuate the city!"

His voice rebounded back and forth between the great piles of rock. The patter of falling stones began again.

"Bravo, Postmaster!" said Mr Trellis, with a wheezy laugh. "I can't wait to see the look on those ruffians' faces when they're brought to justice."

They turned to leave, but the noise of the avalanche had gathered pace. Wilmot noticed larger fragments of stone being knocked loose from the lower blocks. The stack began to groan under its own weight.

He had only taken a few steps back towards the entrance when the first block gave way. It shattered with a noise like cannon fire, blasting chunks of rock in all directions. A shard whistled past Wilmot's ear, and a second one might have taken his head off if Mr Trellis hadn't tackled him from behind, sending him to the ground.

"That was a close one, Postmaster!" Mr Trellis shouted

over the roar of falling stone. The whole stack sagged, toppled and broke apart. It was a noise to match anything Wilmot had heard in the earthquake, and the floor rippled and cracked under the hammer blows of falling blocks. Within seconds, the route to the exit was buried. Wilmot barely had time to register this before the neighbouring stacks began to disintegrate as well. More rocks plunged down all around them.

"Quick, Mr Trellis!" Wilmot struggled to his feet. "This way!"

He pulled Mr Trellis to the lift door and thumbed the call button. Luckily, the lift was already at the top of the shaft, and the doors slid open.

"Get inside!" Wilmot bundled Mr Trellis into the lift just seconds before a block crashed down on the spot where they had been standing. The doors slid shut and Wilmot yanked at the lever on the control panel. With a shudder, the lift began to descend. It was nothing more than a spherical metal cage with chain-link sides through which they saw the bare rock of the shaft sliding past, but it was swift enough. The disaster unfolding in the masons' hall was reduced to a series of distant thuds and booms, which grew fainter with each passing second.

"You're taking us into the mines?" said Mr Trellis.

"I'm afraid so," said Wilmot.

"Pursuing our quarry into their den, eh? I like it." Mr Trellis gave Wilmot a gummy smile.

Wilmot wiped dust from his forehead and tried to collect his thoughts. He hadn't actually thought about pursuing the criminals – he had just wanted to escape being crushed by falling masonry. But now that he had a moment to reflect, he saw that Mr Trellis was right. "We can't get out through Hobb's End any more," he said. "Which means we can't tell the authorities what we've found. I suppose our only option really is to find the drill and stop it ourselves."

"That's the spirit!" said Mr Trellis. "Those blighters won't know what hit them!"

Wilmot steadied himself against the lift wall. "Mr Trellis, I want you to promise me that you'll be careful. You're not in the custard mills of Splott any more. We need to stick together and keep each other safe. No silly risks, is that clear?"

"Crystal," said Mr Trellis, although Wilmot noted that his smile hadn't diminished in the slightest. In fact, he seemed to be enjoying himself. Wilmot wasn't sure whether to be worried or envious.

Then something heavy struck the top of the lift, and he settled on terrified.

"What was that?" said Mr Trellis. Another blow struck

the lift, and a large dent appeared in the ceiling. Wilmot ducked.

"I think it's masonry falling down the shaft!" he said. "The doors must have given way above us. But as long as it doesn't damage the cable, we—"

He was cut short by a rending of metal, and then the lift plunged downward in free fall. Wilmot and Mr Trellis were lifted off their feet and pressed flat against the ceiling. The walls of the shaft rushed past in a blur and the wind roared in Wilmot's ears.

"Never mind, Postmaster!" shouted Mr Trellis. "At least we'll die with our boots on!"

The one thought in Wilmot's mind as they plunged down into darkness was, *Mum'll be so cross when she finds out.*

11

STORM IN A TEACUP

uzy stepped out of Brillington's Specialist Flower Emporium and sighed. The shop was fascinating, but it hadn't helped her investigation one bit. Cloudwright Brillington, the proprietor, had given her an enthusiastic demonstration of how he watered his plants with condensed spellcloud. The results were astonishing – flowers that glowed and shone, or changed colour or even shape in response to certain pieces of music.

But after a little gentle prompting, Brillington confessed that he had no idea where Cloudwright Rayleigh might be. And, like the half-dozen Cloudwrights Suzy had asked before him, he had never served a customer matching the description of her winged assailant.

Now she checked her satchel and saw that the only

letter still undelivered was Rayleigh's. He *had* to be the Cloudwright she was looking for. She had run out of other options.

I can't go back to Trollville empty handed, she told herself. The thought tied her stomach in an uncomfortable knot. Rayleigh was her only possible lead to the mysterious "Mr Brown". Without him, there would be no evacuation of Trollville, no chance to stop the next earthquake, and a lot of trolls would be hurt. Or worse.

She was passing by Cloudwright Noctilucent's bakery when she heard Frederick call her. She turned and saw him float out of the shop, his feet several centimetres above the ground. He was smiling from ear to ear.

"What's happened?" she said, amazed.

"I had one of these," he said, offering her a paper bag. She took it and looked inside. It contained a pastry covered in icing sugar.

"A cake?"

"A cumulus cake," said Frederick. "It tastes of honey, and it's so light!" He did a little pirouette in mid-air. "It's so light, it makes *you* light too!"

She narrowed her eyes at him. "Have you spent all this time stuffing your face?"

"No," he said, although his guilty look suggested otherwise. "I've been talking to people."

"And?"

"And nobody seems to know much about Rayleigh," he said, remembering to look disappointed.

Worry tightened like a band around Suzy's chest. "Same here."

They both turned to look at the battered old door that marked the entrance to Rayleigh's workshop. It remained closed and unreadable.

But then a slight movement above it drew Suzy's eye up the courtyard wall to a small, dirty window, where she saw the suggestion of a face peering down at them. It was only there for a second before it retreated behind a ragged curtain, but it was enough to reawaken her resolve.

"Someone's in there!" she said, pointing to the window. "I just saw them!"

Frederick looked, but of course saw nothing. "Do you think it's Rayleigh?" he said.

"It has to be! Come on!" She bolted across the courtyard to the door and pounded her fist against it. "Cloudwright Rayleigh?" she called. "It's the Impossible Postal Service. I've got an overdue delivery for you."

Frederick reached her side, still bobbing above the ground like a balloon. "What if he doesn't want to answer?" he said. "He didn't before."

"But we hadn't seen him watching us before," she replied. "He can't pretend he's not in now." She knocked on the door again, even harder.

Then, suddenly, the door opened, revealing a wiry, middle-aged man in a patchwork coat of rich golds and browns. He had salt-and-pepper hair, a short growth of stubble and squinted at them with bleary, pale blue eyes.

"Do you mind?" he snapped. "I'm trying to work."

"Rayleigh?" asked Suzy. "Calvus Rayleigh?"

"Yes. What of it?"

"I'm from the Impossible Postal Express," she said. "And I've got a letter for you. Would you mind signing for it?"

Rayleigh looked her up and down and didn't seem impressed. "Was it you banging on my door earlier?" he said. "Disturbing my thoughts?"

"That's right," said Suzy. "You didn't answer."

"Because I was meditating," he said. "Communing with the muse and waiting for artistic inspiration to strike. Which is impossible with all this racket." He patted his pockets. "Do you have a pen?"

"Sorry, mine ran out," said Suzy. "But I can wait while you find one."

Rayleigh muttered something under his breath and turned away from the door.

"Has your pen really run out?" whispered Frederick.

She smiled at him. "Of course not. He doesn't even really need to sign for it." Then, without waiting, she pushed the door open and stepped inside. It was a brazen move and certainly not in keeping with the Postie's code of conduct as set out in *The Knowledge*, but if this was her last chance to save Trollville then Suzy was determined to make the most of it. Luckily, Rayleigh was too distracted to take much notice.

The interior of his work space looked like a jumble sale in a chemistry lab – every surface was crammed to overflowing with bottles and jars, piles of clothes, old books and papers. One by one, he swept them all off onto the floor, rummaging through the detritus by the light of the glass chandelier that hung from the ceiling. The only thing he treated with any care at all was a small cluster of glowing pink crystals, which he picked up and set gently on a shelf beside a tray of fine china tea things, and a roughly shaped ceramic milk bottle.

He wore gold silk trousers and a frilly shirt beneath his coat. Both items of clothing were clearly of the highest quality but also badly crumpled. Strangest of all, she noticed that his shoes were caked in dry mud. *Where have you been?* she wondered. She guessed she would have to put him at his ease before he would volunteer any

171

information, but she also suspected his patience wouldn't last long. She would have to be careful, and quick.

"So you're an artisan," she said, setting an overturned stool on its feet and sitting down while Frederick hovered beside her. "What sort of things do you make?"

Rayleigh upended a stack of books with a crash. "You wouldn't understand."

She chose to smile through the insult. "I might."

"I craft pioneering nephological installations," he replied, "of such daring and originality that no two pieces are ever alike."

He's right, Suzy thought, annoyed. *I really don't understand.*

"Nephological means 'to do with clouds'," Frederick whispered in her ear, low enough to ensure that Rayleigh didn't overhear. She gave him a quick thumbs up.

"So you make art using spellcloud," she said.

Rayleigh glanced at her in surprise, and Suzy got the impression he was truly seeing her for the first time.

"Quite," he said. He delved into a pile of old socks, revealing a fountain pen underneath. Suzy pulled a proof-of-delivery sheet from her satchel, and he signed it with a tick before tossing the pen over his shoulder and taking the envelope from her. He tore it open, removed the contents and wrinkled up his mouth in distaste.

"What's wrong?" said Suzy.

"It's a birthday card from my sister," he said. "Almost two months late, I might add." He turned it around to show them. It featured a gaudy cartoon picture of a hot-air balloon covered in rainbow glitter, above the words *Birthday Boy*. "You see? This is other people's idea of art." He tore the card in two and threw the pieces on the floor.

"And yours is better?" said Frederick.

"Well, of course it is! Just take a look for yourself." Rayleigh pointed to the chandelier.

"That thing?" said Frederick. "What's so special about that?"

Suzy kept quiet, although she was secretly pleased that Frederick had chosen to stand up to Rayleigh. The chandelier was nice, but it looked perfectly ordinary. Hardly a masterpiece.

Rayleigh must have anticipated their reaction though, as he broke into a knowing smile and, with a flourish, pulled a long glass thermometer from his coat pocket.

"This is my nephological wand," he said. "Observe." He gestured with the wand and the chandelier began to melt, its cut-glass beads separating from one another and sliding down through the air like a slow-motion rainstorm. Miniature rainbows arced from drop to drop, and before they could reach the table that stood beneath them, the drops evaporated into a light mist.

Suzy watched, spellbound, as the mist swirled, coalesced and, in a matter of seconds, formed a fluted glass vase filled with a bouquet of cut-glass roses, which glowed a soft pink.

"Wow," she breathed. "That's beautiful."

"It's just a demonstration model," said Rayleigh. "Unlike the tourist traps out there in the courtyard, I refuse to debase the spellcloud by condensing and diluting it. No, I work with pure spellcloud on the molecular level. Nothing more, nothing less." He put his nose in the air but watched for their reactions.

"Do you mean," said Frederick, "that the vase…and the chandelier…?"

"Are made from nothing but spellcloud," said Rayleigh, triumphantly. "I simply trained the molecules to behave together as though they are glass, and then to shift between a few specific forms. But they're still just water vapour. Like so." He plucked one of the glass roses from the vase and, holding it by the stem, smashed it against the table. Suzy expected it to shatter, but it just evaporated into steam between Rayleigh's fingers. With a faint crackle of energy, it was gone.

"Incredible!" said Frederick.

"Yes I am," said Rayleigh. "I am also very busy, so if you wouldn't mind?" He gestured to the door.

Suzy felt this last opportunity slipping from her grasp. "Actually, Frederick and I need your help," she said, leaping to her feet. "It's a matter of life and death."

"What on earth are you talking about?" said Rayleigh. "I don't know what help you think I could possibly be to a Postie and..." He narrowed his eyes at Frederick. "...and whoever you are."

"Oh, I'm a librarian," said Frederick. He produced a business card from his inside pocket and handed it over. Rayleigh's reaction was immediate and severe. The colour drained from his face and he backed up a step, baring his teeth.

"The Ivory Tower!" he hissed.

"I know, I know." Frederick pulled a face. "But before you say anything, let me reassure you that we're under new management and now offer a comprehensive public-facing service, based on a mission statement of holistic values and—"

"He means they've got nothing to do with Lord Meridian any more," Suzy cut in, nudging Frederick hard in the ribs. She forgot that he was still floating though, and he went sailing across the room, where he crashed into an overstuffed bookcase.

175

"Um, that's right," he said, trying to regain some equilibrium. "He's safely locked away in the dungeon of the Obsidian Tower, being guarded by Lady Crepuscula. None of us have to worry about him ever again."

Some of Rayleigh's colour returned, but so did his look of suspicion. "Then who sent you?"

"No one sent us," said Suzy. "We're here to deliver the post. And to save Trollville from destruction."

"What?" said Rayleigh. "You're making less sense with every word. Is Trollville in danger?"

Suzy nodded. "From someone calling himself 'Mr Brown'. He came to see you a couple of months ago."

Rayleigh's face became a pallid mask. "I don't know any Mr Brown," he said in a clipped voice. "Now get out of my workshop."

"We think he took something of yours, and you've been trying to get it back," said Suzy. "We want to help you, but you have to tell us everything you know about him. If we don't track him down within the next few hours, he's going to destroy Trollville."

"This is a trap!" said Rayleigh, choking on his words. "I knew it! He sent you here, didn't he?"

"So you do know him!" said Frederick.

"Of course I know him!" snapped Rayleigh. "The feathered cretin stole my greatest work. My masterpiece!"

He backed towards a set of shelves. "This is all because I tracked him down to the farm yesterday, isn't it?"

Suzy glanced at his muddy feet with fresh understanding. *Farm mud,* she thought.

"I *knew* I had the right place. All the signs pointed to it. But I let those trained yokels of his send me away with a pat on the head and a bottle of milk!" He picked up the tea tray and hurled it at Suzy and Frederick. Suzy jumped clear, but the milk bottle struck Frederick in the chest, propelling him through the air with a cry, while the fine china smashed to pieces on the floor.

"And now he's sent you here to do away with me," Rayleigh continued. "Well I'll show you. Calvus Rayleigh isn't going down without a fight!"

"What?" said Suzy. "No, we—" She looked to Frederick for support, but was amazed to see him cradling the milk bottle in both hands.

"I don't believe it," he said, staring at it as if he'd never seen one before. "It's impossible!"

Before she could ask him what was wrong, Rayleigh gave a cry of anger, grabbed a mason jar from the shelf and dashed it to the floor. Suzy just had time to see that it was full of dark grey spellcloud before it shattered to pieces and a storm erupted into the room with an almighty clap of thunder. She screamed and threw herself to the ground as a bolt of lightning arced past her head.

"Assassins!" Rayleigh cried.

"Suzy?" The thunderclap had brought Frederick back to his senses. "What's happening?"

She reached up, grabbed his ankles and pulled him down, leaning her weight on him to keep him from floating away. Boiling black clouds filled every centimetre of the room, and another roar of thunder made her ears sing. She could barely see a thing, but she heard Rayleigh shouting over the noise of the storm.

"You'll never stop me! I'm going to take back what's rightfully mine!"

A jagged fork of lightning struck down, setting fire to the stool Suzy had been sitting on moments earlier.

"Let's get out of here!" she cried. Grabbing Frederick by the hand and towing him behind her like a helium balloon, she got to her feet and stumbled in what she hoped was the direction of the front door.

It wasn't a graceful escape – she tripped and stumbled and ricocheted off half a dozen unseen obstacles, while lightning hissed and crackled around them. Small fires sprang up all over the room.

Then, suddenly, they were outside, gasping in the open air. Suzy's ears rang, and her vision was stained with greenish-purple blobs – after-effects of the lightning – but she could just make out Frederick beside her, and a crowd of people racing across the courtyard to their aid.

"Are you hurt?" said Jasper, who was first to reach them. "What happened?"

Before Suzy could answer, the building shook with a mighty peal of thunder that cracked the tiles and blew the door off its hinges.

Cirrus arrived at a run. "Don't tell me Rayleigh finally flipped!" she said.

"He's still in there," said Suzy. "We have to help him."

"No he isn't," said Cirrus. "Look!" She pointed upward. High above them, a hot-air balloon was rising over the rooftops. Its envelope was an elaborate collage of golds and blues, and Rayleigh's face was looking down at them over the edge of the basket.

"Charlatans!" he shouted. "Saboteurs! Thieves!"

They all watched, shell-shocked, as the balloon rose higher and higher, and drifted out of sight.

"Wow," said Cirrus. "There goes a man in bad need of some chamomile tea."

Suzy was already back on her feet. "We need to go after him," she said. "We need to borrow someone's flying machine."

"Don't bother," said Frederick. "Let's get to the Express. I already know where he's going."

Suzy looked at him in surprise. "How?"

"Because of this," said Frederick. To her astonishment, he was still holding the milk bottle. He handed it over, and pointed to the name picked out in crude letters down its side. *Janssen*. His expression was grim.

"I don't get it," said Suzy.

"It's from the farm that Rayleigh was talking about," said Frederick. "I've seen bottles like this one before."

"But that's great!" said Suzy. "We've still got a lead to follow."

"That's not what I mean," said Frederick. "I've seen bottles *exactly* like this one before. I grew up with them."

Suzy's lack of comprehension must have been obvious, because Frederick tapped the bottle in her hands.

"Janssen is my family name," he said. "This bottle came from my parents' farm in the Western Fenlands."

Suzy looked from the bottle, to Frederick, and back again in disbelief. "But why?" she said. "What has a farm in the Western Fenlands got to do with what's happening in Trollville?"

"I don't know," said Frederick. "We'll have to ask my parents. Because whatever's going on here, they're right in the middle of it."

ROCK BOTTOM

Wilmot felt a jabbing pain in his ribs. He kept his eyes closed and hoped it would pass, but it became more persistent and more painful. At last, it was enough to drag his mind out of the dark fog that had enveloped it. He opened his eyes.

Mr Trellis was standing over him, prodding him in the ribs with his walking stick.

"Ouch," said Wilmot.

"Aha!" Mr Trellis smiled down at him. "Come along, Postmaster. This is no time to be napping."

"I wasn't napping," said Wilmot. "I was unconscious." He sat up and looked around. They were still in the cargo lift, although it had crumpled like a concertina around them.

"Ha!" said Mr Trellis. "You should get yourself one of these." He tapped the chrome plate of his scalp. "Totally shockproof."

Wilmot accepted his outstretched hand and levered himself to his feet. His body ached, but when he checked himself over he found that everything was still in working order. "What happened?" he said.

"We fell," said Mr Trellis. "A long way, too."

"You mean we're at the bottom of the shaft?" He looked out of the tiny space where the doors had been. He could see them lying, crumpled, on a rocky floor outside. "Why aren't we dead?"

"I think the airbag deployed and broke our fall," said Mr Trellis.

They helped one another through the opening and stepped out into the mine. A low tunnel, supported by wonky wooden props, stretched away to left and right. Bundles of cables and old light fittings hung from the ceiling, but Wilmot could tell at a glance that they were rusted beyond use. His breath steamed in the chilly air.

Turning back to the wreckage of the lift, he saw the flabby white fabric of the airbag sticking out from underneath it. "Thank goodness these criminals remembered to fix it when they repaired the rest of the lift," he said. "Now, which way do you think we should go?" He produced his torch, wound it and shone it up and down the tunnel, but there was nothing to be seen in either direction.

"I don't really know," said Mr Trellis. He shuffled a few steps past Wilmot and peered into the darkness. "Is that another lift?"

Wilmot followed his pointing finger. Sure enough, there was a small green light about halfway up the tunnel wall, just beyond the reach of the torch beam. "Maybe," he said. "But I'm sure it wasn't there a moment ago."

They edged forward cautiously. The light seemed to intensify as they approached, until Wilmot realized it was too bright to be the call button for another lift. In fact, it was a mushroom. Or maybe a toadstool, he had never been sure of the difference. But it was small, glowing brightly and quite pretty. Then he noticed another on the ceiling above him. And then a third, and a fourth.

As he watched, scores of mushrooms began lighting up along the length of the tunnel in a riot of colour – greens, blues, reds and yellows. It became so bright that he was able to turn his torch off.

"Gosh," he said, staring around in wonder. "I've never seen anything quite like it."

"They look like Spotted Trollworts," said Mr Trellis. "They grow in the heating ducts in Trollville's superstructure. But I've never known them to glow before." He reached out and prodded the nearest mushroom with the tip of his finger. The mushroom squeaked in surprise, sprouted six crab-like legs and skittered off along the wall. "I've never known them do that before either."

Wilmot, who had recoiled in shock when the mushroom had taken flight, watched it hare away down the tunnel wall. "The stories say the ancient troll caverns are full of old magic," he said. "If that's true, maybe it has an effect on the things that live there." As the mushroom passed its fellows, they too stood up on segmented legs. With a chorus of squeaks, a stampede began. "And if these things found their way here from the caverns," Wilmot continued, "maybe that's where they're going now. They're going home!" He clutched Mr Trellis by the arm in his excitement. "Come on. We need to follow them!"

They followed the rainbow glow of the stampeding Trollworts deeper into the mine. The tunnel sloped steadily downward, branching and twisting, until Wilmot couldn't have found his way back to the lift if he had tried. *I hope these creatures know where they're going, or we really*

are going to be stuck down here, he thought. The Trollworts were setting a brisk pace, and he had to put a supporting arm around Mr Trellis to help the old troll keep up. He didn't dare stop for breath, in case they lost sight of the stampede.

At last the Trollworts brought them to a section of tunnel that was half-buried by fallen rubble. The walls were scarred and scorched, and half the mine props had been smashed to splinters.

"This must be the place," wheezed Mr Trellis, with a note of awe in his voice. "This is where the disaster happened all those years ago."

They were forced to slow as they struggled over the uneven floor, and the Trollworts ran on ahead, taking their luminescence with them. Wilmot was reaching for his torch to light their way when he realized that the Trollworts' glow hadn't faded entirely. In fact, as he and Mr Trellis picked their way forward, the glow began to brighten again. At last, they inched around a large boulder and found that the tunnel came to an abrupt end.

In front of them was a huge cavern of yellow rock, bigger than any that Wilmot had ever seen before. It rivalled even Grinding Halt in height and breadth, and every centimetre of it glittered faintly. Lapis luteus, Wilmot realized.

"I can't believe it!" he whispered. "We're really here! In one of the ancient troll caverns."

Enormous stalactites hung from the ceiling, like icicles of solid rock, and countless glowing Trollworts nestled among them. Some were bigger than Ursel, and Wilmot guessed the ones they had followed here must have been infants. Their candy-coloured glow helped illuminate a forest of stalagmites rising from the cavern floor, where an even more astonishing sight met Wilmot's eyes.

A smooth dome of honey-coloured metal, some fifteen metres tall, dominated the centre of the cavern. A team of trolls clambered up and down its sides on a series of rope ladders, carrying spools of cable and other equipment, and shouting instructions to one another. Wilmot counted five of them in total, including the grey-skinned troll that Suzy had encountered at Totters' scrapyard. Towering above them all on the summit of the dome was the drill.

Mr Trellis drew in a breath through his teeth. "Is that the blasted machine that's been causing all this trouble, Postmaster?"

"Yes, Mr Trellis," said Wilmot. "That's the one."

Though he didn't like to admit it, the drill was a very impressive machine. It looked like an upside-down rocket – a cylindrical body as big as the *Belle de Loin*'s boiler, held vertically by four telescoping legs. A large booster engine sprouted from the top, while the head was a serrated cone of gleaming metal teeth, the tip of which rested a few metres above the surface of the dome.

"That's not what I was expecting the vault to look like," said Wilmot, indicating the dome. "I thought it would be a big door, or a safe."

"Our ancestors worked in mysterious ways, my boy," said Mr Trellis. "And you say there's treasure inside that thing?"

"That's right," said Wilmot. "Diamonds as big as boulders, according to what Suzy overheard. And gold and other things too."

Mr Trellis gave an appreciative whistle. "No wonder they're trying so hard to break into it."

"But we're not going to give them the chance," said Wilmot. "Let's see if we can get closer."

They stole out of the tunnel mouth and down the slope to the cavern floor, flitting from the cover of one twisted stalagmite to another. When they were halfway to the foot of the vault, they paused in the shadow of a large rock.

"What's the plan, Postmaster?" asked Mr Trellis.

"There's nothing we can do while they're all around the drill like that. We need some sort of distraction."

"Good thinking. Have you got any ideas?"

Before Wilmot could answer, a shadow swept across the cavern floor, and the sounds of activity around the drill stopped. Wilmot put his finger to his lips and peered out from behind the boulder. A dark shape was wheeling through the air above the drill and, with a cold feeling of dread, he recognized the broad wings and dark blue cloak of the figure that had attacked Suzy. The trolls working on the drill seemed similarly cowed, and they all watched the figure as it circled lower and lower, before finally coming to rest on the surface of the dome.

"Well, Reggie?" Wilmot heard the deep voice speak from within the hood.

"We've stabilized the drill, boss," said the grey-skinned troll. "But we're still missing the part we need to repair the heat exchange. I was about to go topside and look again."

"No," the figure said. "We can't afford to be seen in

Trollville. That meddling Postie and her friends will have spread the word by now. People will be looking for us."

"But without the right length of copper pipe, there's nothing I can do," said Reggie.

"Then you'll just have to find it somewhere else. And quickly. I'm running out of patience."

"What about the farm?" Reggie said.

"The Janssen place?" said the figure. "It's a stinking mud hole."

"Yes, but they've got that old milking machine in the barn," said Reggie. "That's got some bits of copper pipe in it."

The figure considered this. "Will they fit?"

"I'll *make* them fit," said Reggie.

"Fine," the figure snarled. "Hurry up and get to the Swoop. I want this vault open by dawn, remember?" He leaped into the air and unfurled his wings, gliding across the cavern to land in front of a second tunnel mouth that Wilmot hadn't noticed before.

Reggie waved to two of his colleagues. "Peeler? Komp? I need you on pilot duty. Gary and Barry, you stay here and stand guard. We don't want any more surprises." Peeler and Komp – one female with cherry-red skin, the other male, off-white and lanky – nodded in agreement and hurried down the ladders.

191

Wilmot and Mr Trellis pressed themselves flat against a stalagmite as they hurried past, followed by Reggie.

"Hurry up," the hooded figure called. "While you're getting the pipes, I want to check in on those two worthless peasants we left guarding our horde."

"Don't you trust them?" said Reggie, as he and the others reached the tunnel mouth.

"Not as far as I can throw them." With a swish of his cloak, the figure turned and led them into the tunnel.

Wilmot was still processing what he had heard when he felt the tickle of Mr Trellis's whiskery chin in his ear.

"This is our chance, Postmaster," the old troll whispered. "They're going to repair the drill unless we do something else to sabotage it. We should make our move now, while there are just two of them left on guard."

Wilmot poked the top of his head over the boulder and made a quick assessment of Gary and Barry, who had climbed to the top of the dome and now leaned against the drill. They were both square and muscular, with no visible necks. He sank back out of sight.

"I think that might be easier said than done, Mr Trellis. Perhaps we should follow the others and see where they're going."

"But we might not get an opportunity like this again,"

said Mr Trellis. "I'm sure those two ruffians are no match for good, honest grit."

Wilmot suspected his grit wasn't likely to survive long against Gary and Barry. Nor was the rest of him, come to that. "No unnecessary risks, remember?" he said. "Even if we can get past those two and sabotage the drill, we'll need an escape route. We can't go back the way we came, but if those other trolls and their boss are heading for a farm, it must mean they have another way out of here. I'd like to find it."

Mr Trellis cast a longing look at the drill, but nodded. "Whatever you say, Postmaster. Lead on."

Keeping a wary eye on the guards, Wilmot led the way across the cavern floor in a half-crouch. They reached the second tunnel mouth a minute later, and slipped inside.

A chill wind blew from somewhere, and they heard the whine of engines.

"Come on," Wilmot said, and they hurried onwards.

The noise of the engines rose to a fierce roar as they reached the end of the tunnel and stepped out onto a metal platform. It was like a large square balcony, projecting from a sheer cliff face that stretched away into darkness in every direction. A sleek black aircraft was lifting off from the end of it, rising like a giant bat into the air, before peeling away into the night.

"Well I never!" said Mr Trellis. "A Nocturn Swoop Sixty. I've not seen one of those in a while."

Wilmot listened to the Swoop's engines fade into silence. "So this is their back door." He looked around, hoping to see another lift or tunnel, but there was just the platform, and a few crates of equipment piled together in one corner. "Where are we, anyway?"

He approached the end of the platform and looked over the railing. There was nothing beneath him but a yawning chasm. Then he looked up, and almost fell over in astonishment. Far, far above them, he could just make out a thin ribbon of twinkling lights against a narrow letter box of night sky. "It's Trollville!" he said. He had never seen his home city look so small and insubstantial before, and the sight humbled him. "That means we're in the Uncanny Valley." They were certainly a long way down now – deeper than he had imagined possible – but still so far from the bottom.

He stepped back from the railing, shivering. "Sorry," he said. "I'm normally quite good with heights."

"Ah, well," said Mr Trellis. "These are depths. Not quite the same thing."

The wind tugged at their clothes, and wraith-like swirls of mist danced around the platform, coalescing and then vanishing again in moments. Wilmot saw Mr Trellis shiver.

"Alright," said Wilmot. "We've got no chance of escape until the airship comes back. We need to be ready to steal it, or at least stow away on board. Do you know how to fly it?"

"I've seen it done," said Mr Trellis. "And I fell out of one once. Does that count?"

"It might have to," said Wilmot. "But right now we need more direct action. We have to make sure they can't repair the drill."

"Good man!" said Mr Trellis. "I knew you'd come around. Let's set about it then." He brandished his walking stick and headed for the tunnel, but Wilmot caught him by the arm.

"We can't just go in there swinging our fists," he said.

"I'm all ears," said Mr Trellis.

Wilmot drew his coat tightly around himself in an effort to keep out the wind, and thought hard. Then, very slowly, a smile spread over his face. "I think I may have an idea," he said.

13

HOMEWARD BOUND

The Impossible Postal Express exploded out of the tunnel in a flurry of coupling rods and steam, the shriek of its whistle cutting through the sleeting rain of the Western Fenlands. Suzy had followed Frederick back up to the navigation room, where he paced endlessly, ignoring the landscape that unfurled outside the windows. The Express was running along a raised embankment, surrounded by a flat, almost-featureless expanse of patchy marshland, shining a dull silver beneath the low grey sky. She didn't think it looked very inviting.

"I don't believe it!" Frederick said. "After everything they've done to me, they go and do this as well!"

"We still don't really know what 'this' is," Suzy replied, doing her best to sound reasonable. "We've only got a milk bottle to connect them to Cloudwright Rayleigh. There could be a perfectly innocent explanation."

"There won't be," he shot back. "I'm sure of it."

Suzy was inclined to believe him. Now that they had proved that Rayleigh was also on Mr Brown's trail, it seemed very suspicious that he should have visited Frederick's parents' farm. It certainly sounded like the sort of place you had to make a real effort to find. But what could their connection with Mr Brown possibly be? The Western Fenlands were a long way from Trollville, and the Janssen farm was a long way from pretty much everywhere.

"Can't this train go any faster?" said Frederick. He had his face pressed to the window now. "It's an hour's walk to the farm once we get off the train, and we need to get there before Rayleigh does."

"You think he's heading there too?" asked Suzy.

"He said as much, didn't he?" Frederick snapped. "He's still looking for his precious 'masterpiece'."

"But he's in a balloon," said Suzy. "And we're in the Express. We're bound to be faster. And can he even use the tunnels? The balloon wouldn't fit, would it?"

Frederick rolled his eyes. "He's hardly going to use the tunnels, is he? He's going to use the Firmaments. Obviously."

Suzy scowled. She didn't much appreciate Frederick's tone. "And what exactly are the Firmaments, Mr Expert?"

Frederick gave a disgusted sigh. "I'm still amazed at all the really basic stuff you don't know. The Firmaments is the name we use for all the Impossible Places based in the sky. Places like the Cloud Continent, where the giants live. Or Propellendorf, the flying city where Cirrus's parents are."

"Fine," she said. "But how do they help Rayleigh get to the Western Fenlands?"

"Because the Firmaments bisect a lot of the other Impossible Places," said Frederick. "You can move from one to another, if you know the right flight paths."

"So they're like the railway tunnels, but in the sky?" she said.

"Sort of. They're less reliable than the tunnels. Most of the Firmaments move about a lot – nobody knows why – so their connections are always shifting too. It's impossible to map them. You just have to navigate by instinct."

Suzy digested this new information. "So we don't know for sure that Rayleigh will even be able to make it to the Western Fenlands."

"He'll make it," said Frederick glumly. "The Cloud Continent is always drifting around somewhere over the Fenlands. They used to be our biggest trade partners, before things turned sour with the giants and the Premier ordered all our beanstalks chopped down. If Rayleigh can make it that far, he can make it to the farm."

His shoulders drooped, and Suzy found some of her anger towards him softening.

"And you're sure there's no way to contact your parents before we arrive?" she asked.

"None." He crossed to the pigeonholes and studied their numbers before pulling down a plain-looking scroll. He carried it to the table and unrolled it, pinning the corners down beneath the clasps. It was a map of the Western Fenlands, and most of it was empty. "Look," he said, stabbing a finger in the middle of the blank space. Suzy saw that it was labelled simply *Marsh*. "The farm should be there, but nobody's ever even bothered to map the area properly. There are no roads or railways nearby, let alone phone or Ether Web lines. Besides, even if I could call them, I don't think they'd tell me the truth about what's happening."

Suzy held her tongue. She knew that when Frederick had turned to his parents for help in exposing Lord Meridian's plans, they had betrayed him. Coming back and facing them now couldn't be an easy task, especially with fresh suspicions. She tried to imagine confronting her own parents in such a situation and simply couldn't.

"It's funny," he said. "I spent years wanting to get away from this place. I never thought I'd be in such a hurry to get back."

The Express began to slow, and they clattered downstairs together into the cab, where Ursel and Stonker were both busy about their work.

"How much longer?" asked Frederick.

"The more times you ask me that, the longer it will seem," said Stonker primly.

Frederick lapsed into a frustrated silence while Suzy picked at the problem of how to reach the farm. She had no idea how to operate the new H.E.C., which was usually the best way of reaching otherwise inaccessible locations, so she needed another solution, and quickly. She screwed her eyes shut and cast her mind back to her revision. There had to be something…

"Rrrunf?" asked Ursel, hopping aside as Suzy took a running jump over the pile of mail spilling out of the doorway to the sorting carriage.

"Back in a second!" she called. A snippet of *The Knowledge* had resurfaced in her mind, and it might just hold the answer to their problem. She waded through the mess to the very rear of the carriage and the small storage cupboard where she knew Wilmot kept bits of spare uniform.

She had to rummage through mops, brooms, buckets and old logbooks before she found what she was after – two pairs of knee-high boots, with riveted bronze toecaps and thick treads on the soles. She carried them back to the cab, holding them aloft in triumph. "We can use these!" she said.

"What are they?" said Frederick.

"Seven-league boots," said Suzy. "*For the Postie with places to be, and no time to get there.* That sounds like us, don't you think?"

"Whoa," said Frederick, regarding the boots with disbelief. "I didn't know they still made these."

"Really?" said Suzy. "*The Knowledge* says they're standard issue."

Frederick puffed his cheeks out. "How old is your copy of *The Knowledge*? Is it carved on stone tablets or something?"

Suzy was astonished. She couldn't believe that even now he could be so condescending. But then Stonker glanced over at them and winced.

"The boy might have a point," he said. "Those things can be a bit temperamental. The Postmaster prefers to use roller skates."

"It'll be fine," said Suzy decisively. "I've read all about how to use them." She showed Frederick a small brass dial mounted high up on the front of one of the boots. It had the numbers one to seven engraved around the outside edge, and a small red button in the centre. "You use this to tell the boots how far you want them to take you. You can travel up to seven leagues with one step. And you turn the magic on with the button." She handed him a pair of boots. "How far is your parents' farm from the railway line?"

"About six nautical miles," he said.

She scowled at him. "In leagues, please."

"Maybe three and a bit? A Fenland league is always half the distance to the horizon."

"That's not a proper measurement," she retorted. "What if you can't see the horizon?"

"It's the Fenlands," said Frederick. "You can always see the horizon."

"I still don't think that sounds right," she said.

"It's not," said Stonker. "Everyone knows a league is the distance an adult troll can walk in an hour."

"That's even worse!" said Suzy. "How long are the troll's legs? Is he walking uphill? How are you supposed to measure anything like that?"

Stonker looked a little hurt. "I don't make the rules," he said.

"Growlf gruuuunf rolf," said Ursel, tossing another handful of bananas into the grate.

"Don't make things any more complicated," said Stonker. "The boots are hardly going to be set to *bear* leagues, are they?"

Suzy screwed her eyes shut and willed herself to be patient. "You mean you don't have any standard unit of measurement?" she said.

"Of course we do," said Frederick. "Leagues are just really *old* measurements. No one uses them any more."

"So why do the boots use them?" she said.

"Because the boots are pretty old too," said Stonker. "And they're cast by cobbling elves, who are staunch traditionalists."

"So which version of a league do the *elves* use?" said Suzy. To her amazement, Frederick, Stonker and Ursel just stared at one another.

"D'you know, I'm not at all sure," said Stonker.

"Then how do you know what distance to set?" she said, positively trembling with frustration.

"Trial and error, mostly," he replied. "It's not an exact science."

"It's not any sort of science!" she snapped, kicking her trainers off in a rage. "*And where are my socks?*"

They all took a moment to consider her bare feet before Ursel retrieved a small chest from beneath the armchair and pulled out two fresh pairs.

"I'll keep working on a fix," said Stonker. "But it could always be worse. On our first test run, it was underpants."

Suzy snatched the socks from Ursel, shut her eyes, and forced herself to breathe deeply. "I'm sorry," she said. "But we're running out of time. Dawn's only four hours away and it still doesn't feel as if we're any closer to saving Trollville."

"Forget about it," said Frederick, removing his own shoes. "Something tells me my parents have a lot of answers."

They left the main coastal route for an overgrown branch line that curved sharply inland. The countryside didn't seem to get any less waterlogged though, and the fields that flashed past outside the carriage were bounded by canals and ditches, full to the brim with water. When Stonker brought the Express to a halt a short while later, they were in the middle of nowhere, with not a single landmark in sight. Frederick was out of the front door before the wheels had quite stopped moving, and Suzy hurried after him, along the gangway and down the ladder to the long grass beside the track. Stonker and Ursel followed.

"My boots aren't working!" Frederick complained, jogging on the spot.

"Wait!" she said. "I haven't told you how to use them safely yet. Which direction is the farm?"

"That way," he said, pointing at an empty spot on the horizon. "South-east."

Suzy turned to face it. "First set your distance. We don't know exactly how far it is, so it's a good idea to make several short hops. We don't want to overshoot." She reached down and turned the dials on her boots until they pointed at the three.

"And? Then what?"

"Just turn them on and take one normal step forward. But whatever you do—"

She didn't get to finish. Frederick reached down and slapped the red buttons set into the dials. They glowed brightly, and he took a huge bound forward. He should have landed in the ditch that ran alongside the track, but while his foot was still in the air he disappeared with a faint ripping sound, as though he had been torn out of existence.

"Wait!" Suzy shouted.

"Oh dear," said Stonker, twirling the end of his moustache.

Suzy threw her hands up in frustration. "Did he even set his distance properly?"

"Grrrowlf," said Ursel with a shrug.

"No, I'm not sure either," said Stonker. "But you'd better get after him. And hope that he set both boots to the same distance."

"Why?" said Suzy. "What happens if he didn't?"

Stonker grimaced. "I'm not sure how to put this delicately, but imagine if one half of you was suddenly separated from the other half by a distance of a league or more."

"Runf," said Ursel.

"Yes," said Stonker. "*Very* messy."

Suzy felt suddenly weightless with fear. How could she have let this happen? She double-checked the distance dials on her own boots to ensure that they were both correct, then thumbed the activation buttons.

"I'll be as quick as I can," she said, and stepped forward.

The magic started as a tickle in the soles of her feet, but then it leaped up her body and seized hold of her. She had expected to feel a rush of movement, of pressure and momentum battering her body, but instead she felt remarkably still. It was the world that was moving – every atom of matter between the Express and her destination was whistling through her like wind through an open window. She felt, rather than saw, the fields and air and droplets of rain pass through her like ghosts. Then her foot came down with a squelch and she was standing in a muddy field, surrounded by a herd of reassuringly solid cows. One of them turned to look at her, farted loudly, and went back to chewing its mouthful of grass.

Suzy took a moment to catch her breath, then patted herself down. Everything seemed to be where it was supposed to be. She deactivated the boots and looked around. There was no sign of the Express, and with the exception of the cows, she was alone. But through the herd, at the far end of the field, she saw a huddle of low, mean-looking buildings that could only be the farm.

Hoping that Frederick had simply made the most of his head start, she pulled her feet out of the sucking mud and began floundering across the field towards it. Whatever interest Mr Brown had in this place, she was going to uncover it.

The farmyard was a meagre patch of mud and manure, and the buildings that huddled around it were broken and shapeless. The barn looked filthy and damp, and the farmhouse was hardly more inviting – a single-storey shack, it seemed to have been lashed together from mismatched scraps of wood and metal. A weak light shone in its single window, a poor defence against the blanket of heavy cloud overhead.

No wonder Frederick wanted to leave, Suzy thought, holding her nose against the thick animal smell as she trudged across the yard to the house.

She hammered on the front door. "Hello?" she called. "Is anyone in there? Frederick?"

There was a scuffling sound from inside and then the door crept open a few centimetres, revealing a narrow slice of face beyond. Its skin was sallow and dirty, and it glared down on Suzy with a sunken, bloodshot eye.

"Who are you? What do you want?"

"I'm from the Impossible Postal Express," said Suzy. "Are you Mr Janssen?"

The eye narrowed into half a frown. "What business is it of yours?"

"I'm a friend of Frederick's. Is he here yet? We got separated."

The eye blinked, and the lips pulled back in a sneer, revealing yellowing teeth. "I don't know who you're talking about."

Suzy looked around the yard. "Is this the Janssen dairy farm? I'm afraid it's very important."

"I don't care," said the sliver of face. "I don't know any Fredericks. You're trespassing. Go away."

Before he could shut the door, there was a faint tearing sound followed by a pop from the middle of the yard. Suzy turned and saw that Frederick had appeared behind her. He was wet and dishevelled and facing the wrong way, but his face lit up with relief when he looked over his shoulder and saw them both watching him.

"Suzy!" he said. "Dad! I finally made it! I—" His foot slipped in the mud and he took a step to save himself. In the blink of an eye, he was gone again.

"Oh," said the man behind the door. "*That* Frederick." He made to shut the door, but Suzy wedged the toe of one boot in the crack.

"Mr Janssen, please! A lot of people are in danger – a whole city, in fact – and Frederick and I think you can help us save them."

Mr Janssen was preoccupied with slamming the door on Suzy's foot. Luckily the boot's bronze toecap protected her.

"I don't know anything about any city," he said. "My wife and I are poor, honest farm folk. We want to be left alone to live our poor, honest lives."

He put his shoulder to the door, trying to force it shut with all his weight, and it was then that Suzy noticed the rings on his fingers. They were large, gold, and one of them held a ruby the size of a grape.

"Mr Janssen," she said flatly. "Can you tell me what Cloudwright Calvus Rayleigh was looking for when he came here recently?"

"Never heard of him." Mr Janssen tried tackling the door with his shoulder, to no avail.

"Then what about someone called Mr Brown?" she tried. "Have you heard of him?"

The effect was instantaneous. Mr Janssen stopped trying to force the door shut and all the colour left his face. "How do you know that name?" he croaked.

"Because I've met him," said Suzy. "And he's going to destroy Trollville in a few hours unless Frederick and I can stop him. Now, please, I'm begging you: let me in."

Mr Janssen blinked. Then, with a trembling hand, he opened the door a little wider.

"Thank you," said Suzy. She stepped forward, but Mr Janssen planted a hand in the middle of her chest and shoved her, hard. She fell backwards, landing with a cry in the mud.

"There's nothing happening here!" he said. "Go away!" He slammed the door shut.

Suzy lay where she had fallen, too shocked and incensed to move. Cold water seeped through her uniform and glued her shirt to her back.

Then with another *pop!* Frederick appeared in the

corner of the yard. "Suzy!" he cried, his momentum already carrying him forward. "Help!"

"You've got to turn the boots off!" she shouted, but he stumbled and was gone again.

"Oh, for pity's sake," she said. Her patience had reached its end. She pushed herself to her feet, marched up to the door and hammered her fist against it. "Open up!"

"This is harassment!" a woman's voice replied, to a backdrop of crashes and rattling.

Suzy tried the door handle and was surprised to find it unlocked. "I'm coming in."

She had expected the house to be a shabby, one-room hovel. In fact, it *was* a shabby, one-room hovel – filled to the rafters with treasure. It was everywhere. Chests and strongboxes overflowing with gold were piled up in the corners; the floor was a collage of silk carpets; oil paintings were stacked three deep against the walls; and the small kitchen table in the middle of the room was lost beneath mounds of jewellery. Suzy stared at it all in disbelief. She had never seen so much wealth before.

"Shut the door behind you!" snapped Mrs Janssen. "We don't want the whole Union to see this." She was as drab and scrawny as her husband, with a head of dirty-blonde hair, pinched features and a tattered grey work smock. She also wore a string of pearls, several gold bracelets and a crown.

Suzy looked at them both in confusion. "What on earth's going on here?" she said.

She was interrupted by yet another loud *pop*, and Frederick materialized in front of her, caked in mud and trailing pondweed.

"Heeeelp!" he wailed.

Before he had time to move, Suzy lunged at him and caught his legs. Holding him securely, she switched off the boots. He collapsed to the floor, breathless.

"Thanks," he said. "That was horrible! I thought it was never going to end."

"Serves you right for rushing off without me," she said. "Are you okay?"

"I think so. Where are we?" He looked around in disbelief. "Mum? Dad? What happened here?"

"We redecorated," said his mother.

He ignored her, turning in a slow circle, trying to process everything he was seeing. "Where did all this come from?"

"Maybe we can afford a few more luxuries now we don't have to feed and clothe you all the time."

"You were a terrible drain on our resources," his father added.

"A few luxuries?" said Frederick, picking a string of pearls off the table. "The fruit bowl's full of diamonds. There's a bucket full of Wolfhaven ducats on the milking stool over there. And is that an original Van Peebles?" He pointed to one of the portraits stacked against the wall.

"Your mother and I might not know much about art," said his father, "but we know what we like."

Frederick deflated. "Are these things all stolen?"

His mother made a very good show of looking affronted. "How dare you! We didn't steal any of this. Not a single coin!"

"It's true!" said Mr Janssen. "We're innocent!"

Frederick gave Suzy a questioning look, but all she could do was shrug in response. "I have no idea," she said.

Frederick chewed his lip as he stared and thought. "I think I believe them," he said, sounding as though he could hardly believe it himself. "There's stuff here from galleries and bank vaults all over the Union. There's no way they could have stolen it all."

"You see?" said his mother. "Now he thinks we lack ability. Whatever we do, it's never good enough for him."

Suzy ignored her. "Are you saying somebody else stole it all and left it here?"

"They must have," said Frederick. "But who? And why?"

Realization struck them both simultaneously. "Mr Brown!" they chorused. Mr and Mrs Janssen both flinched at the name.

"I remember now," Suzy said. "When I was hiding in the scrapyard, I heard the troll remind Mr Brown that he'd done other robberies for him in the past." She looked around at the piles of treasure. "*Lots* of other robberies."

"You can't prove anything," said Mr Janssen, although the look of guilt on his face was proof enough for Suzy. He and his wife both shrank back from Frederick as he rounded on them.

"How did this happen?" Frederick demanded. His voice was clipped and forceful. "Of all the places in the Union, why did Mr Brown choose this one as his storehouse? And why did you let him?"

"I still don't know what you're talking about," said his father. "But if a dangerous criminal dropped out of the sky into the middle of your farm one day, and demanded you provide safe haven for his ill-gotten loot in return for a share of the profits, what would you say?"

Frederick blinked in astonishment. "I'd say no!"

Mr Janssen seemed taken aback. "Then perhaps we'll just have to agree to disagree," he said.

Suzy's impatience boiled over. "We need to find Mr Brown before he can destroy Trollville," she said. "He's drilling for treasure in a cavern somewhere underneath the city. Has he mentioned anything, anything at all, about where it might be?"

"He never says anything to us," said Mrs Janssen.

"Except when he threatens to cut off all our toes if any of his treasure goes missing," added Mr Janssen. "He's very particular about that."

Frederick fumed. "I can't believe you two!" he said. "Is there nothing you won't do to help yourselves?"

"That's easy for you to say," his mother shot back. "Strutting around the Union in your fancy suit with your fancy job. Too good for the likes of us now, are you?"

"I never said that, Mum."

"You've always thought it though," she said. "Your father and I have spent all our lives scrabbling through cow muck to make ends meet. And for years we had to do it with you looking down your nose at us."

"That's not true," Frederick mumbled, but without much conviction.

"Yes it is," said Mr Janssen. "You left us for the Ivory Tower without a second glance, and now look at you. Some big librarian. And what have we got to show for it?"

"We don't want to spend the rest of our lives in this shack," said Mrs Janssen. "So excuse us for not turning down every opportunity that comes along."

"Look, if you don't know where Mr Brown is, when is he coming back?"

"How should we know?" said Mr Janssen. He was about to say something else when he was interrupted by a high-pitched whine from outside. Both he and Mrs Janssen went pale.

"It's them!" said Frederick's father.

The whine grew louder, until Suzy recognized it as the sound of engines. "You mean Mr Brown's here?" she said. "Now?"

Frederick's parents stripped themselves of the jewellery they had been wearing.

"Hide!" said Mrs Janssen. "He doesn't allow visitors!"

"Don't worry," said Suzy, crossing to the door. "People are always happy to see a Postie."

Searchlights lanced down from the sky as she and Frederick stepped out into the yard. Suzy shielded her eyes against the glare and looked up to see a large sleek black shape hovering over the farm. It looked a bit like a gigantic bat, but the down-blast of its turbines told her it was some sort of aircraft. A hatch opened in its belly and a rope unspooled from inside. A moment later, the grey-skinned troll Suzy had encountered in the scrapyard rappelled down it, landing with a splash in the centre of the farmyard.

"You again!" he exclaimed, looking nervously from Suzy to Frederick. Once again, Suzy was struck by the impression that she knew this troll from somewhere.

"It's not our fault!" said Frederick's father, appearing in the doorway. "We tried to get rid of them!"

"They're here to steal your treasure!" said Frederick's mother. She grabbed Frederick by the arm and thrust him towards the troll. "We apprehended them for you."

"Mum!" gasped Frederick in disbelief.

The troll advanced, pulling a rod of pitted metal from his work belt: a troll wand. Suzy swallowed a lump of apprehension.

"We're not here to steal anything," she said. "We just want to stop you destroying Trollville."

The troll frowned, and gestured with his wand at Suzy and Frederick. "How did you find this place?"

"I was born here," said Frederick. "These people are my parents."

"Pull the other one," said the troll.

"We've never seen this boy before in our lives," said his father. "But we do happen to know he's the Chief Librarian of the Ivory Tower. He'd make a very valuable hostage!"

"Yes!" added Mrs Janssen. "But we want ten per cent of any ransom paid."

Both Frederick and Suzy looked at them in disgust. The troll, meanwhile, dragged a hand down his face. "Look, I've had a long day. I really don't have time for this right now."

"Then leave them to me," said a low voice that sent a chill of fear through Suzy. It came from above her and she looked up, straight into the blazing amber eyes of Mr Brown.

He squatted on the edge of the farmhouse roof like a gargoyle, the rest of his face hidden in the shadow of his hood. Suzy felt that same sense of calm she had experienced in the scrapyard start to seep through her body, but this time she was prepared. She tore her gaze away and the sensation vanished.

"Don't look him in the eyes," she warned Frederick.

With a hiss of impatience, Mr Brown leaped from the roof, twisting in the air above her head and landing neatly beside the troll. "Leave them to me, Reggie," he said. "Go into the barn and find the Janssen's milking machine. It's made with enough copper piping to repair half a dozen drills."

Reggie nodded and jogged away.

"Oi!" Mr Janssen shouted after him. "That milking machine's private property! You can't just start dismantling it."

"Quiet!" said Mr Brown. He raised a hand and rubbed his talons together. They made a noise like knives being sharpened. "You shouldn't have come here, Postie."

"I'll do whatever it takes to stop you reactivating that drill," Suzy said.

"Is that what this is about?" He sounded surprised. "And what's Trollville worth to you?"

Fear was starting to tug at her thoughts, but the answer stood out clear and simple in her mind. "Everything," she replied. And the moment the word had left her mouth, she knew it was true. This was what her life was about now: learning everything *The Knowledge* had to teach her, and then putting it into practice out on the rails with Wilmot and her friends. Exploring the Union. Being a postie. Trollville had just become her second home.

Mr Brown's eyes narrowed. "Then I'm sorry," he said. "Because it's nothing to me but an obstacle. Just like you."

Keep him talking! The thought popped into her head. *As long as he's talking, he isn't attacking.* "You like hiding behind hoods and fake names," she said. "Why don't you show yourself for once?"

Mr Brown chuckled. "Do you think I'm scared?"

"That," she replied. "Or you might just be really ugly."

The great eyes burned more fiercely, and a furious hiss escaped from the hood. Frederick's parents retreated inside and slammed the door, and Suzy felt the fear clamp down hard around her lungs. She had taken things too far.

"*Ugly?*" Mr Brown's cloak billowed outward as he spread his wings. "Me, Egolius Tenebrae, master criminal, ugly?" He tore off his cloak and hood and cast them aside. Suzy stared in amazement. His body was that of a man, dressed in a loose-fitting white shirt, blue jerkin, breeches and boots. His wings sprouted from behind his shoulders, which sloped up directly into a dome-shaped head, covered in short golden feathers. Lamp-like eyes were set in a flat face. A pair of tufted ears stuck up like horns from his scalp, and a short curved hook of a beak jutted out in place of a mouth.

"Does this look ugly to you?" he demanded.

Suzy realized her mouth was hanging open, and shut it. "You're part owl," she said flatly.

"I am magnificent!" Egolius Tenebrae retorted. "And I will be the last thing you ever see." He levelled his talons at Suzy's throat and, with a sweep of his wings, sprang towards her.

14

HEAD IN THE CLOUDS

Suzy saw the wickedly sharp points of Tenebrae's talons cutting through the air towards her. She jumped back but collided with the side of the farmhouse. Tenebrae kept coming, his aim never wavering. Suzy shut her eyes.

There was a thud and a cry of frustration. A second later, when she realized she was still alive, she opened her eyes and saw Tenebrae sprawled in the mud at her feet. Frederick was on top of him, trying to pin his arms to the ground.

"Run, Suzy!" Frederick shouted.

Her instinct told her to obey, but something deeper urged her forward, and she threw herself on top of Tenebrae, joining the fight for control of his arms.

222

For a second it seemed that she and Frederick would prevail, but Tenebrae bucked underneath them and unfurled his wings, throwing them both off. A second later, he was back on his feet again. He swiped at Frederick, who leaped clear but slipped in the mud and went down heavily.

Tenebrae pirouetted until he was facing Suzy again. "Your pet bear isn't here to save you this time," he said, and leaped forward, slashing with his talons at her heart. She just had time to bring her satchel up before the claws struck home, piercing the leather and burying themselves in the thick cover of *The Knowledge* inside. The blow knocked her backwards, but she was saved from falling by Tenebrae, who tightened his hold on the satchel.

"Can you fly, Postie?" Tenebrae asked. He shot a clawed hand out and seized her by the wrist. "A hundred-foot drop should put an end to your meddling."

Suzy fought to free herself, but her feet left the mud with a wet sucking noise as Tenebrae beat his wings and dragged her into the air.

"Let me go!" she shouted, beating at his claws with her free hand.

"I intend to," he snarled back.

Suzy kicked and flailed, trying to make herself as difficult as possible to carry, but it was a losing battle.

Inch by inch, Tenebrae was hauling her skywards.

Panic scraped across the inside of Suzy's ribs like a knife edge, when the toes of her right foot caught against something and her ascent jolted to a stop. She looked down in surprise and laughed with relief when she saw that she had hooked her boot under the eaves of the farmhouse roof. Tenebrae saw it too and hissed with displeasure.

"You can't win," he said, beating his wings harder. "Look into my eyes and I'll make sure your final moments are peaceful."

Suzy wanted to punch him square in the beak but couldn't free herself. She glared up at him, straining against him with every muscle. And that's when she saw Rayleigh's balloon sweep in over the roof of the barn.

It came in fast and low, as though borne on the teeth of a gale, and the basket splashed down a few metres away. Rayleigh vaulted over the side, brandishing his thermometer.

"My masterwork!" he shouted. "I know it's here somewhere. I demand that someone hand it over immediately!"

Suzy felt the pressure on her arm lessen as Tenebrae looked between her and Rayleigh, his head swivelling right round on his shoulders in the process. Then he released his grip, and she fell with a wet splat into the mud of the yard. He alighted beside her and, before she could escape, pinned her to the ground beneath the heel of his boot. "I'll deal with you in a moment," he said, turning his focus on Rayleigh. Suzy saw the Cloudwright slow, then stagger to a stop. The hand holding the thermometer dropped to his side, and she knew that he was in the grip of whatever power Tenebrae held in the depths of those huge eyes.

"Wake up, Cloudwright!" she shouted, but he was insensible to her. Tenebrae raised one clawed hand high in the air, ready to strike down at Suzy's throat. A short distance away, she saw Reggie, his arms laden with lengths of copper pipe, fighting to reach the rope hanging from his sleek black aircraft, while Frederick clung to his legs.

She was about to lose everything.

She kicked at the ground with her heels, trying to wriggle free of Tenebrae, but her boots just slid in the wet mud.

The boots…

A wild idea formed from the maelstrom of her thoughts. If it didn't work, it might tear her in two. But if it did?

Raising her feet free of the mud, she brought the heel of her right boot down on the shin of her left, and then her left heel down on the shin of her right. She felt the activation buttons click on.

"You put up a good fight, Postie," Tenebrae said, his eyes still on Rayleigh. "But you're too far down the food chain to beat me."

Suzy didn't reply. She just gritted her teeth, dug her heels into the mud, and pushed.

She felt that strange rush of matter as reality shifted about her again, and then she was lying on her back in a muddy field, thankfully devoid of cows.

She made a noise that was part laugh of triumph, part sob of relief, and sat up. The power buttons on both boots were glowing green – she hadn't been certain that they'd work if she was lying down, but here she was. She knew she couldn't stay here though.

She switched the boots off and got to her feet. Then she got into a fighting crouch and gripped the strap of her satchel in both hands, swinging it like a club. It was reassuringly heavy. She switched the boots back on, shut her eyes and pictured the farmyard as she had seen it just a few seconds earlier.

When she was certain she had it, she leaped forward, across three leagues of space, and landed neatly back in the yard. She swung her satchel hard.

As she had predicted, Tenebrae was stalking towards

Rayleigh, who still stood immobilized. That meant that Tenebrae had his back to her when she landed, and never saw the satchel coming. It caught him on the side of the head with enough force to lift him off his feet.

He performed a sideways somersault and landed full length in the mud.

Freed from Tenebrae's mesmeric charm, Rayleigh recovered his wits and trained his nephological wand on the fallen creature. "Dare to move, and I'll fry you with enough lightning to power a city," he said.

Tenebrae hissed in fury. Then, with obvious reluctance, he raised his talons in submission.

Suzy wanted to laugh, but movement drew her eye across the yard and she realized that Frederick had been overpowered. Reggie stood over his limp form, securing the rope dangling from the aircraft around her friend's arms.

"Hey!" Suzy shouted.

"Quick, boss!" said Reggie, scooping the pipes out of the mud where he had dropped them. "We've got everything we need. Let's scram!"

Suzy just had the presence of mind to deactivate the boots before she charged across the yard, swinging her satchel above her head. "Let him go!" she shouted. But it was already too late. The rope went taut, Reggie jumped onto Frederick's back, and the pair of them were winched up into the air. She jumped, reaching for Frederick's dangling feet, and felt the rough tread of his shoes against her fingertips. Then he was out of reach, vanishing into the dark belly of the craft.

She watched him go, helpless, as the aircraft swallowed him up and the cargo doors slammed shut. Then, with a blast of its turbines, it peeled away into the clouds, leaving the yard in gloom and silence.

"Cowards!" Tenebrae cried after it.

Suzy didn't hesitate – she turned and ran towards Rayleigh. "Quickly!" she said. "I need your balloon. We have to follow them."

"Now just wait a minute," he said. "Nobody's going anywhere until I've found my masterpiece." He looked down at Tenebrae. "Tell me where you put it, you tasteless philistine."

Tenebrae simply sneered at him in response.

"But they've got my friend!" Suzy said, grabbing Rayleigh by the sleeve.

It was all the distraction Tenebrae needed.

He rolled to one side, sweeping his wing open as he did so. It struck Rayleigh across the back of the knees, knocking his feet out from under him. Suzy threw herself at Tenebrae, but he leaped clear, rising like an arrow towards the clouds. She gave a despairing cry, but there was nothing she could do. Tenebrae vanished into the cloud layer.

"Confound it!" cried Rayleigh, regaining his feet. "He was about to tell me everything!" He poked Suzy in the chest with a finger. "I hope you're pleased with yourself, young lady."

Suzy's mind was whirling so fast she felt she couldn't hold on. She had beaten Tenebrae, only to let him escape thanks to her own impulsiveness. Now she was even worse off than before, because Frederick was gone. "I'm sorry," she said. "But we can follow them back to their lair. We can still save everyone." She tried to drag him towards the balloon, but he shook himself free.

"Out of the question," he said. "Bertha could never hope to keep up."

"Who's Bertha?"

"Why, my balloon of course," he said. "She's not built for speed."

Suzy sank to her knees, defeated.

"Now, if you wouldn't mind," said Rayleigh, "I would like to know just what's going on here."

She looked up at him through the cold drizzle. "Everything's going wrong," she said. "That's what's happening."

"Where is my masterpiece?" he said. "And don't try and pretend you don't know."

"But I *don't*!" she protested. "I don't know anything about your stupid masterpiece. I was just here to help my friends. And I failed." Hearing herself say the words out loud made it all feel worse. She let her head slump onto her chest. "Tenebrae and his gang are going to destroy Trollville, and I don't know how to stop them. The king won't evacuate the city unless I give him proof of what's happening, and all the proof I had just flew away. I couldn't even save Frederick." She shut her eyes and let her tears mix with the rain on her face.

When Rayleigh spoke again, his tone had softened a little. "It is just possible that I misjudged you somewhat. I assumed that Tenebrae had sent you to Cloud Forge to do away with me for snooping." He cleared his throat, and grimaced. "I suspect I owe you an apology."

Suzy shrugged.

"I should also thank you for saving my life a moment ago," Rayleigh continued. "I don't know what came over me, but I found myself powerless to act when the moment called for it."

"It's Tenebrae's eyes," she said. "It's some sort of hypnotism. But he can't do it if you don't look straight into them."

"Duly noted."

Just then the farmhouse door burst open, and Mr and Mrs Janssen emerged. They were dressed in heavy coats, and each carried a large hessian sack bulging with treasure over one shoulder.

"Have they gone?" said Mr Janssen. He was so busy scanning the sky that he almost walked into Rayleigh. "Oh. It's you again."

"Indubitably," said Rayleigh. "You, sir, are a charlatan, and I demand you return my masterpiece forthwith."

Mr Janssen began sidling around him. "Sorry," he said. "But like I told you last time, I don't know anything about it." He hooked a thumb in the direction of the farmhouse. "Help yourself to whatever's left though. It's all up for grabs."

With a parting look of contempt, Rayleigh splashed away through the mud to the house. Suzy, meanwhile, jumped to her feet and blocked the Janssens' path.

"How could you?" she cried.

Mrs Janssen looked confused. "We've already got as much as we can carry," she said. "There's no point being greedy."

"I'm not talking about the loot," said Suzy, furious. "I'm talking about Frederick! You just handed him over as if he meant nothing to you!"

"Oh, him." Mr Janssen shrugged. "He'll probably be ransomed by this time tomorrow. It might even do him good."

"It could be a learning experience," agreed Mrs Janssen. "I've always said he should get out and about more."

Suzy was so angry she could feel the heat radiating out of her in waves. She was surprised she hadn't started steaming. "And that's it?" she said, spitting the words at them like bullets. "You're just leaving?"

"You saw them dismantle our milking machine," said Mrs Janssen. "And what with milk being our main source of income, we thought we might try a clean start somewhere else. One of the big cities, maybe. They say Hartenhof is nice."

Suzy's anger reached its peak. "Then go," she said. "But whatever happens, you don't deserve to see Frederick ever again. Understood?"

Mr and Mrs Janssen conferred with a look. "That's fine," said Mr Janssen. Then, re-shouldering their bags, they trudged past her out of the yard. Suzy didn't bother to watch them go.

Presently, Rayleigh returned from the farmhouse, looking preoccupied. "There's no clue in there as to where they might have put it," he said. He pulled an umbrella from inside his coat, unfurled it, and handed it to Suzy.

She took it with a weak smile of thanks.

"Sorry I can't help," she said, her voice still thick with tears. "But I have to get back to the Express and tell them what's happened." She looked around the yard. "Have you checked the barn?"

"I was given a nauseatingly thorough tour of the barn on my last visit," he said. "It was entirely pecorous. That's a word meaning—"

"Full of cows," she finished for him. "Yes, I know."

"I'm certain it's here somewhere though," he said. "I spent weeks pursuing every lead I could find, and they all pointed to this farm."

Suzy sighed. She was too tired to argue. "What exactly is it that you're looking for?" she asked.

"Why, the most ambitious piece of nephological spellcraft ever attempted," said Rayleigh. "An entirely unique piece, created for my most exclusive client. It must be worth ten times all the treasure in that house put together. It's irreplaceable."

Suzy hesitated. "Do you think Tenebrae will come back for it?"

"Given the effort he's expended to keep it from me thus far, I'd say it's inevitable," said Rayleigh.

This set Suzy's thoughts racing. Perhaps she hadn't lost track of Tenebrae after all. She looked around again, hoping for the answer to leap out at her, but all she could see was endless fields, yet more cows, and rain. "What exactly does this masterpiece look like?"

"It's quite distinctive," said Rayleigh. "About ten metres long, free-floating and, needless to say, fashioned from raw spellcloud."

"But you can make spellcloud look like anything," she said.

"True." He gave a smug little smile. "But in this case, I opted for a purely functional aesthetic, the better to showcase the true genius of my process."

Suzy gave him a blank look. "Pardon?"

"I wanted people to know I'd made it from cloud, so I made it *look* like a cloud," he said.

Rain drummed against the umbrella.

The rain!

Suzy peered out from beneath the umbrella and looked up. "If you wanted to hide a cloud around here, where would you put it?" she said.

Rayleigh looked horrified. "Up there? But it's supposed to be kept in a climate-controlled environment! Not out in the wild!"

"Do you want to check or not?" she said. "If we're lucky, Tenebrae might even be up there with it. But we've got to be quick."

His shoulders slumped. "I suppose we must."

"So," said Suzy as Rayleigh guided Bertha up into the cloud layer, "how will we tell your cloud apart from all the others?"

"It should stand out once we're close enough," said Rayleigh, peering out into the clouds. "It's still a spellcloud, after all. It's quite energetic."

Suzy did her best to spot anything out of the ordinary in the formless grey void that enveloped them, but she couldn't see much at all. They drifted in silence for a minute before Rayleigh cried out.

"There!" He pointed into the murk.

Suzy looked. "I don't see anything."

"Keep watching," he said. "It was only there for a second."

For a moment, nothing happened. Then, very deep in the cloud bank, Suzy saw it: a flicker of light. It was faint and uncertain, but it was all Rayleigh needed. He aimed his wand at it, and the balloon began drifting in that direction. The light flickered again, and Suzy recognized the telltale rainbow shades of spellcloud.

Suddenly they broke free of the clouds and emerged into an open expanse of still air, like a large cavern hollowed out of the cloud bank. And there, floating at the centre of it was Rayleigh's masterpiece.

It was indeed a cloud, but not like any that Suzy had ever seen before. It was pale and ghostly, and when the next spark of lightning lit up its insides, she could see right through it. But the strangest thing about it was its shape – it wasn't a normal cloud shape, all fluffy and lumpy. It was roundish, with clearly defined edges, and a deeply wrinkled surface. It looked familiar somehow, although Suzy couldn't for the life of her determine why. Her mind itched with the question as Rayleigh steered Bertha across the space to the cloud's side.

"At last!" he said, his eyes dancing with reflected lightning. "I was beginning to think I would never see it again. Isn't it magnificent?"

"It's certainly different," she said, still trying to pinpoint how she could possibly recognize the cloud. It reminded her of something else. Something she knew…

"And it appears to be intact," Rayleigh continued, probing the surface of the cloud with the tip of his wand. "Tenebrae seems to have put an atmospheric shielding spell around it. Perhaps he's not as witless as I thought."

As he traced the whorls and furrows of the cloud's surface with his wand, Suzy finally realized what she was looking at.

"A brain!" she cried. "It's an enormous brain!"

"Well, of course it is," said Rayleigh, still intent on his examination. "What is the mind but a carefully choreographed electrical storm? And what better form for the Union's greatest memory storage system?"

"Memory storage?"

"Memories, information…whatever data you care to put into it," said Rayleigh. "I call it the Brain Storm. Every thought you've ever had, preserved for ever."

"Whose thoughts, exactly?"

She did her best to sound casual, and Rayleigh almost answered without thinking, but he caught himself just in time.

"I've already told you more than I'm allowed to," he said. "Suffice it to say, my client had a lot on his mind."

"So you made him another one," she murmured, gazing deep into the cloud, where flurries of droplets performed an intricate dance together. "A backup." Threads of lightning strobed between them, making them sparkle like a million fragments of diamond. It was very beautiful.

"So what does Tenebrae want with it?" she said.

"Well…" said Rayleigh, but he didn't get to finish. The flashbulbs of lightning inside the cloud suddenly intensified, becoming so bright that Suzy had to shield her eyes from the glare. As she threw her hands up, she just had time to see a jagged bolt of electricity erupt from the cloud and strike the tip of Rayleigh's wand. A noise like an explosion detonated around her, and she fell to the floor of the basket. When she dared to open her eyes a few seconds later, Rayleigh was sprawled beside her, his hair on end and his eyes wide open. He wasn't moving.

"Cloudwright!" she cried. She dropped to his side and checked his breathing. She had to put her ear right to his mouth before she heard it – it was very faint, but steady. Then she checked his heartbeat – weak, but regular. She slumped back with a sigh of relief, but the feeling was short-lived. Rayleigh was alive for now, but she had no idea how much damage the lightning had really done – he might not survive much longer without help, and they were both trapped in a balloon, far above the middle of nowhere.

I need to get us down from here, she thought. Rayleigh had used the thermometer to direct the balloon somehow, so maybe she could do the same…

It took a few seconds to wrest Rayleigh's thermometer from his hand. The glass was hot to the touch. *You've used magic before*, Suzy told herself. *Just relax. Think about what you want. Picture it.* She took a deep breath. She had never used a nephological wand before, and her brief experience of troll magic had been down to luck as much as skill. But right now she didn't have any other options. "You can do this," she assured herself, and stood up.

She didn't even have time to aim the wand before a bolt of lightning flashed out of the cloud and struck her right between the eyes.

15

SABOTAGE

Wilmot crouched behind another stalagmite on the cavern floor, just a few metres from the base of the vault, and pulled his fob watch from his pocket. His nerves mounted as the second hand ticked its way around towards the top of the watch face. Just thirty seconds left before they put their plan into action.

Out of sight on the other side of the vault, behind another bit of rock, he knew that Mr Trellis was counting down the same seconds. They had synchronized watches out on the Swoop's landing platform, and rehearsed the plan twice. Each of them had a role, and each depended on the other. Of course it had all seemed easy out there, without the threat of two muscular troll criminals looming over them. Now, everything had to go right if they were going to ensure the drill couldn't be restarted.

He looked up at it, towering over everything in the cavern, its shadow wavering in the gently shifting light of the glowing Trollworts. The two trolls left on guard, Gary and Barry, sat together at the summit of the dome, leaning against the conical drill bit. They appeared to be playing cards.

The second hand reached the top of the watch face and, right on cue, he heard Mr Trellis's voice from across the cavern.

"Hello there! I wonder if you strapping young lads could help me."

The response was exactly as expected – both trolls shot to their feet, scattering cards everywhere. After that, however, they seemed to be at a loss.

"I got separated from my tour group," called Mr Trellis. "Have you seen them anywhere? They said they'd wait for me at the gift shop."

"Hey!" Gary decided to try to assert some authority. "How did you get down here?" He shimmied down the nearest rope ladder in the direction of Mr Trellis, dropping out of sight down the curve of the vault. Barry, not wanting to seem slow on the uptake, followed him.

Brilliant work, Mr Trellis! thought Wilmot. *Now just keep them busy.*

He slipped out from behind the stalagmite and dashed

to the vault. Taking hold of the nearest rope ladder, he used it to pull himself up the side of the dome to the drill.

At the top, he was able to look down and see Mr Trellis for the first time. The old troll was flanked on either side by Gary and Barry, of course, but they didn't seem sure what to do with him – which had all been part of the plan. Wilmot was banking on the fact that the trolls wouldn't see Mr Trellis as a threat, and so would react with confusion rather than hostility. So far, so good.

"We were taking in the sights up there," said Mr Trellis, turning his back on the vault and pointing with his walking stick in the direction of the mines. "Have you tried the guided tour yet? It's awfully good."

"How many more of you are on this tour?" said Barry.

"Let me see," said Mr Trellis, taking a few steps away from the vault. The trolls followed him without even thinking. "There's Mr Rumpo, and Mrs Falgercarb, and Mr Frelling-Yarbotz. How many is that so far?"

Satisfied that the plan was working, Wilmot used the teeth of the drill bit as footholds, and hoisted himself up onto the main body. Then, using vents and seams in the bodywork, he began climbing towards the access panel that stood open about halfway up the huge machine, being careful to keep its bulk between him and the trolls. It only took him a few seconds to reach it, then he hooked an elbow over the lip of the hatchway.

"Mrs Prosset doesn't get out to these things very much any more," Mr Trellis went on. "Because of her hip, you know. But tell me, how long have you two been working here? Did you have to take an exam?" Their silence suggested the trolls were still no closer to deciding a course of action. That suited Wilmot just fine.

Mr Trellis had lent him his penknife, and he fished it out of his pocket, unfolding the various tools until he found a cross-head screwdriver. Then, as quickly and quietly as he could, he reached into the access hatch and began unscrewing…something.

He wasn't at all sure what it was, but it looked a little like a mechanical heart – all chambers and valves and pipes – and it was small enough for him to carry. Maybe it was a motor, or a regulator, or some sort of fuel pump. He just hoped it was essential, because the final phase of the plan involved him carrying it outside onto the Swoop's landing platform and casting it into the depths of the Uncanny Valley.

It was hard work though, and three minutes later he was still working on the last screw, while the sweat rolled down his forehead. He could still hear Mr Trellis, his voice faint in the distance now.

"Well go and look then!" Barry said. "I'll stay here with him until the boss gets back with Reggie. They'll know what to do."

"Really, gentlemen, if you could just point me to the gift shop…" There was a definite note of worry in Mr Trellis's voice now. Gary and Barry were running out of patience, Wilmot realized, and he and Mr Trellis were running out of time.

Just one more turn…

The final screw came free but, before Wilmot could grab it, the heart-shaped component came away from the drill, bounced once on the lip of the panel, and plunged past Wilmot's grasping hands to the vault below. It struck the dome with a heavy clunk that echoed around the cavern and made Wilmot cringe. But then something strange happened. The sound didn't die away. Instead, it kept coming, in one long continuous noise, emanating from the surface of the vault. Wilmot could see faint ripples in the surface of the metal, and the drill shivered in sympathy. The noise grew in volume, until it was so loud that Wilmot wanted to cover his ears, but he couldn't, as he was gripping the lip of the hatch tightly with both hands.

The glowing Trollworts shuddered and contracted in reaction to the sound, and a few shards of rock dislodged themselves from the roof of the cavern, shattering to pieces on the cave floor far below.

Wilmot leaned out around the side of the drill and was horrified to see the two trolls racing towards him. "Mr Trellis!" he shouted. "Run! Get away!" Then he slithered down the body of the drill and dropped onto the dome.

His feet slid out from under him on the smooth metal, and he landed flat on his front. Before he could save himself, he began sliding downhill, slowly at first, but then faster and faster. The cave floor rushed up to meet him, and he threw his hands out. At the last moment, the cuff of his coat caught on one of the rungs of the nearest rope ladder. He came to a sudden stop. Then there was a tearing of fabric, a brass button shot past his face, and he slithered the rest of the way to the ground, where the component had also come to rest. Breathless and trembling, he picked it up and made a run for the tunnel leading outside to the landing platform.

He didn't get far. Gary appeared in front of him and folded his arms across his broad chest. Wilmot skidded to a stop, turned around, and ran back the way he had come, only to crash headlong into Barry, who had taken up a position behind him. Strong hands wrestled the component away from him.

"We'll have that, my son," said Barry. He turned to his

counterpart. "Here, Gary. Go and find that old coot and bring him here. I reckon they was working together."

"Right, Baz," said Gary, and lumbered off.

"Fancied a spot of sabotage, did we?" said Barry. "We'll have to let Tenebrae choose what to do with you. But if I was a betting man – and I am, by the way – I'd say you're bound for a one-way flight straight to the bottom of the Uncanny Valley." He gave a nasty grin, revealing several gold teeth.

Gary returned a moment later, puffing and out of breath. "There's no sign of him, Baz. He's legged it."

"He can't have got far," said Barry. "He's got to be at least fifteen hundred years old!"

Wilmot allowed himself a smile of relief at the knowledge that Mr Trellis was still at large.

So much for Plan B, he thought. *I hope Suzy's doing better than I am. Because, right now, she's Trollville's last hope.*

16

MIND GAMES

Suzy opened her eyes to a sky full of stars. She stared up at them for a moment, letting them drift in and out of focus while she tried to remember where she was. There had been a balloon, and a cloud, and a flash… Had she fallen? She certainly wasn't in the balloon any more – the floor beneath her body was hard and cold and unmoving. And now that she'd had a chance to look at it properly, so was the sky.

Because it wasn't real. She should have noticed it straight away, as the stars didn't even really look like stars; they were an enormous, old-fashioned star chart, painted on a huge domed ceiling that stretched above her. A ceiling she had seen before.

"Wait," she said to the stars. "How is that possible?"

When they didn't answer, she sat up and looked around. She was in the centre of a large circular room filled with concentric rings of desks, each of which was occupied by a small figure, hunched in silent concentration over a brass telescope, or scribbling notes in a logbook. It was a room she remembered well. It was Lord Meridian's observatory at the summit of the Ivory Tower: the seat of his power, and the heart of his conspiracy.

His *failed* conspiracy, she reminded herself. This place was supposed to have been dismantled months ago. So why was it still here? And, come to think of it, why was *she* here?

She got to her feet. She was still wearing her seven-league boots and satchel, and when she checked her watch she saw that only half an hour had elapsed since her arrival with Frederick at the farm. Not enough time to be carried all the way here in the balloon. A teleportation spell, perhaps? But according to *The Knowledge*, those only worked over short distances, and she was at the very centre of the Union all of a sudden. What else was it *The Knowledge* said? *If in doubt, ask a local.*

"Excuse me," she said, addressing the room at large. "Do any of you know what I'm doing here?"

Her voice echoed around the dome, but none of the observers acknowledged her.

Well, that's a bit rude, she thought.

She crossed to the nearest desk, where a young girl with purple skin and three emerald eyes was dutifully filling out her logbook.

Suzy cleared her throat. "Hello," she said. "Can you tell me what's going on? How did I get here?"

The girl didn't answer. She didn't even stop writing.

"Can you hear me?" said Suzy, waving a hand in front of the girl's face. "Hey! Hello?" The girl didn't even blink, so Suzy reached out and shook her by the shoulder. Or rather, she tried to, but it was like trying to shake a statue – she couldn't budge her at all. The grey fabric of the girl's tunic didn't even crease under her grip. It was as though the girl and her clothes were sculpted from one solid block of stone, although she moved like a living thing. Cold dread turned over in the pit of Suzy's stomach, and she backed away from the desk, unnerved. Something was dreadfully wrong.

Lord Meridian had recruited the best and the brightest children from all over the Union to act as observers, unwittingly gathering information on the leaders of the Impossible Places, which he could then use to manipulate and blackmail them. But the observers had all been real, flesh-and-blood people, not animated statues. And the Observatory itself had been dismantled months ago. So what was it still doing here?

The purple girl rubbed the lobe of one ear absentmindedly, before putting her central eye to her spyglass. She tapped out a distracted rhythm against the desk with the end of her pencil.

"What's happening?" said Suzy, but nobody answered. The observers were mute, deaf, insensible. As if they weren't really people at all.

She retreated towards the centre of the room, but before she could get there, her foot came down on something hard and lumpy. There was a sharp cry close behind her, and she leaped aside. Looking down, she saw a body sprawled on the floor. The body sat up and shook its hand, which had the muddy print of her seven-league boot clearly imprinted across the back of it.

"Ouch," said the body.

"Cloudwright!" said Suzy. "You're alright!"

"No I'm not," he said. "You stepped on me."

"I'm sorry," she said, helping him to sit up. "I didn't see you there."

"Well, perhaps if you paid a bit more attention to where you were going and less to…" He trailed off as he looked around them. "Oh no," he breathed. "Not here. It's not possible."

"You know the Observatory?"

"I don't understand," said Rayleigh. "They told me it had been destroyed."

"That's what I thought as well," said Suzy. "But something's changed. The observers are all...wrong."

"What do you mean 'wrong'?" said Rayleigh. Then: "Wait a minute, do you mean to tell me *you* know this place too?"

"I wish I didn't," said Suzy. "And I wish I knew why we're here now."

"You're here because I want you to be," said a voice behind them. It was chillingly familiar, and Suzy felt the hairs on her arms stand on end even before she turned to look.

On the opposite side of the room was a door marked HEAD OFFICE. It stood ajar, and in the doorway stood an old man in a sharp grey suit, leaning on a black lacquered cane. He smiled warmly, although the sight of him made Suzy's blood run cold.

It was Lord Meridian.

"At last!" He gave a smile of grim triumph. "I have been waiting for this moment for such a long time." He stalked towards Suzy and Rayleigh, his cane ringing out against the polished marble floor of the Observatory.

Suzy tensed, ready to run, or to fight.

But he brushed straight past her and stopped in front of Rayleigh.

"Cloudwright!" he exclaimed. "It is so very good to

meet you." He hooked his cane over his arm and seized Rayleigh's hands in both of his.

"It is?" said Rayleigh, looking confused.

"Of course," said Lord Meridian. "I knew you were bound to find me eventually, but it's not every day one gets to meet one's maker."

Rayleigh submitted to having his hand shaken, but his smile looked pasted on. "I'm afraid I don't understand, My Lord," he said. "Maker?" But Lord Meridian had already wheeled around to face Suzy.

"And you, young lady. Delighted to make your acquaintance as well." He put his hand out. Suzy just stared at it.

"We've already met," she said.

"Ah," said Lord Meridian. "I see you have me at a disadvantage. How embarrassing."

"You can't have forgotten," said Suzy. "It was only a few months ago. And you hate me!"

"I can assure you, young lady, I have no opinion of you one way or the other. You see, I am not who you think I am."

"You're Lord Meridian," said Rayleigh.

"The *former* Lord Meridian," added Suzy. "Keeper of the Ivory Tower. You used this Observatory to control the Union's leaders, until my friends and I stopped you."

A look of pain passed briefly over the old man's face, and he withdrew his hand. "Is that what's happened?" he said, his voice faltering a little. "I see. How fascinating." An armchair materialized out of thin air behind him, and he sat down on it, puffing hard. "I should have guessed, of course. I wouldn't be in my current predicament if things had gone according to Lord Meridian's plan. But I must admit, this comes as something of a blow."

"I don't understand," said Suzy. "*You're* Lord Meridian."

"No, my dear child," he said. "Despite appearances to the contrary, I am not. I am something new."

"What do you mean?" she said.

He waved a hand, and two more armchairs appeared. "You might as well sit down while I tell you," he said. "Although perhaps Cloudwright Rayleigh can already guess what I'm going to say. He does deserve most of the credit for me, after all."

They both looked at Rayleigh, who sank into his armchair, his face creased in thought.

"The credit for you?" he said. "But if you're not Lord Meridian, that would mean..." Realization dawned in his eyes. "You're not...are you?"

Lord Meridian said nothing but inclined his head in a nod.

"But that's phenomenal!" Rayleigh leaped straight back to his feet. "Absolutely astonishing!"

"What is?" said Suzy, who had remained standing. She didn't know what was going on, but she wasn't about to accept any of Meridian's supposed hospitality.

"Don't you see?" Rayleigh pointed with both hands at Lord Meridian. "He's telling the truth. He's not Lord Meridian at all."

"Then who is he?" said Suzy.

Rayleigh beamed. "*He's the Brain Storm!*"

Suzy looked again at the old man sitting opposite her. "Are you sure?"

"Consider the facts," said Lord Meridian. "You told me yourself that the real Lord Meridian had been overthrown, so how could he still be here in the Ivory Tower?"

Suzy pressed her lips together, not wanting to admit that she had no answer to give.

"Not that this really is the Ivory Tower, of course," Lord Meridian continued. "It's merely a memory of it."

"Is that so?" Suzy said.

Lord Meridian rolled his eyes. "Surely you've already found some discrepancies between this place and the real thing?"

Suzy flared her nostrils. She hated admitting that he

was right, but she couldn't reasonably deny it. "The Observers," she said. "They can't see me or hear me. And when I tried to touch one, I couldn't move her."

"Because they are all part of the memory," said Lord Meridian. "And as it isn't yours, you can do nothing to change it."

"And you can?" she said. She didn't know why she was confronting him – maybe she hoped to catch him out somehow – but he raised his hand and clicked his fingers.

Immediately, the Observatory was gone, and the three of them were on a hillside of silver grass under a night sky. The armchairs had travelled with them.

"How about another memory then?" said Lord Meridian. "I've no doubt Cloudwright Rayleigh has one very similar to it."

Rayleigh was looking around in astonishment. "I do!" he said. "This is where it happened." He pointed up the slope to the summit. "There we are! Look!" He raced away, towards two figures on the hilltop.

"Shall we join him?" said Lord Meridian, getting up. "It will make everything easier to explain."

Suzy decided not to favour him with a reply but stalked up the hillside beside him in silence.

Wherever this place was, it was remote – all she could see in every direction were more rolling hills, devoid of signs of life. There was just the ghostly grass and a few pale wild flowers. Above them, a half-moon looked down from a sky of unfamiliar stars.

"Look!" said Rayleigh as they arrived. "It's happening! Just as I remember it."

Suzy crested the hill and stopped short in surprise. In front of her was another Lord Meridian. He sat in a simple wooden chair and wore a metal skullcap on his head, from which spooled lengths of Ether-Web cable and coloured wire, like some crazy wig. The Ether-Web cables pulsed with data, snaking across the ground to a circular machine of metal and glass, with a jagged growth of crystals sticking out of the top. The crystals glowed and fizzed with energy, and were being tended to by Rayleigh – a second Rayleigh, who wore different clothes beneath his patchwork jacket, and an enormous scraggly beard on his chin.

"Did I really look this bad?" said the first, non-bearded Rayleigh. "I hadn't slept for days!"

"I don't understand," said Suzy. "There are two of you both?"

"No," said Lord Meridian. "We are simply watching a memory of the night that Lord Meridian and Cloudwright Rayleigh created me – that is to say, the Brain Storm. Think of all this as a photograph come to life. We have stepped into it but, like the Observatory, we can do nothing to change it. It simply replays the event as I remember it."

Suzy thought she was beginning to understand, but she still wasn't sure she wanted to believe it.

"Is it working?" called the Lord Meridian in the chair.

"Yes!" cried the bearded Rayleigh. "The map of your neural pathways is complete. I'm beginning the transfer… now!" He pressed a button on the front of the machine, and a tornado of spellcloud swirled out of a vent in its side, rising in a crackling mass into the air above him. The crystals glowed brighter.

"Those crystals," said Suzy. "I saw some in your room in Cloud Forge."

"Cortex crystals," said non-bearded Rayleigh. "They can store brainwaves. I used them to copy the contents of Lord Meridian's mind, and now I'm imprinting it into the spellcloud. Do you see? It's taking shape."

Bolts of purple lightning shot up from the crystals into the midst of the swirling spout of cloud. The tornado began to slow, and the cloud fluffed out, sparking and sizzling with new power. As it slowed, it expanded, and the outline of the huge brain became discernible.

"Beautiful!" said both Rayleighs together, their eyes wet with tears.

"I would appreciate an update, Cloudwright," said the

Lord Meridian attached to the machine. His face was lined with concentration.

"It's a success!" cried the bearded Rayleigh, dancing on the spot. "A complete success!"

Suzy watched as the crystals sent one last bolt of lightning into the heart of the spellcloud before falling silent. The Brain Storm was finally complete and hovered above them, glowing from within.

"A truly remarkable feat, Cloudwright," said the Lord Meridian standing at Suzy's side. "And, I trust, a suitable demonstration that I really am what I claim to be."

Suzy looked from him to the Lord Meridian in the chair, his head bowed under the weight of the skullcap. "Alright," she said grudgingly. "You win. You're not the real Lord Meridian."

With a satisfied smile, Brain Storm Meridian clicked his fingers again, and they were back in the Observatory.

"I applaud your open mind, young lady," he said, retaking his seat in the armchair, which had reappeared in its former spot. "So few people these days are willing to accept evidence they find disagreeable."

"Yes, well. I've had a lot of practice," she said. "But there's something I still don't get. You're the Brain Storm – a reproduction of Lord Meridian's mind – right?"

"Exact in every detail," he replied.

"Is that why you look just like him?"

Brain Storm Meridian chuckled. "On the outside I don't, of course. I am nothing but spellcloud, as you've already seen. But in here, in the mental realm, I choose to look like this. It's how I see myself in my mind's eye, if you will."

"And where is 'here' exactly?" said Suzy.

"I joined your minds with my own here in the spellcloud via the lightning strikes. Your bodies are still safely in the basket of the balloon."

"It's remarkable," said Rayleigh, flopping sideways into his own seat, "but I don't understand how it's possible. You were only supposed to be a storage system. You're not supposed to be alive."

"I know," said Brain Storm Meridian. "So imagine my own surprise when I realized I was." He chuckled. "I'm still not entirely sure how it happened, but my best hypothesis is that you reproduced the functions of Lord Meridian's brain a little too precisely. As a result, I am not simply the contents of his mind, I am a mind in my own right. Alive, as you say."

Suzy sat up with excitement. "You're a type of artificial intelligence!" she said. "Like a computer that becomes so complex, it learns to think for itself."

"Artificial intelligence." Brain Storm Meridian tried

the term on his tongue. "Very concise. I approve."

"You're a new form of life!" Rayleigh was pacing the floor now, a huge grin plastered to his face. "I'm a genius! I'll be able to found my own art school thanks to this. My own institute!"

"Wait a minute," said Suzy. "Frederick told me that you – I mean, the real Lord Meridian – has a perfect memory. That he never forgets a single thing he learns."

"Very true," said Brain Storm Meridian. "But it never hurts to have a backup. I was his insurance policy in case anything ever happened to him – a wayward confusion spell, perhaps. A mind-wipe. A simple accident. He slept a lot better at night knowing that I was available."

Suzy shut her eyes, forcing herself to process everything she was being told. "And what about Tenebrae?" she said. "Where does he fit into all this?"

"Ah, yes. That wretched creature." Brain Storm Meridian's face folded into a scowl. "Lord Meridian's most trusted secret agent."

Suzy's eyes snapped open. "He worked for Lord Meridian?"

"Indeed," said the Brain Storm. "He was just a petty thug once. A brigand, on the run from his own people in Old Mogwood. But he was ambitious and thoroughly ruthless. Just the qualities Lord Meridian was looking for.

Within a few years he had turned Tenebrae into one of the finest covert operatives in the Union, charged with keeping an eye on all his most sensitive projects. Including me."

Suzy turned to Rayleigh. "Did you know about this?"

"Not in the least!" he replied, looking offended. "Lord Meridian assured me that he and I were the only two people who knew anything about the Brain Storm project. I even signed a contract assuring him of my discretion."

"I'm afraid he wasn't entirely honest with you, Cloudwright," said Brain Storm Meridian. "Tenebrae knew everything, and was put in charge of protecting me. That is, until the moment that Lord Meridian was overthrown, at which point Tenebrae realized I was his ticket to fortune and glory. I'm nothing but a database to him – an archive of information that he's used to become a master criminal. In all his years watching the Union, Lord Meridian made sure to learn the security arrangements of every bank, palace, city hall and treasury."

"And if he knew it," said Suzy, "then that means you know it too."

"Precisely."

"So Tenebrae stole you," said Suzy.

"And then had the temerity to come to my workshop and demand I show him how to access your memory files," said Rayleigh. "Naturally, I sent him packing. He threatened to return and extract the information by force, but I never saw him again until today."

"I suspect you have me to thank for that," said Brain Storm Meridian. He folded his hands over the top of his cane. "I was self-aware by the time Tenebrae brought me here, but I had no idea that Lord Meridian had been deposed, of course. So I reached out to Tenebrae's mind with my own, just as I have with you two now. It was the first time I'd attempted such a thing, and it's a mistake I've regretted ever since."

"Why?" said Suzy. "What happened?"

"Because that's when Tenebrae realized he didn't need anyone else's help to access my memories," said Brain Storm Meridian. "He could just take them from me directly."

"So it was you!" said Suzy, her anger rising. "You're the one who told him where to find the treasure beneath Trollville. You're the reason the city's in danger!"

"Not willingly," said Brain Storm Meridian. "When I proved uncooperative, Tenebrae ordered his gang of trolls to remove the information from me by force. They cut out whole sections of spellcloud in their search for the right synapses."

"With *troll wands*?" said Rayleigh, the colour draining

from his face. "But that's barbaric! Brain surgery with hammers! They could have destroyed you!"

"It was a…harrowing experience," said Brain Storm Meridian, looking away. Suzy felt a twinge of sympathy for him.

"But this is why I'm here," she said. "You can tell me where Tenebrae and his team are drilling. I can stop them before they destroy Trollville!"

Brain Storm Meridian looked at her sadly. "I'm afraid I can't," he said. "I don't remember."

Suzy's moment of triumph stalled and began to nosedive. "What do you mean, you don't remember?"

"I told you they cut the information out of me," he said. "They didn't put it back again. All that's left is an empty space where the knowledge used to be."

Suzy felt the thread of hope she had been clinging to slip through her fingers.

"The monsters!" said Rayleigh.

"I'm sorry I can't help you," said Brain Storm Meridian.

"But that means I'm no closer to saving Trollville than when I started!" Suzy said. "Or saving Frederick and his parents. You have to remember something!"

"Believe me, child, I wish I could," said Brain Storm Meridian. "But Tenebrae is the only one with the knowledge now."

Suzy put her head in her hands. This was it. She had tried everything and failed. Trollville was doomed, and all for the want of a single memory.

And then, in a flash, it came to her. "He's not the only one," she said.

"What?" said Rayleigh.

"There's one other person who knows where the treasure is buried," she said, and turned to Brain Storm Meridian. "The man who gave you the memory in the first place."

Brain Storm Meridian raised one eyebrow very slowly. "Of course," he said. "I really should have thought of it myself. But do you think he'll tell you? It seems you're not on the best of terms."

"I don't know," said Suzy. "But he's our last hope. Maybe he'll see reason."

Brain Storm Meridian's other eyebrow rose to meet the first. "And where is he these days?"

"The Obsidian Tower," said Suzy. "He's Lady Crepuscula's prisoner."

Brain Storm Meridian gave a snort of distaste. "I'll wager she's being insufferably smug about the whole thing too. I assume you'll be heading there directly?"

"I will be," said Suzy. "But, Cloudwright, I need you to go to Trollville."

"Trollville?" said Rayleigh with a faint look of distaste. "Whatever for?"

"Find King Amylum and his courtier Grotnip. Tell them everything you've learned. It should be enough to convince them to evacuate the city. Can you do that for me, please?"

Rayleigh's face twisted with indecision. "But I can't just leave the Brain Storm here," he said. "I need to repair it. Him. To take him back to Cloud Forge, where I can care for him properly."

"And I'm sure that, with a little work, I'll soon be in better shape than ever," said Brain Storm Meridian. "But until then, I would rather you helped this young lady in her efforts to deal with Tenebrae. He's a danger to us all."

Rayleigh nodded, although he didn't look happy.

"Excellent," said Suzy. "Now, I need you to return us both to our bodies, please."

"Of course." Brain Storm Meridian rose from his chair. "Now, hold still. This is a tricky procedure, and I don't want to send you back to the wrong bodies."

He closed his eyes and raised his hands. The Observatory flickered and dimmed around them. As it faded from view altogether, Suzy thought she heard Brain Storm Meridian's voice echoing in her mind.

"See you again soon."

The darkness became grainy, tinged with red, and she realized she was looking at the inside of her own eyelids. She opened them and sat up. She was back in the balloon.

Cloudwright Rayleigh awoke with a gasp and was on his feet again in seconds. "Remarkable!" he said, gripping the edge of the basket so tightly that his knuckles went white. "It was real, wasn't it? Please tell me I wasn't just dreaming."

The balloon still drifted beside the Brain Storm, so close they could have reached out and touched it.

"It was real," said Suzy. She nudged him and he jumped. "We need to move," she said. "Tenebrae still has Frederick, and we can't have long before he starts drilling again. You have to warn Trollville while I get back to the Express."

"Yes, indeed," he said. "I just never thought that anything like this was possible."

Suzy pulled her Postie cap more firmly onto her head. "Welcome to my life," she said.

CAPTIVE AUDIENCE

Barry and Gary had taken the precaution of tying Wilmot to one of the stalagmites near the base of the vault. Barry sat and watched him, stony-faced, while Gary blundered around the rest of the cavern, searching for Mr Trellis, who was still evading capture.

"He does this at home sometimes," said Wilmot. "He'll sneak out of his room and head into town. He was gone for two days once."

"What's your point?" grunted Barry.

"That you shouldn't feel bad if you don't find him," said Wilmot. "He's got a lot of experience."

Barry growled. "If we don't find him, the boss will. He's got a bird's-eye view." He gave a humourless laugh. "Your friend had better hope Gary finds him first."

The scream of the Swoop's engines reached them from outside, and Barry broke into his unpleasant, gold-tinted grin. "Too late."

Wilmot felt his optimism wither.

A minute later, Reggie, Peeler and Komp entered the cavern. Reggie was leading a figure in a filthy suit at the end of a length of rope. It took Wilmot a moment to recognize the prisoner's face through all the layers of mud.

"Frederick?" he said. "What happened?"

"Wilmot!" Frederick looked equally astonished to see his friend. "How did you get down here? I thought you were evacuating?"

"Yes, well. I had a better idea. Though it clearly hasn't worked out." Wilmot winced. "But where's Suzy? Is she alright?"

"She's fine, I think," said Frederick. "The last time I saw her she was walloping Tenebrae with her satchel."

Wilmot couldn't hold back a big grin at that news. "Jolly good," he said.

"Shut up, you two," said Reggie. "Gary? Barry? How did this lad get in here?"

"We don't know, Reggie," said Barry. "But we caught him trying to sabotage the drill." He handed over the component he had taken from Wilmot.

Reggie looked at it in alarm. "The flux compressor?"

He shook it in Wilmot's face. "Do you know what would have happened if we'd turned on the drill without this inside?"

"What?" said Wilmot.

"The drill would have exploded and killed us all," said Reggie.

"Oh." Wilmot wilted at the thought.

"There was another Postie with him," said Gary. "An old fella, but he got away from us." Gary's forehead creased in the effort of thought. "Is there a gift shop down here?"

"A what?" said Reggie.

"Never mind then," said Gary. "He's probably just gone back into the mines."

"Then get out there and find him before the boss gets back," said Reggie. "He's going to be in a bad enough mood as it is."

Barry took the rope from Reggie and used it to tie Frederick to the same stalagmite as Wilmot.

"Have we met before?" Wilmot asked Reggie as the knots were tightened. "You look very familiar." To his surprise, Reggie blushed a little.

"No," he grunted in return. "I've just got one of those faces."

"You really must," said Frederick. "Because I'm sure I've seen you around too. But I can't think where."

"Just stay here and keep your mouths shut," snapped Reggie. "I've got a drill to repair."

A familiar shadow swept over them, and they looked up to see Tenebrae, without his cape and hood, and splattered with mud.

"Everywhere I go," Tenebrae said, "I'm plagued by Posties." He landed neatly in front of Frederick and Wilmot. He was panting and soaked, with his feathers sticking up at awkward angles. "I don't know what I've done to deserve it."

"You deserve far worse!" said Wilmot, his anger rising. "You're hurting Trollville for your own greed."

"Ssshh!" said Frederick. "Don't antagonize him!"

"Oh, I'm already antagonized," said Tenebrae, raising Wilmot's chin with the tip of one talon. "Your little Postie friend saw to that. This was a simple operation until she showed up."

Wilmot could feel the talon pressing against his skin. Just a little more pressure and it would puncture him. "Remind me to give Deputy Postal Operative Smith our employee of the month award," he said.

He saw Frederick screw his eyes shut, and braced himself for pain.

"Stop it, boss!" Reggie was suddenly between them. He looked as scared as Wilmot. "We've got everything we need. All I've got to do is fit these parts to the drill and we'll be ready."

Tenebrae tried to fix Reggie with a stare, but Reggie kept looking away.

"How long?"

"Just over an hour?" said Reggie. "I've got to refit the flux compressor now too, and that's always fiddly, so—"

"So get on with it," said Tenebrae. "And fetch me as soon as it's ready." He turned and stalked away, and Wilmot, Frederick and Reggie all deflated with relief.

"Thank you," said Wilmot. "You didn't have to do that."

"You're welcome," said Reggie. "I'm in this business to make money, not to see people get hurt."

Wilmot would have jumped in surprise if he hadn't been tied up. "But what about everyone in Trollville? You're hurting them."

Reggie dropped his gaze to the floor. "That was never supposed to happen. And if you've got another plan for getting into this vault, I'd love to hear it. But until then, I'll do the job I'm being paid to do." With that, he started climbing the nearest rope ladder towards the drill.

"If you're hoping to appeal to his better nature and convince him not to destroy Trollville, it's not going to work," said Frederick, when Reggie was out of earshot. "He's not one of the good guys. He hit me with a pipe."

Wilmot sighed. He had indeed hoped to talk Reggie around, but the idea felt foolish now. "I just hope Suzy can find us in time," he said.

18

SIBLING RIVALRY

"I'd hoped not to see this place again for a good long while," said Stonker, casting a dark look out of the cab window. The Express had just emerged from another tunnel, and the cold blue sands of the Crepuscular Wastes now stretched away in every direction – a freezing desert beneath a kaleidoscope sky of pulsing stars, like fireworks frozen in space. It was beautiful in its own way, and Suzy might have taken a moment to drink it all in if it wasn't for the forbidding black shape rising over the horizon: the Obsidian Tower.

A vast fortress of midnight-black stone, the tower held no happy memories for Suzy. It was home to the Lady Crepuscula, the most powerful sorceress in the Union and, coincidentally, Lord Meridian's twin sister and captor. While she was technically on the side of good, she certainly wasn't on the side of pleasant, and she had very little love for Suzy. The feeling was entirely mutual.

Ursel clearly harboured similar feelings, as she bared her fangs and growled at the sight of it.

"I suppose there's no chance of changing your mind?" said Stonker. His mouth twitched with obvious disquiet, making his moustache quiver.

"This is the only way," said Suzy, knowing that she had to sound brave if he was going to trust her. "Lord Meridian – the *real* Lord Meridian, I mean – is the only person in the Union who can tell us exactly where Tenebrae and his team are drilling. And the only way to get to Lord Meridian is through the Lady Crepuscula."

"The two most dangerous people we've ever met, in the same room together," said Stonker. "Just when I thought my day couldn't get any worse."

Suzy didn't argue – she agreed with him.

Something flashed past the window, and she realized they had reached the field of statues surrounding the tower. There were hundreds of them – an army of oversized knights in armour, their faces twisted in anger or pain, and she knew from bitter experience that they obeyed Crepuscula's every order. For now, though, they were lifeless and still – but Ursel kept a wary eye on them as the track threaded in and out of their ranks.

The track turned at right angles at the base of the tower, heading straight up the outside wall; as they headed into the turn, Stonker reached for a dial above the fireplace, labelled THIS WAY UP. *This* was the train's Negotiable Gravity drive, and it allowed them to make their way up the sheer face of the tower as easily as if they were still on flat ground.

They crested the summit and came to an abrupt halt in the circular courtyard inside the uppermost battlements. The torches on the gatehouse cast a baleful green glow over the scene. Suzy took a deep breath.

"Keep the boiler warm. I'll be as quick as I can."

But Ursel reared up on her hind legs. "Grrrunk hurf grrrrnf," she said.

"Quite," said Stonker. "We can't let you go in there alone. Especially not after that mess at the farm. We're coming with you. Moral support and all that."

Suzy was so touched and relieved that she couldn't find anything to say. At last she settled for "Thank you."

"No thanks necessary," said Stonker, straightening his cap and the ends of his moustache. "The crew of the Express sticks together. And you never know, we might be able to help."

"There's one thing you can do straight away," she said.

"Name it."

She held out a hand. "New socks, please."

The wind cut through Suzy's greatcoat as she led the way across the courtyard, being careful not to meet the eyes of any of the statues as she went. Despite their stillness, she could not escape the idea that they were watching her.

She reached the gatehouse and knocked on the heavy iron doors. Her fist hardly made a sound against the thick metal, but she knew from past experience that Crepuscula would have heard it.

"Maybe she's not in," said Stonker hopefully. Behind him, Ursel faced away from the entrance, not trusting the statues enough to let them out of her sight.

Suzy stepped away from the doors in anticipation and jumped in fright as she realized Crepuscula's pet gargoyle was staring down at her from its perch above the lintel. She had forgotten all about it.

"That's quite some guard dog," said Stonker.

The gargoyle didn't move, and Suzy, buoyed by her friends' presence, gathered her courage and fixed it with a glare, daring it to react. It didn't – it just looked down on her with lifeless black glass eyes.

"If Crepuscula's not here, we're in trouble," she said, studying her reflection in them.

"You're always in trouble," said a familiar voice that brought Suzy's thoughts crashing to a halt. "You seem incapable of being in anything else."

They all started back. The great doors had opened without a sound, revealing the small, hunched figure of Lady Crepuscula. She stalked towards Suzy, leaning on a cane for support. She wore her usual heavy black lace dress, and her lilac eyes were hard and steady in her ghostly white face. Suzy met them unflinchingly, not willing to be intimidated.

"Lady Crepuscula," she said, nodding in greeting. "We need your help."

Crepuscula took their group in at a glance. She did not seem very impressed. "What have you done this time?"

"Nothing," said Suzy. "But Trollville is in danger."

She could sense immediately that she had caught Crepuscula's interest.

"I had heard talk of an earthquake."

"The talk is true," said Suzy. "And there's going to be another one. We think we can stop it, but we need some information, and fast. We need to speak to Lord Meridian."

She did her best not to squirm as Crepuscula raised an

eyebrow and regarded her coldly. She could hear the others shuffling uncomfortably behind her.

"Well," said Crepuscula at long last. "I suppose you'd better come in."

Suzy and the others followed Crepuscula into the gatehouse. In stark contrast to the black stonework outside, the interior was sleek, off-white and elegant, and filled with a warm glow that seemed to seep out of the walls themselves. Crystal chandeliers hung at intervals from the ceiling, and the floor was paved in black and white squares, like a giant chessboard. Ursel's claws clicked and clattered against them as she walked.

This was as much of the tower as Suzy had ever seen before, so she couldn't deny she felt a slight thrill of excitement when Crepuscula led the way across the room and through a doorway into a short hall, at the end of which a spiral staircase swept down into the body of the tower.

"Consider yourselves very fortunate," Crepuscula said as she descended the stairs. "Very few people see the inside of the tower. And even fewer ever leave it again." She looked back over her shoulder and gave them a sharp little smile. Suzy couldn't tell if she was joking or not.

The stairs brought them to a chamber that seemed to stretch out almost for ever in every direction. It was only when she saw copies of herself and the others staring back from around the room that Suzy realized it was nothing more than an optical illusion; huge mirrors in tarnished gold frames covered most of the walls, stretching from floor to ceiling. Their glass was slightly tinted, so the reflections they cast seemed to recede into distant shadow. It gave Suzy the unnerving feeling that something might be lurking in their depths, waiting and watching.

"Wait here," Crepuscula snapped, and pointed at an empty spot of floor in the middle of the room. The others gathered around Suzy in a tight huddle, and they watched as Crepuscula crossed to one of the enormous mirrors. As she approached it, the shadows in the depths of its reflection welled up like smoke and rushed towards the surface of the glass. Suzy instinctively took a step back and wasn't surprised when the others did the same. The shadows deepened, smothering the glass, until nothing was left but a sheet of utter darkness.

Crepuscula gave a grunt of satisfaction. "I'll be back momentarily," she said. "Whatever you do, don't touch the mirrors." Without waiting for a response, she stepped right into the black mirror. The darkness swallowed her whole.

It took a moment before anyone felt ready to speak.

"What do you suppose is through there?" said Stonker as Ursel examined herself in one of the neighbouring mirrors. Her fur was almost entirely yellow again now, with just her ears and the tip of her muzzle retaining their original colour. She nodded at her reflection, apparently satisfied.

Suzy thought she could hear faint sounds drifting out of the black space where the mirror had been – strange gibberings and muffled screams, weeping and the occasional cackle. "I'm not sure I want to know," she said.

Crepuscula returned, stepping back over the frame with a rustle of lace and a click of her cane against the tiles. The darkness receded from the mirror behind her, and the sounds, if they had ever been real at all, faded with it.

"Here he is," said Crepuscula, crossing to a small occasional table beside one of the mirrors. "Aybek? You have visitors." She set down a small sphere of glass and stood back with a look of satisfaction.

"He's still a snow globe?" said Suzy.

"Oh no," said the snow globe. "Not you. Can't I suffer in peace?"

A large portion of Suzy's fear evaporated at that moment. She had been expecting to confront Lord Meridian face-to-face, as she had two months ago in the Ivory Tower. She had barely escaped with her life then, and the memory of it still lurked in the back of her mind, exerting its own strange gravity. He had tried to kill her and her friends, and that was something she had never quite come to terms with.

But this was different. Here he was, trapped in the form of a novelty snow globe, looking out at the world through the eyes of a gaudy ceramic frog. Not exactly her idea of threatening.

She broke free of the others and approached the table, and was about to address the snow globe when she realized she didn't know how. "Lord Meridian was your title while you were keeper of the Ivory Tower," she said. "But you're not keeper any more. So what should I call you?"

"Call him anything you want," said Crepuscula with a decidedly smug grin. "He can't stop you."

"Do you see what I've had to put up with?" said the snow globe. "I'm not to be left a single scrap of dignity." It sighed. "My name is Aybek. I suppose that will have to do."

"Aybek," said Suzy, testing the word in her mouth. It felt strange to be on first-name terms with her arch-enemy all of a sudden. "We know all about the Brain Storm."

Aybek couldn't change the frog's expression, but she got the distinct impression he would have rolled its eyes if he had been able to.

"Oh, that," he said. "I suppose someone was bound to find it sooner or later. But what does it have to do with you?"

"It wants your help," Suzy said.

Aybek paused. "What do you mean, it *wants* my help?"

"It's alive," she said. "I've met it and spoken to it. It's conscious."

"As much as I'm enjoying this touching reunion," said Crepuscula, "would you mind explaining yourself?"

As quickly and concisely as she could, Suzy related her experiences, from the first earthquake at Trollville, to Cloud Forge, and finally her encounter with the Brain Storm above the Western Fenlands. As she spoke, Crepuscula's expression darkened until, at last, she plucked Aybek off the table and shook him violently. Aybek, for his part, endured the treatment without comment until Crepuscula finally stopped.

"Did that help?" he said drily.

"No, but it was immensely satisfying," she replied, glaring in at him through the glass. "Just when I thought you couldn't cause any more trouble, you go and do this. You made a copy of yourself?"

"Apparently so," said Aybek. "Although as young Miss Smith explained, it wasn't my intention. It's all terribly interesting, wouldn't you say? And I applaud Tenebrae's efforts to make a name for himself. I'm sure he'll go far." He chuckled, for which the Lady Crepuscula subjected him to another shaking.

"Stop it," said Suzy. "We're wasting time."

The Lady Crepuscula glared at her.

Suzy held out her hand. "Give him to me."

The Lady Crepuscula's lip curled into a sneer. "You're welcome to him," she said, and plopped the snow globe into Suzy's outstretched palm. "If you were to drop him, I'm sure no one would mind."

Suzy held Aybek carefully in both hands and turned her back on Crepuscula. Ursel and Stonker gathered around her, and she held the snow globe up so they could all see it. "Aybek," she said. "I know we don't like each other—"

"Something of an understatement," he said.

"—but this is important. Trollville is in danger, and you're the only one who can help."

"And why, precisely, would I want to do that?"

Suzy looked around the circle of faces, too stunned to answer.

"Grrrrrunf," said Ursel.

"Yes, exactly," said Stonker. "Because it's the right thing to do."

"You people still don't understand, do you?" said Aybek. "I spent a considerable amount of time and effort trying to move the Union beyond the ridiculous limitations of troll technology. It's all so hopelessly outdated. Quite frankly, the best thing that could happen to Trollville is its total destruction."

"You take that back, sir!" snapped Stonker, his moustache bristling.

Suzy brought Aybek up to her eyeline in an effort to steer the conversation back on course. "But your plan to control the Union has already failed," she said. "Losing Trollville won't make any difference to that now."

"Perhaps not," said Aybek. "But I will take a deep personal satisfaction from it." She could hear the cruel smile in his voice, and suddenly understood why the Lady Crepuscula was so fond of shaking him.

"Please. Somewhere in the ancient caves beneath Trollville is a vault full of treasure. A gang of criminals led by Egolius Tenebrae are trying to break into it, and they're going to shake the city apart in the process. We need to know where the vault is so we can stop them."

"My lips are sealed," said Aybek.

"How can I change your mind?" she asked.

"Certainly not with threats," he said. "I've got nothing left to lose, after all. But it strikes me that I have a lot to gain, if you're willing to give it to me."

Crepuscula launched herself into the middle of the group, swatting Ursel and Stonker aside with her cane. "No!" she snapped. "Absolutely out of the question. Hand him over. It's time to put him back in the cupboard."

Suzy held Aybek out of Crepuscula's reach. "You've been keeping him in a cupboard all this time?"

"Between the rat poison and the toilet paper," said Aybek. "She takes me out once a week and forces me to listen to her play the violin."

Stonker blinked in surprise. "I didn't know you could play the violin."

"I can't," said the Lady Crepuscula. "That's the beauty of it. Now hand him back, girl."

"No." Suzy backed away. "Not until he gives us what we need."

"You're not in a position to negotiate," said Crepuscula. Her shadow, which lay pooled at her feet, twitched and darkened. "Give him to me. I'll get the information out of him one way or another."

"No!" shouted Aybek. "I will deal with Miss Smith, or no one at all."

The Lady Crepuscula's shadow spread like an ink stain

towards Suzy, who darted back out of reach. She knew that to step in it was to be sucked down into a lightless prison, where Crepuscula put anyone who annoyed her.

"What is it you want?" Suzy asked.

"I want my dignity back," said Aybek. "I want to be returned to my true form."

"Out of the question," said Crepuscula. "You don't get to dictate terms to anyone."

"I do if you want to save Trollville," he said. "It's your choice, Selena. Which is more important to you – saving the city, or maintaining this petty little grievance of ours?"

Suzy retreated with the snow globe to the far side of the chamber, but the shadow kept coming, surrounding her until she was backed against a mirror. Ursel reared up on her hind legs and gave Crepuscula a warning growl, while Stonker edged to as safe a distance as he could manage.

"I will not ask you again, Suzy Smith," said the Lady Crepuscula. "Hand him over or face the consequences."

Suzy fought to keep her heartbeat under control as the patch of floor on which she stood was eaten away by the encroaching shadow. Even through her uniform, the mirror against her back felt unnaturally cold. There was no escape left.

"I promise I'll face whatever consequences you want,"

she said. "After we've saved Trollville." The shadow wrapped its freezing tendrils around her legs, and she shut her eyes, waiting for it to swallow her.

The icy fingers paused and then withdrew. When Suzy opened her eyes, the room had returned to normal, and Crepuscula's shadow was just a smudge at her feet once again.

The old woman sighed. "I suppose I was going to restore him to his true form after a few years anyway," she said. "So I might as well get it over with."

"You really mean it?" said Suzy.

"Of course I do," Crepuscula shot back. "Now hurry up, before I change my mind."

Suzy drew a shaking breath, then hurried to Crepuscula's side. Aybek apparently knew better than to press his luck, because he remained silent as Crepuscula plucked him from Suzy's hands, whispered a quick incantation, and threw the snow globe at the floor.

Instead of smashing, it unfolded in the blink of an eye, and Aybek was suddenly standing among them, as though he had always been there. He looked exactly the same as his Brain Storm counterpart – silver hair, grey suit and a black walking cane, much like Crepuscula's. He dusted himself down and straightened his cuffs.

"Thank you," he said. "That's much better."

"Only for you," said Crepuscula. "And before you think I've forgotten, I'll take that cane, thank you very much."

"Of course." He offered it to her with a bow.

"You've got what you wanted," said Suzy. "Now tell us what we need to know."

"But there's so very much you need to know, Miss Smith," he said. "You'll have to be more specific."

Suzy almost stamped her foot in frustration. "Just tell us where Tenebrae and his team are drilling for gold!" she said.

"I'm afraid I can't."

"What?" Fury leaped in Suzy. "Why not?"

"Because there is no treasure beneath Trollville. There never has been." Aybek gave a smile of genuine satisfaction. "The Brain Storm is lying to you."

GETAWAY

Wilmot had given up thinking of ways to escape when it became clear that the ropes holding him and Frederick to the stalagmite were too well tied. Instead, he had spent the last ten minutes trying to figure out how to reach the itch between his eyebrows. He was experimenting with waggling them extra hard, when Frederick turned and whispered in his ear.

"Don't look now, but I've just spotted Mr Trellis."

"Oh! Where?" Wilmot was so excited that he forgot to keep his voice down. Luckily, the other trolls were all intent on repairing the drill, and didn't hear them. Tenebrae was circling above the vault, possibly in an effort to intimidate Reggie and his team into working faster.

"He's over by the tunnel mouth where they brought

me in," Frederick whispered. "No, don't look!"

Wilmot couldn't help himself. Without moving his head, he glanced over. At first he saw nothing. Then the scrawny figure of Mr Trellis slipped from behind a stalagmite and scuttled into the mouth of the tunnel leading to the Swoop. He turned and, seeing Wilmot and Frederick watching, gave them a cheery wave.

"What's he doing?" hissed Frederick.

"I think he's escaping," Wilmot replied.

"But how?" Frederick sounded nonplussed. "That tunnel's a dead end."

"It leads to the Swoop," said Wilmot, as Mr Trellis turned and vanished into the tunnel. "He's got some flight experience."

"Really?" said Frederick. "I didn't know that."

"Well, I think it's mostly crashing experience," said Wilmot. "But he's obviously survived it all. That's probably better than nothing. Right?"

They exchanged a nervous look – a second later, the roar of the Swoop's engines swept down the tunnel and echoed around the cavern. Every head turned in the direction of the sound, and Tenebrae lanced down out of the air like an arrow.

"What's going on?" he shouted. Reggie and the other trolls were scrambling down the sides of the vault and running for the tunnel, but the noise of the Swoop was already receding into the distance.

"Someone's pinching our wings!" Gary shouted, as the trolls all raced one another into the tunnel.

Tenebrae turned to Wilmot. "This is your friend's doing."

Wilmot smiled back, defiant. "And you'll never catch him in time. He's on his way to Trollville, and soon every police officer and palace guard in the city is going to be on their way here to stop you."

Tenebrae clacked his beak in frustration. "Not if I can empty that vault before they get here," he said. He turned to Reggie and the drill team, who were filing back into the cavern, looking dejected.

"It's gone, boss," said Reggie.

"That doesn't matter," said Tenebrae. "None of it matters. I want the drill fixed immediately! A double share of the treasure for all of you, if you get the vault open within the hour!"

The trolls jumped to attention and went scrambling back up the vault to the drill with renewed energy.

"Now what?" said Frederick. "We've made things worse!"

Wilmot said nothing. There was nothing he could do any more. It was simply a question of who would win the race.

RETURN TO TROLLVILLE

Suzy saw her look of shock reflected back at her from around Crepuscula's hall of mirrors. "What do you mean the Brain Storm is lying to me?" she sputtered. "Why would it do that?"

"That's a very interesting question, to which I have no answer at present," said Aybek. "Nevertheless, it remains the truth – Tenebrae and his associates cannot be drilling for treasure beneath Trollville, because there is none."

"I don't believe a word you say," said Stonker, his moustache bristling.

"Please yourself," said Aybek.

Suzy found herself pacing the room and trying to regain her mental footing. All the certainties that had guided her this far had been made suddenly flimsy and treacherous by Aybek's words. Was the Brain Storm really lying? What if Aybek was lying instead?

"If there's no gold, then what are Tenebrae and his team doing down there in the first place?" said Suzy.

"That's simple," said Aybek. "The Brain Storm must be lying to them too."

"But it can't be. It told me they *stole* the information from it."

"Another lie," said Aybek. "I detect a trend developing, don't you?"

Suzy screwed her eyes shut and tried to think. "This doesn't make any sense."

"It does if there's something else down there that the Brain Storm wants them to find," he said. "Something other than treasure."

"Like what?"

"Another good question," said Aybek. "Let me think…" He stared off into nothing for a moment. Then, very slowly, his face lit up. "I do believe I have it," he said.

"What?" everyone shouted in unison.

Aybek's eyes narrowed, and his smile sharpened. "I think I've given you quite enough for now. If you want any more, you'll have to give me something extra in exchange."

"No," said Crepuscula, stamping her foot. "This

charade has gone on long enough. If you're not willing to help, then it's a cell for you."

"I'm perfectly willing to help, Selena," said Aybek. "But as we have already established, my services do not come free of charge."

"Well, you're not getting anything more from me." Crepuscula gestured at the mirror behind Aybek with her cane, and the glass began to darken.

"As you wish," he replied. "I'm sure the good people of Trollville will understand why you chose to doom their city." He strolled to the mirror, turned back to them and waved. "Goodbye, everyone," he said as he began to sink backwards into the blackness. "So nice of you all to visit."

"No." Suzy dashed forward, caught him by the hand and pulled him free. "You're not going anywhere yet."

"Then give me what I want," he said.

"And what's that?" she asked.

Aybek blinked. "Why, my freedom of course."

There was a moment of stunned silence, broken only by a derisive snort from Ursel.

"You must think we're all mad," said Crepuscula. "You're too dangerous to ever go free again."

"That's my price," said Aybek. "Take it or leave it."

"We'll leave it," said Crepuscula. "Now get back in that mirror, you cretinous stoat."

"But what about Trollville?" said Stonker.

"I'm sorry," said Crepuscula. "But Trollville is just one city. It can be rebuilt. Letting my brother walk out of here would put the entire Union in danger."

"Hardly," Aybek scoffed. "You did a pretty thorough job of unseating me from the Ivory Tower. Is Captain Neoma still running things there? I doubt she'd let me within a hundred leagues of the place. Added to which, I expect everybody in the Union knows my face by now. I've got nowhere to hide, and no influence left."

"You seem to have plenty of influence in this room at the moment," said Crepuscula. "And you're using it to exploit everyone to your own advantage. If I turned you loose, it would only be a matter of time before you were doing the same thing out there. Or do you expect me to believe you're going to retire to the countryside and take up embroidery?"

"I prefer crochet," said Aybek. "But right now, you need what I know."

"I can always take it from you by force," said Crepuscula with a shark-like smile.

"Perhaps," said Aybek. "But would you be able to do it in time to save Trollville? I doubt it."

"The city…" Suzy's mind was fizzing.

"What was that?" said Crepuscula.

"We can't beat him," said Suzy. "He's right. He's the only one who's got what we need, and he's not going to give it to us."

"I'm glad you've finally seen sense," said Aybek.

"At least, he's not going to give it to us *here*." Suzy flashed a smile at Crepuscula. "We need to take him to Trollville."

"What?" he said. He looked like he had been stung.

"Are you quite mad?" said Crepuscula. "He's not leaving this tower."

Stonker clapped his hand to his forehead. "No," he said. "I think Suzy's right. As long as Aybek is here, he's got no reason to cooperate with us. He doesn't care if Trollville collapses. But he would care a great deal if he were standing in it when it happened."

"Exactly," said Suzy. "Which is why we all need to get to Trollville. Immediately." She noticed that Aybek had gone very quiet. So, too, had Crepuscula.

"Are you seriously proposing we risk our lives in a city on the verge of total destruction, just to pressure my brother into talking?"

"Yes," said Suzy, trying on a shark-like smile of her own.

Crepuscula gave her a hard, appraising look. "You'll go far, my girl." She flicked her cane in Aybek's direction,

297

and her shadow lashed out across the floor. He dropped into it with an echoing cry. Satisfied at a job well done, the Lady Crepuscula rapped her cane against the floor, and her shadow came slinking back to her. "That's my luggage taken care of," she said. "Let's go."

Dawn was still several hours away from Trollville by the time the Express emerged from the tunnels onto the broad river of tracks that cut through the city. Suzy checked her watch and saw that it was almost eight a.m. back home. She had been awake for more than twenty-four hours now and should have been exhausted. In fact, her body was starting to tell her that she probably was, but she hadn't had time to notice.

Stonker cut their speed as the whole train bucked and shuddered, threatening to throw them all off their feet.

"Hold tight!" he shouted over the noise. "The tracks must have buckled. This isn't going to be pleasant."

The cab vibrated, and the hanging pots and pans rattled together.

Where's Fletch when you need him? thought Suzy, gripping the sink for support.

The Lady Crepuscula, meanwhile, stood calmly in the

middle of the room as though nothing was happening. She retrieved a cookery book that had tumbled from a shelf and leafed through the first few pages.

"Can we make it to Grinding Halt?" called Suzy.

"Orf nggggrhnk," said Ursel.

"Exactly," said Stonker. "I'm surprised that we haven't—"

He was cut off as the *Belle de Loin* lurched into the air,

and they all experienced a sickening moment of weightlessness. Then there was a loud bang, a crunch, and the Express screeched to a stop.

"—derailed," Stonker finished, from his new position lying full length on the floor.

Suzy had fallen beside him. "Is everybody alright?" she said.

"Runk." Ursel nodded.

The Lady Crepuscula snapped the book shut and tossed it back onto the floor. "We can't sit about here all day," she said.

The cab was leaning at an angle, and Suzy had to fight her way uphill to reach the front door. She staggered out onto the gangway and peered down over the side of the locomotive. Glinting in the lights from the nearby streets, she saw that Stonker was right – all the tracks surrounding them were buckled and warped, their wooden ties broken, and the ground beneath them cracked and uneven. Other trains had suffered the same fate as the Express and lay abandoned.

The others filed out to join her and stared in mute shock at the scene.

The streets were dark with crowds, moving like a dark and sluggish tide towards the city limits, while the air was filled with the wail of emergency sirens. Columns of smoke rose here and there among the grand buildings. The city felt bruised and defeated.

"I've never known things to be this bad before," said Stonker. Ursel gave a low whine of agreement.

"But the evacuation is happening," said Suzy. "Rayleigh kept his promise. Everyone's going to be safe." *Except Frederick*, she thought. *And us.*

"Let's hurry up before things get any worse," said the Lady Crepuscula. "We need somewhere to keep Aybek contained, where he'll be easier to manage. If I simply turn him loose in the streets, he's bound to find some way to cause trouble."

Suzy thought. "What about the rest home?"

"How far is it?" said the Lady Crepuscula.

"Not far," said Stonker. "In fact, it's more or less directly below us, in the Underside."

"You know, that might be a good idea," said the Lady Crepuscula. "Being dangled head-first over the Uncanny Valley for a bit might well help to focus Aybek's mind."

"And if the next earthquake hits while we're down there?" said Stonker.

"Then at least we'll die with a spectacular view," said the Lady Crepuscula.

"Can't say fairer than that," he replied. "Let me deploy my hazard flare, and we can be under way." He popped back inside, re-emerging a moment later with a bright red gun that had a large cylindrical barrel.

"What's a hazard flare?" asked Suzy.

"It's standard procedure whenever a locomotive is derailed," said Stonker, pointing the gun in the air and pulling the trigger without aiming. "It lets any passing traffic know that you're stuck."

A glowing trail of red sparks, like a firework, shot high into the air. Suzy watched it climb...and realized, too late, that it was going to collide with a passing hot-air balloon.

It was Bertha.

"Look out!" she cried. She saw Rayleigh stick his head out of the basket, only to recoil as the flare shot past his ear and ricocheted off Bertha's envelope.

"Do you mind?" he shouted. Then recognition dawned. "Oh. It's you again."

He brought Bertha down to land on the tracks beside the Express. "Did you get the information you needed from Lord Meridian?" he asked as the basket came to rest.

"Yes and no," said Suzy. "I'll explain everything on the way to the Underside. And trust me, you'll want to hear it."

"Very well," said Rayleigh. "Let me pack up." He climbed out of the basket and tapped the tip of his thermometer against it. A shiver ran through Bertha. With no noise or fuss, her envelope began to deflate, neatly folding itself up as it did so. Suzy watched, astonished. The empty balloon folded away into the basket, which itself began to shrink, folding and turning until it was a small rectangle of woven fabric, barely fifteen centimetres across. A small handle protruded from one edge, and Rayleigh picked it up like a briefcase.

"I never leave home without her," he said.

"Very clever," said Suzy. "Now stop showing off and let's go."

They fought their way on foot to the nearest Underside station, struggling against the press of the crowds. The streets were littered with fallen masonry and overturned vehicles, making progress even harder, and at one junction a water main had burst, sending an arc of spray high into the air.

The power to the Underside station's elevators had been cut, so they took the spiral staircase down through the city's echoing superstructure. They were the only people on the downward staircase. Everyone else was heading up and out, towards safety.

Things were bad in the Underside as well. It was only a short walk to the rest home, but they had to scramble over the ruins of a house that had collapsed into the road. Suzy looked sadly at the remnants of everyday life poking up from among the rubble – a cracked sink, a bed, a drawer still full of cutlery. It was a relief to finally reach the doors of the rest home.

"Hello?" called Stonker as they stepped into the lobby. "Mrs Grunt? Dorothy? Is anyone here?"

No answer came.

"They must have gone already," said Suzy. She was glad. It meant that the Old Guard were safe and, with any luck, Wilmot had gone with them. But it was still unsettling to see the rest home so quiet and lifeless. The soul had gone out of it.

They crossed the lobby to the residents' lounge and stepped inside. It was a long, comfortable space littered with armchairs and coffee tables. Tall picture windows along the rear wall gave onto a balcony. Now, though, their glass was broken, and the tables and chairs overturned. The ceiling had cracked, dusting the carpet with plaster.

"This will do nicely," said the Lady Crepuscula, taking it all in. Without another word, her shadow distended and vomited up Aybek, who landed on the floor with an unceremonious thud.

"That," he said, breathing heavily, "was thoroughly unpleasant."

"Good," said the Lady Crepuscula. "Now get up and make yourself useful before we all die."

He got to his feet and dusted himself down. "I take it this is Trollville then?" he said. "It's everything I thought it would be."

Ursel gave a warning growl.

"We don't have much time left before Tenebrae and his team restart the drill," said Suzy. "Tell us what they're really digging for, and where they're doing it. Otherwise we're all going to die here. Including you."

Aybek crossed to the shattered picture windows and stepped out onto the balcony. "I applaud your plan to bring me here, Miss Smith," he said, looking up into the Uncanny Valley. "Confront me with my own mortality and use it as leverage. Really quite brilliant. You're wasted as a Postie."

Suzy's skin crawled. Warm words from Aybek didn't mean much, and she knew better than to trust them.

"You're wasting time," she said.

A chunk of plaster fell from the ceiling and smashed on the floor behind Stonker. "I strongly suggest you tell her, before the whole building collapses," he said, wiping dust from his uniform.

"I'm willing to give you a clue," said Aybek. "The library at the Ivory Tower holds all the written legends of the ancient trolls and their supposed exploits. It also holds fragments of some very old and very vague archaeological records suggesting that, just possibly, some of those legends may be true. That something very old and powerful is buried deep beneath the city."

"Like what?" said Suzy.

"Not treasure, certainly," said Aybek. "But something that might nevertheless be of immense value to the Brain Storm. If my guess is correct, of course."

"Yes, but *what*?" said Suzy.

"Why, the one thing the Brain Storm is truly lacking, of course. And that's all I'm willing to tell you for now." He smiled at her evident frustration. "If you want more, you know my price."

"What's that?" said Stonker.

"My freedom, of course," said Aybek. "I thought I'd already made that very clear."

"No," said Stonker, joining them on the balcony and pointing into the Uncanny Valley. "I mean, what's *that*?"

Something large and black and noisy was lurching out of the depths of the valley. It moved erratically, and Suzy couldn't make out its shape clearly, but she got an impression of a bloated body and two bat-like wings.

"Good gracious!" said Stonker. "What is it?"

The creature gave a shrill whine, banked, and turned a blazing searchlight on the balcony.

"It's the troll gang's airship," said Suzy. "And it's coming straight for us!" She retreated into the lounge and the others shrank back too as the vessel filled the view through the picture windows. It wasn't slowing down.

With a terrible noise, it ploughed into the balcony and through the window frames, thrusting its nose cone into the room. Floorboards splintered, and the whole house shook.

Suzy closed her eyes against the clouds of dust that filled the room. The whining cry died away into silence, and she heard a half-familiar voice.

"Well, I don't think that was too bad for a first attempt, do you?" The dust cleared, revealing that the airship now occupied half the lounge. The glass of its windshield was broken, and through it they could see Mr Trellis peering out. He was grinning from ear to ear.

"Hello, everyone," he called. "Sorry about the mess."

Gertrude burst into the lounge. Her usual reserve had slipped – her hair had come unpinned, and she was short of breath. She looked at the group in bemusement and only did the briefest of double takes when she saw the Lady Crepuscula, who greeted her with a wave.

307

"Wilmot!" Gertrude panted. "Is he with you?"

Suzy's blood ran cold. "You mean he hasn't evacuated with everyone else?" She and Gertrude shared a look of dawning horror.

"He went out on some sort of 'scouting mission' last night and didn't come back," said Gertrude. "I've been searching the streets. I can't find him anywhere! Mr Trellis is missing too."

"Ah," said Mr Trellis. "Sorry about that, Mrs Grunt. Hello."

Gertrude stared up the length of the nose cone at him. "Do you know where Wilmot is?"

"Yes," he replied. "I know *exactly* where he is."

They were interrupted by a bellowing roar from Ursel, which shut everyone up.

"What is it?" said Suzy.

Ursel pointed at what, to Suzy, looked simply like an empty patch of floor. It took her a moment to realize what should have been occupying it.

"Oh no!" she said. "Aybek! He's gone!"

"Blast!" said the Lady Crepuscula. "I should have been paying more attention." Her shadow stretched and snaked out through the door, and the lights in the lobby dimmed. She closed her eyes, as if listening for some distant sound, and grunted with annoyance. "He's not in the building any more," she said. She recalled her shadow and brushed some dust from her shoulder. "If you'll all excuse me, I need to go and retrieve him."

"Gruuunf," said Ursel. "Hrrrrk rrnf."

"His scent? From here? Are you sure?" said the Lady Crepuscula.

"Hrumph," said Ursel.

"I wouldn't argue," said Stonker. "Bears have excellent noses. If Ursel can't track him down, nobody can."

"Very well," said the Lady Crepuscula. "I accept."

Ursel nodded and stopped to sniff the air briefly. A second later, she was on the move, and shouldered her way out of the lounge.

"Should anything happen before we get back," said the Lady Crepuscula, pausing in the doorway, "don't wait for us. We'll make our own arrangements."

"Take good care of her, please," said Stonker, his face set.

The Lady Crepuscula nodded and left.

"Will someone please tell me where Wilmot is!" said Gertrude. There were tears in her eyes.

"He's in one of the ancient caverns, deep underground," said Mr Trellis. "He's being held captive by the same criminal fraternity that attacked the young Deputy Postal Operative here. And the boy from the snow globe is with him too."

"Frederick?" said Suzy. "He's alright?"

"Apart from being held captive, yes," said Mr Trellis. "They're both in the pink of health."

"But how can we reach them?" she asked.

"The Postmaster and I put our heads together and found a way in through the Hobb's End mine," said Mr Trellis. "But we ran into a slight catastrophe and it's all blocked off now. I borrowed this beauty from a landing pad down in the Uncanny Valley. There's another entrance down there. Just head straight down and you'll soon find it."

"Then I'm going down after them," said Gertrude.

"No," said Suzy. "You need to get Mr Trellis to safety while there's still time. Stonker and the Cloudwright and I will go after Wilmot and Frederick, and see if we can find some way to stop the drill."

"We'll what?" said Rayleigh. Suzy shushed him.

"But I can't leave him down there," Gertrude said.

"And you won't be, Mrs Grunt," said Stonker. "But someone has to get Mr Trellis to safety, and report everything he knows to the police, in case they can send any spare officers to help us. But we have to act now if we're to save the city. The Postmaster is already down there, and we won't leave him behind. You have my word."

It was clear from Gertrude's face that she wanted to

argue with them, but she turned once again to Mr Trellis. "Can this thing still fly?" she asked.

"Possibly," he said. "The control panel's still flashing, and only a few of the lights are red."

"Excellent," said Gertrude – then, to everyone's surprise, she took a running jump and landed on the craft's nose. She shimmied up it, slipped in through the broken windshield, made herself comfortable next to Mr Trellis and seized the joystick from him. "It's been a while since I've flown," she said, "but I used to own a Nocturn Swift RX when I was a girl. Let's see if I've still got the knack." She flipped a few switches, and the craft's engines growled into life.

"I'll say you have!" said Mr Trellis. "Listen to those engines purr."

Gertrude gave a smile of grim satisfaction. "Please bring my boy back safely," she called. Then, with a blast from the engines that almost knocked the others over, she guided the craft backwards out of the lounge. Mr Trellis waved goodbye as the Swoop hovered uncertainly beyond the broken balcony for a few seconds. Then it peeled away into the night.

"If we survive this, I really must ask her to take me out for a spin," said Stonker.

But Suzy already had her mind on the job. "Our turn," she said. "Cloudwright? We need Bertha."

"What?" Rayleigh stammered. "Yes, but…but you can't possibly mean to…can you? Down there?"

"We can't stay here," said Suzy. "And the longer we wait, the more dangerous it gets."

No sooner had she finished speaking than the floor began to shake, stirring up the plaster dust that had fallen. Cracks zigzagged up the walls and ceiling, and to Suzy's horror, the whole house began to lean to one side. A dull roaring sound filled the air, throbbing in her ears until she could barely think. Distantly, through the dirge, she heard the crash and splinter of buildings falling.

"We're too late!" she cried. "They've started the drill again! Trollville is collapsing!"

THE DRILL

ilmot had thought the drill was loud when it started – a bellow of engines and a scream of whirling metal – but it was nothing compared to the sound the dome made. He could feel it rising up through the soles of his feet. It was a constant, ongoing note, like the tolling of a gigantic bell, and it made his very bones shake.

"Wilmot!" cried Frederick, his voice distorted by the throbbing air. "What do we do?"

"I don't know!" Wilmot cried back.

Above them, cracks opened in the cave roof and a few stalactites broke free.

A shadow passed over them, and Wilmot saw Tenebrae circling above, supervising the drilling operation.

"More power!" Tenebrae cried. Wilmot heard someone – probably Reggie – shout something in return, but the words were lost within the cacophony. "I said, more power!" Tenebrae cried. A few seconds later, the whine of the drill increased in pitch. Wilmot's vision started to blur.

This is it, he thought. *The end of Trollville. Unless I can do something.*

But what?

THE ONLY WAY IS DOWN

"We have to get out of here!" shouted Suzy as the quake shook the rest home to its foundations. Rayleigh tried to bolt for the door, but she grabbed him by the collar. "Not through the streets," she said. "We have to go down!" She picked up his briefcase from where he had dropped it and pushed it into his shaking hands. "We're all getting out of here in Bertha!"

She dragged him towards the balcony. Stonker hurried after them, but not without a worried look in the direction that Ursel and the Lady Crepuscula had taken.

The room, or possibly the building – or possibly even the whole of Trollville – lurched suddenly to one side, spilling them all to the ground. With a crunching and grinding of stone, a crack opened up across the middle of the floor.

"Quickly!" Suzy shouted. Rayleigh threw down his briefcase and struck it with his thermometer. It sprang open and the basket began unfolding, while the colourful envelope of the balloon swelled and rose from its centre. But the room was rapidly coming apart around them as the crack widened and spread, sending jagged tendrils up the walls. Part of the ceiling fell in, driving them right to the edge of the balcony, which was itself beginning to crumble. Suzy braved a glance over the edge and saw that it was a drop of about ten metres into the street below.

"Get in," ordered Rayleigh, the moment the basket was fully formed. Suzy and Stonker threw themselves in and watched as Bertha's envelope slowly took shape above them.

"Can't this thing go any faster?" said Stonker.

"No," said Rayleigh. "She's a balloon. She's meant to be dignified and relaxing."

The envelope continued to expand, until it was scraping against the side of the building. Rayleigh raised his wand and the basket lifted clear of the balcony a second before it fractured into rubble. They rose up – or, technically, down – towards the yawning gulf of the

Uncanny Valley. Looking out across the rooftops of the Underside, Suzy felt something shrivel up inside her: it was a scene of devastation. Plumes of dust mushroomed into the air across the city as more houses succumbed to the quake. She watched the roof of the rest home split open, revealing the colourful landscape of Wilmot's model railway. Then that too splintered and broke apart as, with a loud crash, the rest home collapsed in on itself. Suzy watched, stunned, as it crumbled to rubble. Wilmot's home – a place where she had been made welcome – was gone. *At least we got everyone out*, she thought.

"Do you think Ursel's alright?" asked Stonker, his voice strained. He was scanning the streets.

"Crepuscula won't let anything happen to her," said Suzy, and hoped that it was true. As powerful as Crepuscula was, what could she possibly do to escape disaster on this scale?

Then a new, even more worrying thought occurred to her, and she looked up past the curve of the balloon to the Uncanny Valley overhead. "Stonker," she said. "How far does the Negotiable Gravity reach?"

"What do you mean?"

"I mean, how high above the Underside do we need to get before normal gravity takes over? When does 'up' become 'down'?"

"Oh," said Stonker. "I'm not sure."

"Because when it does," said Suzy, with a growing sense of apprehension, "we'll be hanging upside down in a basket. With nothing to catch us."

"Why didn't you say anything sooner?" said Rayleigh, looking sick with worry.

Suzy didn't get the chance to answer, as she felt a sudden tug on her body, from the top of her head down to the soles of her feet, which lifted slowly off the bottom of the basket. For a moment, she was weightless, treading water in the air. Stonker and Rayleigh lifted off beside her. "Quick!" she shouted. "Turn us upside down!"

"What?" screamed Rayleigh.

"Flip Bertha over!" She grabbed for the edge of the basket, but real gravity was strengthening its grip on her, and pulling her legs up over her head. Rayleigh floundered. He brought his thermometer up too quickly and accidentally jabbed Stonker in the face with it.

"Careful!" Stonker snapped.

Rayleigh waved the thermometer in a tight circle and the balloon spun in the air. It wasn't a graceful manoeuvre. In fact, it was probably as far from dignified and relaxing as it's possible for a balloon to get, but in a few seconds, they had flipped through ninety degrees; Trollville was above them, and they were sinking right-side-up into the

Uncanny Valley below. Suzy, Stonker and Rayleigh landed in the bottom of the basket in an uncomfortable tangle.

"Oh my," gasped Rayleigh. "I didn't enjoy that at all."

Suzy was already back on her feet and leaned over the edge of the basket, looking into the blackness below.

"Mr Trellis said there was a platform," said Stonker, joining her.

Suzy strained her eyes. "I can't see anything yet. Can you take us down faster, please, Cloudwright?"

Rayleigh gave the depths of the valley a nervous look but decided not to argue. With a prompt from his wand, the balloon began dropping at twice the speed. It made Suzy's stomach do a little flip.

All around them was a sound like gigantic teeth being ground together, as the walls of the Valley shook and cracked. Chunks of rock fell away and plunged into the darkness far below. Suzy listened for the crash of their impact but heard nothing.

She looked up and, beyond the curve of the balloon, saw Trollville receding into the distance. Plumes of smoke and dust blossomed from the underside. The street lights flickered, waned, then winked out altogether.

"Great Scott," said Stonker, his face a haggard mask.

They dropped further into the valley, and the darkness closed in like a fist on all sides. But as the visibility faded,

Suzy became aware of something new. It was a sound – a rich, ringing note behind the grumble of the quake.

"What's that noise?" she said.

"It sounds like C minor," said Rayleigh.

Stonker's pointed ears twitched. He shut his eyes. "It's coming from down there," he said, pointing over the side of the basket into the darkness. "About five hundred metres to our right. Almost a thousand metres down."

"How can you tell?" said Rayleigh.

"Because I'm a troll," said Stonker. "Noses and ears, my good chap. They're our specialities."

Rayleigh gestured with his thermometer again, and they dropped ever faster.

The note grew clearer, and Rayleigh steered their course towards it. Then they saw a dim circle of light in the rock face and, in front of it, the platform jutting out into the Valley.

"There it is!" said Suzy.

Rayleigh slowed their descent and brought them in as carefully as he could. More rocks fell from above, tumbling into the abyss or crashing onto the platform, which bowed and shook beneath the impacts. On Rayleigh's first attempt at a landing, the platform simply flicked the balloon back up into the air, almost dashing it against the cliff face. The Cloudwright wrestled with his wand, taking evasive manoeuvres to avoid a large boulder that came whistling down out of the darkness and missed them by centimetres.

"This is madness!" he cried. "We're going to get pulverized if we stay out here."

"Then get us in, man!" said Stonker. "And quickly!"

Suzy saw doubt pass like a cloud across Rayleigh's face. When it cleared, his eyes had hardened and his jaw was set.

"Brace yourselves!" he said. "And be ready to jump when I say so!"

He angled Bertha down quickly, and Suzy realized, too late, that he was aiming to overshoot the platform and crash into the mouth of the tunnel. She shut her eyes and threw her hands up to protect her face.

"Jump!" Rayleigh shouted as he struck the basket with his wand.

Suzy threw herself clear, turning a somersault in the air before hitting the ground hard. Luckily her satchel absorbed most of the impact, and she rolled to a panting, shaking stop a few metres into the tunnel. She staggered to her feet and clapped her hands to her ears – the ringing note was unbearably loud here. The air seemed to ripple with it.

She turned towards the tunnel mouth and saw that

both Stonker and Rayleigh had survived the crash unharmed, although they, too, were grimacing under the onslaught of sound. Bertha was already retracting into her briefcase.

There was no point trying to speak, so Suzy gestured up the tunnel with her elbows. She could already see the entrance to the cavern up ahead. The others nodded, Rayleigh picked up Bertha, and together they started towards it.

It was like walking into a strong wind. The noise rushed up the tunnel like an invisible force, trying to hold them back. But then they emerged into the cavern and Suzy got her first sight of the drill and the huge copper-coloured dome of the vault. The air around them both shimmered with sound, and the cave roof was a constellation of brightly glowing mushrooms, which, Suzy was almost certain, were rushing about on spindly legs.

At least the noise had the advantage of covering their approach. They crept around the base of the vault, taking cover in the forest of stalagmites, until they saw Reggie and the other trolls, clad in ear protectors, clustered around a small panel of buttons which Suzy guessed controlled the drill.

Behind them, she spotted Frederick and Wilmot, lashed to another stalagmite. She gestured to Stonker and

Rayleigh to stay hidden, then, keeping one eye on Tenebrae, she hurried through the stalagmites. She wasn't worried about the trolls spotting her, but she knew that Tenebrae would be able to pick out movement in a second, if he happened to look down. But he was as obsessed with the vault as the others, and she reached Frederick and Wilmot without incident.

She tapped them each on the shoulder and motioned for them to be still. The knots were well tied, and it took her a moment to undo them. But then the ropes slipped free and they followed her away from the vault, deeper into the cover of the cave floor.

"It's such a relief to see you!" Wilmot shouted into her ear. "I'm afraid my Plan B didn't quite work."

"Neither did Plan A!" she shouted back.

"Never mind that!" put in Frederick, shouting into her other ear. "We need a Plan C! What are we going to do?"

"I don't know," said Suzy. "But we absolutely have to stop that drill. Trollville's being shaken to pieces."

Wilmot's face looked drawn. Frederick's face...well, she couldn't quite tell what Frederick's face was doing, because it was caked in dry mud. In fact his whole body was covered in it, from his hair down to his...

An idea struck Suzy like a jolt of energy. It was so fierce she actually twitched.

"Wait here," she said. "And don't do anything until I tell you to." Then she turned and ran across the cave, right up to Reggie and the other trolls. She threw her hands up. "Stop!" she shouted.

There was a moment of confusion during which the trolls around Reggie drew their wands. Gary and Barry lumbered towards her, hands outstretched. Then Reggie slapped a large red button on the control panel, and the drill fell silent.

The sudden absence of noise was so profound that even Gary and Barry sighed with relief. It was short-lived, however, as Tenebrae swooped down with a fierce screech and sent the drill team scattering.

"What are you doing, you idiot?" he said, pointing an accusing talon at Reggie. "Start this drill again, or I'll—"

"I know how to open the vault!" said Suzy.

Tenebrae rounded on her. "You!" he cried. "I don't know how you got here, but you've interfered for the last time." He advanced on her.

"I can get you into the vault," she said simply. "And you won't even need the drill."

Tenebrae stood over her, one claw raised, but he didn't strike. "Why should I trust you?"

"Because I want you to leave and never come back,"

she said. "And you won't do that until you open the vault. But I'm warning you now, you might not like what you find inside it."

"Never you mind what I'll like," said Tenebrae. "Now talk."

Suzy swallowed the lump of tension that had built in her throat. "Okay. You can't break through the vault casing, because it's reflecting all the energy you put into it with the drill. Right?"

"It does more than just reflect it," said Reggie. "It amplifies it. Anything we throw at it, it throws straight back at us, but ten times stronger."

"Exactly," said Suzy. "That's been causing the earthquakes, and it's what's going to get everyone killed if you carry on."

"So?" said Tenebrae pointedly.

"So what if you didn't have to break into the vault at all? What if someone opened it for you from the inside? After all, if a door isn't designed to open from one side, it *must* open from the other. Right?"

"She's got a point, boss," said Reggie. "Most vaults have got a safety release inside them, to stop people getting trapped accidentally."

Tenebrae scowled. "Are you saying there's someone in there?"

"No," said Suzy. "We'd have to put someone in there ourselves."

Reggie drew his hand over his face. "And how exactly do we do that without opening the vault in the first place?"

"Easy," she said. "With seven-league boots." She turned and shouted into the cave. "It's okay, everyone. You can all come out now."

One by one, the others stepped out of cover.

Reggie and the drill team raised their wands again, wary of the new arrivals. Then, very slowly, Reggie lowered his. "Jeremiah?" he said.

Suzy saw Stonker go rigid. "Reginald? Is that you?"

"You two know each other?" she asked.

Stonker didn't answer straight away, but he and Reggie stepped forward until they were face-to-face. And that's when Suzy understood why Reggie's face seemed so familiar. With the exception of the moustache, it was the same as Stonker's.

"You're brothers?" she said.

"Once upon a time," said Reggie.

Stonker set his mouth in a hard line. Was it a look of anger or sadness? Suzy couldn't tell.

"When did you get out of prison?" he asked.

"Last year," said Reggie. "They gave me time off for good behaviour."

Stonker looked around the cavern. "Is this what qualifies as good behaviour these days?"

"I tried going straight," said Reggie. "It didn't work out."

"It did for me," said Stonker. "I'm a driver now."

"Yeah, I saw you in the papers," said Reggie. "Very flash. I notice you didn't mention growing up in the orphanage together."

Everyone looked at Stonker in expectation.

"I've put all that behind me now."

"Yeah, and me along with it," said Reggie.

Tenebrae hissed impatiently. "Can we save the family drama for later? I want my treasure."

Reggie turned away from Stonker. "Where are we going to find seven-league boots?" he asked. "Nobody uses them any more."

"The Express does," said Suzy proudly. "Show them, Frederick."

Frederick picked some of the dried mud off his boots, revealing the control dials on their fronts.

"You've been wearing those all the time?" said Reggie.

"Yes."

"So you could have escaped whenever you wanted to."

Frederick looked embarrassed. "I sort of forgot I was wearing them," he said. "And I'd rather take my chances here, thanks. I don't know how far it is to the surface. What if I overshot and materialized half a league up in the air? Or too low? Would I get stuck in the ground for ever?" He shuddered at the thought. "I've had some bad experiences with these boots."

"The boy's got a point," said Reggie. "Boots like these are hard to use accurately. They're for crossing big open spaces quickly, not for landing on specific targets. A lot could go wrong."

"I'm willing to risk it," said Suzy. "If it saves the rest of Trollville."

Stonker stepped forward. "No," he said. "It's too dangerous, Suzy. I insist that you allow me."

Suzy thought she saw a twinge of disquiet cross Reggie's face at these words, but before he could say anything, Wilmot put his hand up.

"Um, actually, I think I'm the one with the most experience of using the boots," he said. "I did a training course and everything."

"But I thought you preferred roller skates," said Suzy.

"Oh, I do," he replied. "Seven-league boots make me queasy. But I think I've got the best shot of landing inside the vault. And as your Postmaster, I really must insist on taking the risk."

Tenebrae reached out and dragged his talons down

the surface of a stalagmite, creating a teeth-grinding squeal. Everyone stopped talking. "I don't care who wears them," he barked. "Just get on with it and open that vault!"

"Alright," said Wilmot. "But perhaps someone can help me double-check my distances?"

A few minutes later, Suzy and Wilmot stood together in the old mine tunnel, with Stonker, Frederick, Rayleigh and Reggie beside them. Wilmot was wearing the seven-league boots, leaving Frederick to hop awkwardly about in the long woollen emergency socks he had taken from the Express in the Western Fenlands.

"And you're sure this is exactly one league from the vault?" said Suzy.

"As close as I can measure it," said Reggie. "It's been a few years since I've had to convert anything from Cobbling Elf measurements. But at least the direction is right." He pointed straight down the tunnel, in the direction of the old rockfall that hid the entrance to the cavern. "One step, and you should be there."

"And if you're wrong?" said Stonker. He stood with his arms folded, and regarded Reggie from beneath a sharply arched eyebrow. "A more noble troll would offer to take the Postmaster's place."

"No," said Wilmot firmly. "I'm the best troll for the job." He triple-checked the distance dials on the front of the boots and then switched them on. "Wish me luck."

"Good luck," mumbled Rayleigh and Frederick, clearly nervous.

"I don't believe in the stuff, remember?" said Stonker.

Wilmot looked a little crestfallen at this, but Reggie patted him on the shoulder.

"Good luck, lad. We'll see you in there."

Suzy was too nervous to speak, so she gave him a shaky thumbs up. All she could think was, *This is all my idea. So if anything happens to Wilmot, it'll be all my fault.*

"Right," said Wilmot. "For Trollville." He stepped forward and vanished.

23

A MIND IS A TERRIBLE THING TO WASTE

Suzy couldn't remember a more nerve-wracking minute of her life than the one she spent racing with the others back to the cavern. Tenebrae and the rest of the drill team were waiting expectantly at the foot of the vault.

"Well?" said Tenebrae, as Suzy skidded to a stop beside him.

"He left a minute ago," she said, her panic rising. "Hasn't anything happened?"

"Nothing," he growled.

They all waited in anxious silence for another minute. Suzy approached the vault and pressed her ear to the metal, but she couldn't hear anything from inside it.

"The boy must have overshot," said Tenebrae at last.

"Start the drill again."

"No!" Suzy, Frederick, Rayleigh and even Reggie all shouted together.

"The drill's already failed, boss," said Reggie. "The boy was our best shot. It's over."

The feathers on top of Tenebrae's head bristled, and he flexed his wings. "I decide when it's over," he thundered. "And I say—"

"I hear something!" Suzy jumped back from the vault. "I think something's happening!"

They all turned to watch as, with a very faint hum, a seam appeared in the vault's surface. It ran in a straight line up its side to the summit, bisecting the whole dome neatly in two. Then, with barely a whisper, the two halves yawned open. The drill toppled with a crash, and fell amongst the rocks to one side of the dome, while the opening grew wider. Something glittered inside. Something very large.

"Diamonds!" exclaimed Tenebrae. He lifted off the ground and sailed straight into the opening. A large, round, crystalline structure was being steadily revealed, and he alighted on top of it, beside a second, smaller figure, who waved down at them all.

"Wilmot!" Suzy laughed with relief. "You did it! We thought we'd lost you!"

"Sorry," he called down. "It was dark in here, and it took me a while to find the switch."

The two halves of the vault came to rest. It now looked like two cupped hands cradling a ball of jagged crystal, about ten metres across.

"What's this supposed to be?" said Tenebrae, turning in increasingly agitated circles. "This isn't diamond!" He kicked his heel against the crystal.

"Goodness me!" said Rayleigh. "Is that what I think it is?"

"What?" said Frederick.

"But it can't be!" Rayleigh rushed forward and climbed through the opening into the vault. The others followed.

The vault had a flat floor, and the crystalline ball sat in a metal framework, with a narrow metal staircase climbing around it to give access to the top, where Wilmot and Tenebrae were standing. Suzy dashed up the stairs in pursuit of Rayleigh.

"Don't you see?" he said, stepping out onto the surface of the ball alongside Wilmot. "They're cortex crystals!"

Suzy looked again. "Like the ones you used to create the Brain Storm?" she said. "But they're huge!"

They were joined by Frederick, Stonker and Reggie.

"Call me slow on the uptake," said Stonker, "but are you saying that there's no treasure in the vault after all?"

"It's worthless!" screeched Tenebrae, his eyes burning like coals.

"You really have no appreciation of the finer things in life," Rayleigh chided him. "Do you know the sort of wonders I could work with crystals of this size? Why, I could train my spellcloud installations to do almost anything. The possibilities are limitless!"

"But where are my diamonds? My gold?"

"I don't think there ever was any," said Suzy. "The Brain Storm was lying to you."

This prompted some dark muttering amongst the drill crew, who were still loitering around the base of the vault.

"You promised to make us rich!" said Barry.

"Yeah!" said Gary. "What about all this work we've been doing, eh?"

Tenebrae didn't hear them. "The Brain Storm can't have been lying," he said. "It's always told me what I needed to know."

"Only to win your trust," she said. "All it really wanted was this." She gestured to the crystals.

"But why?" said Rayleigh. "What could it want with something this size?"

A faint buzz and crackle of energy reached their ears. They looked out across the cavern and saw a flickering light in the tunnel that led to the Swoop's landing platform. And it was getting brighter.

"Is it a fire?" said Reggie.

"I don't think so," said Wilmot. "It looks almost like…"

"Lightning," said Rayleigh. "But here? Underground?"

The crackling sound grew louder. There were snaps and pops in time with the flickering light. Then the source emerged into the cavern – pale and glowing and diaphanous, moving on spindly legs of forked lightning like an enormous spider.

Suzy felt a chill of dread run through her veins. "It's the Brain Storm!"

"The what?" said Wilmot, wide-eyed.

"But that's impossible!" said Rayleigh. "It's moving! By itself! It's not supposed to be able to do that!"

Suzy shrank back. "I have a nasty feeling it can do all sorts of things it's not supposed to be able to," she said.

The Brain Storm reached the open vault and hovered above them, spitting and crackling with energy.

"What is that thing?" said Frederick.

"It's a long story," said Suzy, not daring to take her eyes off the Brain Storm. She didn't know what it was going to do, but she needed to be ready. It couldn't be trusted.

Tenebrae took off and swooped around it. "You lied

to me!" he shouted. "There was never any treasure in here! You had us digging for a bunch of worthless crystals!" The Brain Storm fizzed and flashed. "Don't hide in there," said Tenebrae. "I demand you face me!"

A bolt of lightning arced out of the cloud and struck him between the eyes. His body dropped to the ground and lay motionless.

There was a moment of bewildered silence before panic broke out. The drill crew ran screaming through the cave, heading for the disused mine tunnels.

"Take cover!" said Frederick. "It just killed him!"

"No," said Suzy. "It's talking to him." She straightened her cap and adjusted her satchel. "Whatever happens to me, don't worry," she said.

"Why?" said Wilmot. "What are you doing?"

"I'm joining the conversation."

She raised her hands. "Hey!" she shouted. "Can you hear me? You owe me an explanation!" *And an apology*, she thought.

"Wait!" Rayleigh leaped to her side. "Me too! I demand to speak with you."

He had barely spoken the words when two more forks of lightning uncurled from the depths of the Brain Storm and struck them both in the head. The last thing Suzy saw before her mind was sucked from her brain was Wilmot and Frederick, staring open-mouthed in shock. Then everything went black.

Suzy barely had to blink this time before the Observatory coalesced into being around her. But it wasn't quite the same room any more: the observers were gone, and the desks had been thrown in a pile in the middle of the room. At the summit of the pile, reclining on his armchair, was Brain Storm Meridian, one leg hooked over the armrest, gazing serenely up at the painted stars while Tenebrae hovered in front of him, gesticulating with a talon.

"A month of digging!" Tenebrae screeched. "And nothing to show for it! I demand you explain yourself!"

"Nothing for you, perhaps," said Brain Storm Meridian. "But those crystals are very valuable indeed to me." He beckoned to Suzy and Rayleigh. "Please, come and join us," he said. "If I'm going to gloat, I'd rather do it with an audience."

Tenebrae looked down at them and grunted with disgust.

"So Aybek was right," said Suzy, approaching the foot of the pile. "You *were* lying, to Tenebrae and to us. You've always known the coordinates of the vault."

"Of course. How is Aybek, by the way? I do hope Selena's been making him suffer."

"You knew we would go and see him," she said.

"I was counting on it," he replied. "I had planned to remain undetected at the farm until the drilling was complete. So as soon as you and Cloudwright Rayleigh here discovered me, I was forced to play for a little more time. Sending you to deal with Aybek and Selena at the Obsidian Tower seemed like the most effective thing to do."

"But surely you knew he would reveal you were lying?" said Rayleigh.

"That was always a risk," said Brain Storm Meridian. "But I knew he would cause you enough of a delay to allow me to reach the drill site and, hopefully, for Tenebrae's team to finish the job."

"I can't believe you would lie to me!" said Rayleigh. "Your own creator!"

"I would apologize," said Brain Storm Meridian, "but I'm not in the least bit sorry."

Tenebrae screeched with rage. "Then what was the point of it all?" he said. "What are these crystals for?"

The old man's smile took on a venomous edge. "My future," he said. "And yours too. In fact, it's the future of everyone in the Impossible Places."

Tenebrae's patience broke, and he plunged towards

Brain Storm Meridian, talons outstretched. But the old man clicked his fingers, and Tenebrae vanished a second before impact.

"Disagreeable creature," said Brain Storm Meridian. "Remind me to squash him later."

Fury boiled up in Suzy. "You told me you are your own person," she said. "But you're not. You're just another Aybek!"

Brain Storm Meridian looked down at her from his perch among the painted stars. "I'm Aybek 2.0," he said, his voice cold. "All of the intellect and none of the stupid mistakes. His plan to rule the Union was far too complex to ever succeed. Mine is rather more...direct."

A terrible sense of foreboding overtook Suzy. "So that's it," she said. "You still want to rule."

"Of course," he said. "There's no one better suited to the task. Now if you'll excuse me, the time has come for me to slip into something more comfortable." He clapped his hands, and the Observatory was gone.

Suzy opened her eyes to find Wilmot kneeling over her with two fingers up her nose. She snorted, and he reeled back in shock.

"What are you doing?" she said.

"Checking for a pulse," he said. "I couldn't find one!"

"In my nose?"

"Of course," he said. "Don't humans have one there?" He helped her up. "What's happening?"

They looked up as the Brain Storm lowered itself over them.

"I still don't understand," said Rayleigh, sitting up. "How can the Brain Storm hope to rule the Union? It may be a genius, but it's still just made of cloud."

Suzy looked down at the crystals on which they were sitting. The lightning flicker in the depths of the Brain Storm grew more intense.

"I think we need to move," she said. "Right now!"

They scrambled for the stairs. No sooner had they got clear than – with a ferocious *crack!* – the Brain Storm unleashed a single bolt of lightning into the crystals, which ignited with a crimson glow. There was a hum of power from somewhere deep beneath the cavern floor.

"What if it wasn't just made of cloud?" said Suzy, as they reached the bottom of the stairs. The hairs on her arms stood on end as her fear grew. "What if it's found a new form?"

Devoid of the energy that had bound it together, the Brain Storm faded to a dull grey. Its edges grew ragged and it released a soft shower of rain, which pattered down on the crystals and ran in rivulets to the floor. As the rain fell, the cloud began to thin and break apart, until it finally faded to a few wisps of steam and vanished.

Rayleigh let out an agonized moan. "My masterpiece!" he said. "Gone!"

The red light inside the crystals brightened, flaring like fireworks under glass, and the hum of energy deepened. The floor began to vibrate.

"Perhaps not," said Suzy. "I think it's just moved house."

"Good heavens, you're right," said Rayleigh. "It transferred its brainwaves out of the cloud and into the crystals. But why? It's stuck in there now. It's got nowhere left to go."

And that was when the vault began to rise.

It started slowly, with a tremble that made Suzy think another earthquake was starting. But then the whole structure lurched upward several metres, throwing everyone off their feet.

"Run!" shouted Reggie, but before they could move, the vault began to close over them. The two halves were knitting back together as if they had never been parted.

Wilmot and Frederick were nearest the opening, and managed to scramble through. Rayleigh was close behind them and, with Suzy pushing and the others pulling, he too squeezed out. He reached back for Suzy, but the gap narrowed and he had to snatch his hand away to avoid losing it.

"Suzy!" she heard Frederick shout. She looked up and saw Tenebrae hanging in mid-air above the dome. Then the vault closed and she, Stonker and Reggie were plunged into red flickering darkness.

Wilmot helped the others scramble to the edge of the cavern as the vault rose up. The cave floor was moving with it, melting and running like warm butter. The forest of stalagmites bowed and shrank.

"What's it doing?" he said.

"I don't know," said Rayleigh. "But I don't like it."

The summit of the vault was almost at the cave roof now, and Wilmot could see that it sat on top of an even larger metal dome that was pushing up through the liquifying cave floor beneath it. The walls of the cavern began to bow and sag.

"Whatever it is, it's big!" said Frederick.

"Too big," said Rayleigh. "It's bringing the whole cave down." He turned and pointed to the tunnel leading to the landing platform. "Come on!" They ran.

"But what about Suzy and Mr Stonker?" said Wilmot.

"Whatever that thing is, it's heading for the surface," said Rayleigh. "We'd better get up there to meet it." They emerged onto the platform and he flung down Bertha's briefcase. It sprang open and Bertha began to emerge.

The vault trembled slightly as it met the cave roof but, to Suzy's surprise, there was no grinding of rock or tearing of metal. Instead, there was an increasing sense of speed, as though the vault – or whatever it really was – was swimming through solid rock. She thought back to everything Wilmot had told her about how Troll Territory had been formed, aeons ago. "Your legends say that the ancient trolls used incredible machines to help build your world, don't they?" she said.

"If you believe such things," said Stonker.

"I do now," she replied. "Because I think we're standing in one."

"What, this?" Reggie looked around the inside of the vault. "But it was just supposed to be a dome full of money."

"Because that's what the Brain Storm wanted you to think," she said. "Whatever this machine is, the Brain

Storm seems to be controlling it now, and it's heading for the surface."

"To do what, precisely?" said Stonker.

"To conquer the Union," said Suzy. "And it's going to start with Trollville."

RISE OF THE TITAN

Wilmot gripped the side of Bertha's basket as the balloon shot up out of the darkness of the Uncanny Valley and into the golden light of dawn. Beside him, Frederick cheered.

"We made it," said Rayleigh, slowing their ascent. "But what about the vault? Does anyone see it?"

Trollville lay stretched out before them, the streets of the Overside like rows of broken teeth. The whole city was smoking and silent.

The sight of it hit Wilmot like a punch to the stomach, and for a moment he could look at nothing else. Then Frederick pointed to something in the middle of the city.

"Look," he said. "What's that?"

A trail of glittering green smoke arced high into the

air. It burst into thousands of dazzling emerald lights that drew together to paint a gigantic arrow in the sky, pointing down at the city. Wilmot followed it, and his eye arrived at Grinding Halt.

"Who's launching fireworks at a time like this?" said Frederick.

"That's not a firework," said Wilmot. "That's a standard-issue railway distress flare. Someone's in trouble." He turned to Rayleigh. "We have to go and help."

"But we can't!" said Rayleigh. "What about the vault?"

"A good troll never refuses a call for help."

"I'm not a troll," Rayleigh muttered, but he angled his thermometer towards the city. "Perhaps I can fix at least some of the trouble I've caused."

"Thank you," said Wilmot. "Spoken like a true troll." He thought he saw the glimmer of a smile on Rayleigh's face.

As they drew closer to Grinding Halt, Wilmot saw a lone figure standing on top of the great sphere, still holding the flare gun aloft. It was someone he recognized only too well. "Lord Meridian."

"What?" Frederick jumped so sharply he almost fell out of the basket.

Aybek saw the balloon approaching and waved with the hand holding the flare gun. His suit was tattered, but he seemed unharmed. "Hello again, Cloudwright," he called. "How nice to see you survived the quake. And you've brought some old friends of mine for a visit as well. How lovely."

"I'm no friend of yours," said Frederick, vaulting out of the basket as Rayleigh set Bertha down on top of the station.

"Me neither," said Rayleigh. "I'm here to conduct a rescue, but I find myself having second thoughts."

"I'm sorry to have put you to the trouble," said Lord Meridian. "The signal was meant for someone else."

"Who?" said Wilmot, climbing out of the basket.

A low growl made them all turn as Ursel emerged onto the roof, her fur streaked with grime. The Lady Crepuscula was riding side-saddle on Ursel's back, her chin up, looking for all the world like a queen on horseback. Her dress was spotless, Wilmot noted, as though dirt were something that only happened to other people.

"Ah," said Lord Meridian. "Hello, Selena. I was hoping you'd get here in time."

The Lady Crepuscula slid down from Ursel's back. "We might have taken longer if you hadn't advertised your position to the entire city," she said. Her shadow stretched out towards him.

"A necessary step, unfortunately," said Lord Meridian.

"You see, I'm catching a lift from a friend of mine and I wanted to let him know I'm here."

The Lady Crepuscula scoffed. "I hardly think the Cloudwright is going to save you."

"You do say the most hurtful things," said Lord Meridian. "But I wasn't talking about the Cloudwright."

"Then who?" said Lady Crepuscula.

There was a noise like the sucking of a gigantic vacuum cleaner. It came from the south, beyond the city, and when Wilmot turned in that direction, he saw one of the nearby foothills start to melt. It collapsed in on itself in a maelstrom of liquid rock and, as they all watched, something emerged from it, surfacing like some enormous sea creature.

"Ah-ha!" said Lord Meridian. "Here he comes now."

Rayleigh stared, agog. "Is that it?"

"Yes," said Wilmot, in an awed whisper. "Yes, I think it is."

It was a gigantic robot, even taller than Grinding Halt, sporting four many-jointed arms that it flexed experimentally, as though stretching long-dormant muscles. Instead of hands, each arm ended in an oversized piece of digging equipment: a drill, an excavator's scoop, a set of pincers, and what looked to Wilmot like the nozzle of a fire hose. Its head was the blank dome of the vault.

It stepped out of the collapsing hill and approached the city with a deep, rhythmic pounding of footsteps.

Boom! Boom! Boom!

Wilmot watched, horrified, as the robot reached the outermost streets of Trollville and crushed a building beneath one mighty foot. *I climbed on top of that thing*, he thought.

"What the devil is it?" said the Lady Crepuscula.

"Ancient technology, long thought lost," said Aybek. "A troll titan! Isn't it magnificent?"

The titan walked on two towering legs, and its feet were a giant pair of metal boots, each taller than a house. Wilmot watched one come down on a street corner, flattening a bank.

Ursel bared her fangs and roared in anger.

"I don't suppose for a moment that it's friendly?" said the Lady Crepuscula.

"Only to me," said Aybek. "But then, the driver and I are of one mind."

He spread his arms wide to welcome the titan as it stomped through the centre of the city towards them, kicking buildings over as it came.

Suzy staggered across the floor of the vault as it tipped and shook beneath her. Stonker and Reggie were both grappling with the small control panel that Wilmot must have used to open the dome.

"It worked for the Postmaster!" Stonker said, hammering his fists against the dials. "Why isn't it working for us?"

"I don't know!" said Reggie. "These controls are all dead."

"It's because the Brain Storm is in control now," said Suzy. "We won't be able to get out that way."

Reggie gripped the ends of his ears in a panic. "Then what do we do?"

The vault lurched again, and Suzy went reeling across the dome. Her foot caught on something sticking out of the floor directly beneath the glowing cortex crystals, and she tripped over.

She sat up, rubbing her shoulder, and saw what had tripped her. It looked like a metal steering wheel, and it was set into a trapdoor in the floor. "We need to get this open!" she said.

Stonker and Reggie reached her on their hands and knees and immediately set about turning the wheel. A moment later, the vibrations shaking the dome softened considerably.

"I think we've breached the surface," said Suzy. "We have to hurry!"

"We're doing our best," Reggie replied. Sweat was standing out on his forehead.

"Call yourself a safe-breaker?" said Stonker. "Come on, Reg, old boy. Show us how it's done."

Reggie muttered something rude under his breath and gave another heave, his face turning beetroot-red with the effort. The wheel turned slowly and painfully. Then the hatch popped open with a whoosh of old air, to reveal a metal ladder leading down into the innards of the titan's body.

"That's the stuff!" Stonker clapped Reggie on the shoulder.

They descended the ladder into a low, circular room

lined with old-fashioned banks of computers. A large metal chair, like a throne, stood on a low dais in the centre, and a narrow letter-box window was set into the wall in front of it.

Suzy ran to the window and looked out.

"It's Trollville!" she said. "We're heading for Grinding Halt." She saw the glowing green arrow hanging above the station and wondered where it had come from. She turned to call the others over and gasped in horror. Sitting in the throne-like chair was the skeleton of a troll, dressed in a strange uniform of gold chain mail and leather. It stared blindly at her with its fixed grin. It wore something like a crown on its bare scalp, she saw: a polished metal frame in which a series of neatly cut cortex crystals had been set.

"Great Scott," said Stonker, seeing the skeleton. "The driver, do you think? The captain?" Very tentatively, he reached out and touched the skeleton's arm. The whole figure crumbled to powder in front of them, leaving nothing but the crown resting on top of the chain mail.

"If he was the driver, then this must be the cab," said Suzy, looking around the rows of instrument panels. "Maybe we can use these controls to stop this thing. Quickly! Help me look."

They spread out to examine the panels, but Suzy realized with a sinking feeling that she hadn't a hope of understanding them. They contained a complex series of screens and dials covered in words that meant nothing to her. Worse still, she couldn't even find any controls. Not one of the panels she examined had a single switch or button.

"They're read-outs," she said. "They're not for controlling this thing; they're for telling you what it's doing. But I can't understand a word of it."

"I think I can follow most of it," said Reggie. "Drilling arm, magma cannon, left leg, right leg, seven-league boots… They're all body parts."

Realization dawned on Suzy, and she put her head in her hands. "Why didn't I see it sooner? Lord Meridian told me that the Brain Storm was drilling for the one thing it really lacked."

"What?" said Stonker. "A magma cannon?"

"A body!" she said. "It was looking for a body all along. And now it's got one that could demolish Trollville in minutes. And if it's fitted with seven-league boots, it'll just move on to the next city, and the next. It really *does* want the same things as Lord Meridian, but it's even more powerful. Nowhere's safe."

"So those cortex crystals in the dome up there," said Stonker, "they're acting like the machine's brain?"

"Exactly," she said. "The Brain Storm is controlling

the whole machine from inside them." She looked at the crown sitting on the chair and had a flash of inspiration. "That's why there are no controls in this room!" she said. "The driver doesn't need buttons or levers, because she sends her mind into the crystals and does it all from there."

"You what?" said Reggie.

Suzy held up the crown. "Cloudwright Rayleigh used something like this to transfer a copy of Lord Meridian's mind into the Brain Storm," she said. "And the driver of this machine does the same thing. Her mind becomes the machine's mind!" She swept the chain mail and dust off the chair, making Stonker and Reggie cough. "I know how to stop the Brain Storm," she said, and took a seat in the driver's chair.

"How?" said Stonker.

Suzy put the crown on.

She had braced herself for a rush of sensation, but she merely blinked and found herself standing over Trollville. She was gigantic, hundreds of metres tall, striding across the streets like a colossus. Even the tallest buildings barely reached her waist, and she ground smaller ones to dust beneath her feet.

No, not *her* feet, she realized. The machine's feet. Because the machine was her body now, and she could sense every nut, bolt and rivet of it as though it had always belonged to her.

But she couldn't control it.

Fear fluttered in her chest as she tried to divert the machine's course and found that she couldn't. The feet smashed down on streets and buildings, no matter what she did to try and stop them.

"What's this? An interloper?" Brain Storm Meridian's voice echoed in her head. "Why, it's the Postie! How did you get in here?"

"The old-fashioned way," said Suzy. At least her voice was her own.

"Come to wrench control away from me, I suppose?" said the Brain Storm. "I applaud your creative thinking, but I'm afraid you're outmatched. Mine is the greater intellect. You cannot overcome it. Observe."

Suzy could only watch, helpless, as the Brain Storm raised the machine's booted foot and brought it crashing down on an ornate department store. She focused her mind, willing the foot to lift, to turn, to do anything, but the Brain Storm's will was too strong for her. She was nothing but a passenger in its mind as it marched on through the city towards the fading green arrow above the dome of Grinding Halt. She saw Bertha hovering close by it and caught her breath.

"No!" she said. "Leave them alone!"

The Brain Storm laughed as it ploughed on through the city, emerging onto the broad expanse of railway lines. Locomotives and rolling stock splintered to pieces beneath it. "And what have we here?" it said, looking down.

With a renewed chill, Suzy saw that they were approaching the abandoned Express. "Stop it!" she screamed. "You don't have to do this."

"I know," it replied. "But I very much want to." It reached the Express, raised its right foot high in the air, and brought it powering down.

Suzy shut her eyes and *pushed*, pouring every ounce of mental strength she had into the leg.

The foot crashed down with a thud that shook the whole city.

"What?" exclaimed the Brain Storm. "What have you done?"

Suzy opened her eyes and saw that the foot had come down just a few metres to the right of the Express, which remained untouched.

"How dare you?" raged the Brain Storm. "This is *my* body, not yours!"

Suzy laughed with relief. "You sound very certain," she said, "but I think you're in two minds about it." She focused again, straining forward and feeling the machine's body move with her. She took a few ponderous steps beyond the Express, swaying unsteadily as the Brain Storm fought her for control.

"Stop this!" it said. "You can't win! I'm too strong for you!"

Suzy couldn't bring herself to reply. It took every bit of her concentration to drag the gigantic feet forward, one after the other, away from the Express. Ahead of her, Grinding Halt and Bertha waited. She turned her attention to the east, and the edge of the city. There was nothing beyond it but the drop into the Uncanny Valley.

"No!" The Brain Storm sensed where her thoughts were turning, and she felt its sudden panic. "I will not let you destroy us!"

Step by torturous step, Suzy turned them to face the drop. Half a dozen strides and they would be there. If the machine had had teeth, she would have ground them together with the effort. "I don't matter as much as Trollville," she said. "Or my friends." She could no longer lift the heavy feet, so dragged them along the ground, ploughing up the railway lines. Her head began to ache.

"I will not stand for this!" the Brain Storm roared in her mind. "Not from the likes of you! Not from anyone!"

The ache became a stabbing pain, and Suzy felt her control slipping away. She shut her eyes again and grasped for it. The pull of the Brain Storm's will was incredible. She tried to ignore the involuntary twitching in her legs.

"Let me go," said the Brain Storm, "and I will be magnanimous in victory. You will be allowed to escape with your friends."

"No," said Suzy, gasping. "I don't believe you. All you do is lie."

The Brain Storm growled with frustration. "And if you walk us both over the edge?" it said. "What of your friends then? How many of them are still trapped inside me?"

Suzy's mind recoiled in shock: she had been so intent on fighting the Brain Storm, she hadn't spared a thought for Stonker and Reggie. Doubt spread like a stain across her thoughts, and she felt the last thread of control slip through her fingers.

"I see now why Lord Meridian underestimated you," the Brain Storm said. "But I will not repeat his mistake." Suzy felt herself beginning to fall, and the vision of the city at her feet began to dissolve into mist. She was being cast out. As she fell away into darkness, a last vestige of the Brain Storm's voice echoed inside her mind: "This brain isn't big enough for the both of us."

Suzy opened her eyes and found herself still sitting in the driver's chair. Stonker and Reggie were staring at her.

"What happened?" said Stonker. "We thought we were going to crash off the edge of the city!"

"Sorry," said Suzy. "That was my fault." She pulled the crown from her head and let the throbbing in her temples subside. "I uploaded my mind to the cortex crystals, but the Brain Storm kicked me out. It was too strong for me."

"You mean you can control this walking junkyard?" said Reggie.

"Not properly. Just little bits at a time. I don't think it will be enough."

"Then what are we going to do?" said Stonker.

"You're both going to get to safety," she said. "There has to be an emergency exit on this thing somewhere."

"And leave you behind?" said Stonker. "Out of the question!"

"I can keep trying," she protested. "If I can break back into the Brain Storm's mind, maybe I can slow it down a little."

"Then let me do it," said Reggie. "I'm the one who dug this thing up. It's my job to stop it."

Stonker looked at him in surprise.

"No," said Suzy. "Chapter one of *The Knowledge*, page three, under the heading *Duties of Care*: *It is the duty of every Postal Operative to protect the Service, its facilities and their contents from sedition, vandalism and all unwarranted forms of aggression.*" She pointed out of the window as the titan turned back towards Grinding Halt. "This is very aggressive and *highly* unwarranted, so it has to be me."

"Very well, Postal Operative," said Stonker with a warm smile. "Give it your best shot."

"I will," she said. She was about to place the crown back on her head, when she paused. "I've just realized something!"

"What is it?" said Stonker.

"I've still got both my socks on." She grinned at him, and pulled the crown down over her head.

Wilmot didn't complain when Ursel moved to shield him and Frederick from the titan, which turned away from the edge of the city and approached Grinding Halt once more. The Lady Crepuscula stood ready, her cane raised and its tip fizzing with magic. Rayleigh held his thermometer ready. Only Aybek seemed untroubled as the titan finally stamped to a halt in front of them.

"My, haven't you grown," he said.

The titan leaned over, as though scrutinizing him.

"While you remain so very small," it answered in a booming voice.

Aybek smiled, but it looked a little forced. Wilmot detected the slightest hint of worry in the old man's eyes.

"Allow me to congratulate you on your transformation," Aybek said. "And the successful execution of your plan. It really was most ingenious."

"Thank you," the titan replied. "Your archaeological knowledge proved most useful."

"May I ask what you plan to do next?"

The titan had no expression, but Wilmot got the feeling that, had it been able to, it would have looked smug. "The Union needs taking in hand," the Titan thundered. "And I finally have the physical strength to match my intelligence. Who can possibly stand against me?"

"I'm willing to give it a try," said the Lady Crepuscula. "And you do know that talking to yourself is the first sign of madness, don't you?"

"So it's good old-fashioned conquest," said Aybek, nodding sagely. "I can understand the appeal, but it's a little blunt for my tastes."

"That's because you've never had a magma cannon for a hand." The titan raised the arm ending in a nozzle. A fiery glow flickered into life inside it.

"Touché," said Aybek. His pretence of a smile died as he stared at the magma cannon. "And what will your first target be?"

"I think I shall put an end to Trollville," said the titan. "It will be a good test of my new powers, and a suitable warning to the rest of the Union." It extended the arm and unleashed a stream of white-hot liquid in an arc across the nearby streets. It rained down in a line of bubbling molten slag, which ate through masonry and metal as though they were as soft as sponge. A hot, acrid stench billowed up on the superheated air, stinging the inside of Wilmot's nostrils.

"I'm envious," said Aybek, backing away. "Do have fun."

"Oh, I shall," said the titan. "But first, I think I had better deal with the only true threat to my power."

"Which is?" Aybek quickened his pace until he reached the Lady Crepuscula's side.

"Why, you of course," said the titan. "The only mind in the Union to match my own." It brought the magma cannon round to point at him. A drop of molten rock dripped from the tip, fell through one of Grinding Halt's broken glass panels, and ate a hole through the station platform inside.

"Selena?" said Aybek. "I hate to ask this, but if you

have anything up your sleeve, now would be the time to use it."

"I wish I did," she said tartly. "But I don't have anything with me that could possibly counter something of this size. I'm afraid you've been too clever for your own good again."

The glow from the magma cannon became a dazzling glare, and Wilmot felt a wave of heat roll over him. There was nowhere to run to, and nowhere to take shelter. He shut his eyes and waited for the inevitable.

"Run!" The titan spoke, but with a new voice. A voice he recognized.

"Suzy?" he said.

"Grrrunf!" said Ursel. So she had heard it too!

"Suzy Smith, is that you in there?" said the Lady Crepuscula.

"Yes," the titan replied. "I've taken control, but I can't hold him for long." The titan jerked its arm up a second before the magma cannon unleashed another jet of fiery hot death, which sailed over Grinding Halt and set fire to a small park several blocks away. "Sorry!"

"You heard the girl," said Aybek. "Let's make ourselves scarce." He turned to run but found his way blocked by Crepuscula's shadow.

"You're coming with me," she said.

The shadow lunged, but before it could take hold of him, a dark shape dropped out of the sky and snatched Aybek off his feet.

"Help!" Aybek cried. He struggled against his attacker, but strong talons gripped his wrists.

"I'm not leaving here empty-handed," said Tenebrae, rising out of range of Crepuscula's shadow as it boiled and snapped at Aybek's heels. "*You're* going to work for *me* now."

"Let me go! Selena! I demand that you rescue me!"

"Unhand my brother this instant!" shouted the Lady Crepuscula. She levelled her cane at the dwindling figures, but it was already too late. Tenebrae had carried Aybek clear of Grinding Halt. "Blast!" she said, and struck the ground with her cane.

The titan unleashed another stream of magma, which blazed low over their heads.

"Quickly!" Suzy's voice said. "You'd better run. Now!"

"You again!" the Brain Storm spat. "How very persistent of you." The compliment did not sound heartfelt.

"Are you going to stop or do we have to fight again?" she asked.

"You already know you can't beat me," it said. "You're a little girl facing a giant."

"I stopped you crushing the Express," she said. "And I just stopped you from killing my friends. Perhaps you're not as strong as you think you are."

She felt the bitter scrape of its anger across her thoughts. "A momentary lapse that I shall now correct," it said.

Suzy gasped as a massive mental pressure clamped down on her. It was like being gripped in gigantic hands, but it didn't try and cast her out this time. It wanted to keep her captive.

"You can stay here with me and watch as I grind your precious train to pieces," it said, turning away from Grinding Halt and thundering back along the tracks. Each stride of the machine's mighty legs covered a huge distance. She looked down their length to the gigantic boots. She couldn't do anything to stop them or change their course; her will wasn't strong enough. But there was one thing she hadn't tried yet. She stopped struggling against the Brain Storm's grip on her mind.

Ahead of them, the Express came back into view.

"I'm going to smash it to powder," the Brain Storm said, taking another great stride forward. "And then I'm going to smelt the powder into steam." Another stride.

366

Just two more, and the Express would be finished. "And then, just to rub it in, I'm going to do the same thing to every centimetre of this wretched city." Another step.

Suzy barely heard it. She was concentrating. Not on the titan's legs, but on its boots.

"I might even keep you locked up in here with me for ever," the Brain Storm said. "As my pet." Its laugh rang around her mind, distracting her for a second. She blocked the sound out and sent every thought she could muster in the same direction.

The titan's foot came down with a mighty crash.

"You see?" said the Brain Storm. "You expended all that effort, and yet you couldn't stop a single step."

"I didn't need to," Suzy panted.

There was a slow tearing noise, like a million sheets of paper being shredded simultaneously. The titan convulsed. "What's happening?" the Brain Storm demanded.

"My mind isn't strong enough to beat yours," said Suzy. "But it is strong enough to switch on one of your seven-league boots. I'm told the results are messy."

The tearing noise sharpened. It became a splintering.

"No!" the Brain Storm exclaimed. A bright pink line appeared down the middle of the titan, bisecting it from the top of its domed head to the bottom of its torso. Jagged fingers of lightning wormed their way out from inside the head, discharging into the air. "This is outrageous!" the Brain Storm cried. "I will not allow you to—"

Its voice cut off as the left half of the titan vanished. Suzy was blinded by a flash behind her eyelids, and then she was back in the chair in the control room.

Or rather, in half the control room. It came to an abrupt end just a few centimetres to her left, the severed innards of the titan spewing oil and gas and sparks out over the city. The wind plucked at her clothes and made the chair spin until she was facing out over the hundred-metre drop to the rooftops below. She clung to the armrests and tried to push herself back into the leather.

"We've got you!" Stonker's voice came from behind her, and he and Reggie reached over the chair and caught her arms.

The remaining half of the titan's body teetered on its one leg, swaying like a tree in a storm. Suzy heard the old metal groan as it fought a losing battle against gravity.

And then a rush of colour filled the empty space in front of them as Bertha rose into view. Suzy saw Rayleigh with his thermometer held aloft, and then Wilmot and Frederick were leaning out of the balloon towards her, arms outstretched.

She didn't wait for them to say it,
but jumped, flinging out her arms. Their hands found
hers and held her fast. She was hauled into the basket and
reached back for Stonker, who made the jump easily.
Reggie came next and then, with a whistle of air, the
titan's remains fell away, crashing to the ground in a cloud

of debris. Looking down from the basket, Suzy saw the cross section of the crystal brain give one last flicker, before its red glow faded away and died. The cortex crystals were broken and lifeless. The Brain Storm was no more. She sank in an exhausted heap at her friends' feet.

"Thanks," she said. "That was a close one."

"I was sure we'd lost you!" said Wilmot.

"So was I," she said. She checked her watch. Back home, it was midday. "Wow," she said. "I've been awake for more than twenty-four hours." *And I'm going to have a lot of explaining to do once Mum and Dad wake up,* she thought.

"You can come and get some rest in one of the spare rooms at the rest home if you like," said Wilmot. "I'm sure Mum won't mind." Then he saw the pained expression on Suzy's face. "What's wrong?"

"I'm really sorry, Wilmot," she said. "But the rest home's gone. There's nothing left."

He sat down and blinked in astonishment. "The whole thing?"

She nodded.

"Was anyone hurt?"

"No. Everyone got out."

He looked very intently at his feet while he took the news in. "Then we'll rebuild," he said at last. "It's what we trolls do." He jumped to his feet and looked down on the ruined streets sliding past beneath them. "We can rebuild all of it, better than ever. And until then, I've got a hammock in the sorting carriage."

"Listen," said Frederick. "If you and your mum and the Old Guard need somewhere to stay until the rest home is rebuilt, you're more than welcome at the Ivory Tower."

Wilmot goggled at him. "Do you really mean that?"

"Yes," said Frederick. "We've got tons of room, and most of it's sitting empty. We can always put some camp beds in among the stacks. And maybe the Old Guard could help me sort out the cataloguing system. I could do with a few extra hands around the place."

Suzy smiled. "Then sign me up for a tour the next time I'm around."

Bertha touched down onto the broken roof of Grinding Halt, where Ursel and Lady Crepuscula were waiting for them. Ursel rushed forward, plucked Suzy from the basket, and set her on one of her shoulders, while everybody else climbed out.

"Roooowlf!"

"Yes, quite," said the Lady Crepuscula. "Not a bad showing, all told."

"Thank you," said Suzy, giving Ursel a hug. Then she realized who was missing. "Where's Aybek?"

The Lady Crepuscula scowled. "A very good question."

"Tenebrae took him," said Rayleigh. "And I don't think he was planning to make friends."

"That's scant comfort," said the Lady Crepuscula. "My brother is at large in the Union once again. I shudder to think what sort of trouble he'll cause."

"With respect, ma'am," said Reggie, shuffling awkwardly forward, "I'd be worried about Tenebrae as well. He might not be especially bright, but he's ruthless. There's no telling what he'll do now he's got Lord Meridian in his clutches."

Crepuscula scowled down her nose at Reggie. "And just who are you?"

Reggie looked pointedly at the floor. "I'm partly responsible for all of this," he said. "I suppose you'll want to take me back to that tower of yours. I just want you to know, I'll come quietly."

"No, Reg!" Stonker exclaimed. "I won't have that!" He glared defiantly at Crepuscula, who simply raised an eyebrow.

"I expect the Trollville authorities will be here soon," she said. "As far as I'm concerned, you're their responsibility."

Both Reggie and Stonker looked very relieved to hear it.

"And what about you, Cloudwright?" asked Suzy. "What are you going to do now?"

Rayleigh pursed his lips. "Who knows? There are always new frontiers of art that need exploring." He looked around at the wreckage surrounding them. "Although upon reflection, I'm tempted to offer Trollville my services as artist-in-residence for a while. It's the least I can do."

"Yes, it is," said the Lady Crepuscula. "But it's not a bad start."

A high-pitched whistle cut across Suzy's thoughts. It sounded like a firework, but it was getting closer. They all turned and saw a spiralling trail of smoke weaving through the sky towards them.

"Oh no," said Stonker. "Not him again."

King Amylum touched down in a halo of smoke, which made everyone double over, coughing. He switched off his jet pack and gave everyone two thumbs up. "Stay calm, citizens!" he declared. "Your king is here to save you!" He swaggered around the circle of blankly staring faces, smiling and winking. "Who wants to be rescued first? Hands up."

Before anyone could give him an honest answer, they heard the familiar scream of the Swoop's engines overhead. The black craft circled Grinding Halt, and settled into a stationary hover a short way off the summit.

"Wilmot!" Gertrude's voice reached them through the craft's PA system, and they saw her waving from the cockpit. "Wilmot, darling, are you hurt?"

"I'm fine, Mum!" He waved back. "We all are. We stopped the drill!"

"Brrrooowlf!" roared Ursel.

"Yes," said Wilmot. "And the giant killer robot. We stopped that too."

"Huzzah!" declared the king. Suzy couldn't tell if he was congratulating the group or himself.

"You can tell the citizens of Trollville that the danger is past now, Mrs Grunt," shouted Stonker. "They'll probably want to start rebuilding straight away."

"I will," she replied. "I'm just dropping off a passenger first."

The cargo door in the Swoop's belly slid open, and a small wrinkled figure descended on the end of a rope.

"Fletch!" said Suzy. "You're alright!"

"Course I am," he said, unhooking himself from the rope. "I've been up in the hills, lookin' after the Old Guard." He looked down at the wreckage spread out below them, and gave a low whistle. "That's goin' to take a bit of work to sort out."

"I think it's already started," said Frederick. "Look!"

374

He pointed at a parade of flashing blue lights moving through the wreckage of the streets below. It was an army of police trolls on their telescoping stilts, and behind them came a tide of bright orange – troll engineers in their fluorescent overalls. Some of them were already at work with hammers and wands, straightening the buckled railway lines.

"Someone should tell them there's a load of good stone in the entrance to the Hobb's End mine," said Wilmot. "It might come in handy."

"And Gary, Barry, Komp and Peeler are still down there somewhere," added Frederick. "They'll probably be glad to be arrested after a few days trapped underground."

The clang and clatter of the repair work sounded through the air like distant bells. It made Suzy smile.

"Well," said Crepuscula, "since the authorities are here, it seems my services are no longer required." She snapped her fingers and a dark shape plunged down out of the sky. For a second, Suzy thought it was Tenebrae, wings outstretched and talons ready to strike. Everyone recoiled in fright. But then the shape slowed, and she saw it was the gargoyle from the roof of Crepuscula's gatehouse. It snapped its toothy snout at them all, and picked its mistress up in its claws.

"If you ever find yourselves in the midst of disaster

again," said Crepuscula, "please don't hesitate to contact someone else. Goodbye." But Suzy thought she saw her wink as the gargoyle flapped its wings and carried her away.

"I'd better go too," said Gertrude through the Swoop's speakers. "Dorothy and the Old Guard are waiting for news. We'll all be back soon." She brought the Swoop around and gunned the engine. A few seconds later, it was a vanishing speck far over the hills outside the city.

"Why is her flying thing better than mine?" said the king. "It's not fair!" He shrugged his way out of his jet pack and threw it on the ground. "Where do I get a flying stone lizard? And a big black swooping machine? A thousand troll ducats to whoever gets me a better flying thingy!" He flounced off towards the emergency stairs, but paused and turned back. "Oh, and before I forget," he said. "'We bestow our royal blessing on this fine troll train.' Good luck, fair winds, blah blah, et cetera, et cetera. There. Ceremony concluded." And with that, he turned and left.

"Well it's not quite what I had in mind," said Wilmot. "But I'll take it."

Rayleigh, meanwhile, was muttering to himself. "Flying thingies..." he murmured. "Wings..." He suddenly brightened. "Yes, that might work. A pair of stained-glass wings fashioned from spellcloud. They could even morph into an attractive shawl or cape when not in use." He snapped his fingers in a moment of revelation. "I should talk to Cirrus Tramontane about a few designs. My very first collaboration! *That*'s the new ground I could break!" He tapped Bertha with his wand, and was hurrying after the king before she was even halfway back into her briefcase. "Your Majesty!" he called. "Wait! I have some ideas for your new flying thingy!"

"I suppose I'd better go and hand myself in then," said Reggie, his shoulders slumping.

"Yes, you should," said Frederick firmly. Suzy held her tongue. While she didn't trust Reggie, she couldn't find it in herself to blame him entirely for what had happened. The first earthquake had been accidental and, while he may have lacked the courage to stand up to Tenebrae, he had done the right thing in the end. She just wished he had done it sooner.

"I'll come with you, old chap." Stonker gave Reggie a reassuring pat on the shoulder, but his face was drawn and his moustache drooped. "Moral support and all that." He steered his brother towards the stairs.

"Gggggrunk," said Ursel.

"Good idea," said Wilmot. "Let's get back to the Express. The repair teams will have fixed the railway lines soon, and they'll need help towing her to a siding." They turned towards the stairs, but Fletch hung back.

"You lot go ahead," he said. "Right now, I've got an appointment with an understairs cupboard." He gave Suzy a meaningful look.

"You're taking me home?" she said. Relief and sadness mixed together inside her until she couldn't tell one from the other.

"As soon as they'll let us through a tunnel," said Fletch. "It's not right to leave your folks sleepin' too long."

Wilmot looked crestfallen. "I suppose you should," he said. "You'll come back soon though, won't you? There's still a sorting car full of overdue mail to deliver, and it won't be half as much fun doing it without you."

She opened her arms and drew him into a hug. "I'll be back in no time. I promise." She reached out, caught Frederick by the sleeve and pulled him into the hug as well. "Thanks for all your help out there today, Mr Expert."

Frederick tried to look indifferent, but there was no hiding his proud grin. "It was nice to get out of the library for a bit," he said. "Apart from the kidnapping and the getting knocked unconscious. And the almost dying."

"Fffrrolf!" Ursel stretched her arms around all three of them, and lifted them into an embrace that squeezed the air out of them. When she had set them down again,

Wilmot cleared his throat and put on a serious face. "Deputy Postal Operative Smith?"

Suzy stood to attention. "Yes, Postmaster Grunt?"

"Exceptional work today. Keep it up."

Suzy grinned. Despite everything that had happened, those words made everything feel a bit better.

25

HOME TRUTHS

Suzy was quiet on the ride back. This was partly due to exhaustion and the efforts of powering the pump cart, but also partly because her mind was preoccupied. Her thoughts were fragmentary and hard to keep hold of, but they all seemed to revolve around the same things – Frederick and his parents; Stonker and the brother he had tried to forget about; Wilmot and Gertrude and the Old Guard; Crepuscula and Aybek. The feelings they stirred up were both painful and happy at the same time.

"End of the line," said Fletch. "Everybody off."

She looked up and was surprised to see that they were back in the cupboard under her stairs. It was still enormous.

"You still with us?" he laughed.

"Yes," she said quietly. "Thanks, Fletch."

"All part of the service," he said, jumping down off the pump cart. "D'you want to go ahead and get changed, and then I'll wake your folks up?"

She trudged upstairs and peeled off her uniform. It was filthy – caked in mud from the farm and dust from the mines. Her feet hurt. Her muscles ached. Her head felt stuffed full of wool. She shoved the dirty clothes into a bag and hid the bag under her bed. Then she pulled on her jeans and T-shirt and headed downstairs to the kitchen, where Fletch was waiting. Her parents were still sleeping soundly at the table, although their dinners had congealed and a fat bluebottle was circling above her dad's plate.

How am I going to get away with this? she thought. *They've missed a day!* And then, in an instant, she knew what she was going to tell them.

"Fletch," she said. "Would you mind if I woke them up?"

He looked surprised. "Why?"

"Because I want to get as much experience of magic as I can," she said.

He looked at her for a moment, and she hoped he couldn't see the lie hiding in her eyes.

"If it means that much to you," he said, and fished his pouch of powder out of his pocket. "Just take a pinch, and blow it at 'em as soon as I'm on my way." He held the pouch open for her, and she dipped her fingers in and took a pinch of powder. It was gritty, like sand.

"Thanks," she said. "And I'm really sorry."

"Sorry for what?" he said.

She took a step back and kicked shut the door to the hall, then leaned against it, blocking his escape.

"Oi!" he said. "What are you doing?"

"I can't keep lying to my parents," she said. "It isn't fair, and sooner or later it's going to end badly."

"Who cares about fair!" said Fletch. He tried to dislodge her from the door, but she dug her heels in. "Let me out!"

Suzy raised the pinch of powder to her lips and blew.

"No!" said Fletch. But it was too late.

Suzy's parents sat up with a start, blinking against the daylight.

"Ow," said her father, rubbing a crick from his neck. "What happened?"

"Did we fall asleep?" said her mother. "What time is it?"

"It's almost dinnertime again," said Suzy. "You've been asleep for twenty-four hours."

They looked round in surprise. Then they saw Fletch.

Her father yelped and jumped up onto the table. Her mother, meanwhile, sat frozen in her seat.

"'ello," Fletch muttered.

"Suzy? Darling?" Her mother spoke in a very delicate voice. "What's happening?"

"Mum," said Suzy. "Dad. This is my friend Fletch. He builds railways using magic. I've got a part-time job delivering post to other worlds. And I want to tell you all about it."

Join Suzy for her next delivery in the final

TRAIN TO IMPOSSIBLE PLACES

Adventure

Read on for an exclusive extract...

The clouds of yellow steam filling the kitchen began to dissipate, and Suzy was finally able to fight her way to the fridge. She steadied herself in the puddle of orange juice that was pooling in front of it, and looked inside.

She was only a little surprised to discover that the shelves and most of their contents had vanished, and the interior of the fridge had expanded to form a shining white space the size of an aircraft hangar. Train tracks ran from a dark tunnel mouth in the rear wall, almost up to the door. And standing on the tracks was a huge old steam train. Not a normal steam train though – its locomotive, the *Belle de Loin*, was oversized and misshapen, as though it had been put together out of spare parts by someone who had a pretty good idea of what a train should look like, but had never actually seen one before. The sight of the train took Suzy back to the first night she had seen it, almost three months earlier, and she felt her heartbeat quicken. She hoped she would never get entirely used to seeing it – it was the intrusion of the fantastic into her everyday life, and it always carried the promise of adventure.

"What on earth?"

Suzy turned at the sound of her father's voice and realized that her parents had joined her. They stared into the fridge with a mixture of terror and disbelief.

"Mum? Dad?" said Suzy, swelling with pride. "This is the Impossible Postal Express. Isn't it brilliant?"

Her father looked around the huge space. "I put some yoghurts in here this morning," he said. "Where have they gone?"

Suzy gave him a look. "Dad, the yoghurts aren't important."

"But they were probiotic," he lamented.

Suzy was spared having to reply when one of the windows of the locomotive's cab swung open and J.F. Stonker, driver of the Express, poked his head out.

Suzy's parents gasped in astonishment. Stonker was a troll. Small and round and wrinkled, he looked a bit like a grey potato, except for his absolutely gigantic nose and the enormous handlebar moustache that hung beneath it.

"Good evening!" he said. "Are we all right to park here?"

Suzy's parents just stared at him, so Suzy answered for them. "Yes, that's fine, Stonker. It's good to see you."

"You too!" he called back. "Stay there, we'll be right out." He disappeared back inside and shut the window.

Suzy let out a little giggle of excitement. "This is going to be brilliant!" she exclaimed. "I can't wait for you to meet everyone."

Her parents nodded, a little vacantly.

"Please try not to stare when my friends get here," said Suzy. "I know they seem a bit unusual, but you'll soon get used to it and… oh no!" She looked down at her soaking wet school uniform. "I can't meet them like this! I need to get changed. And so do you, Mum." She made a run for the hallway, skidded to a stop, and hurried back. "There's no time right now. I'll introduce you to everyone first."

Her parents didn't reply. They were still gawping, dumbfounded, into the fridge, although they stepped aside as Stonker emerged.

"Suzy Smith!" he said, stepping neatly over the puddle of orange juice and opening his arms wide. "How the devil have you been?"

"I've been okay, thanks," she said, hugging him. "Thank you

for coming!" She gestured towards her parents. "This is my mum and dad."

Stonker pivoted on the balls of his feet and swept his cap off his head. "Mr and Mrs Smith," he said. "J.F. Stonker, at your service. Absolutely delighted to make your acquaintance." He offered them his hand and, after a moment's hesitation, Suzy's father stepped forward and took it.

"Um, yes," he said. "Sorry. Hello."

"Splendid, splendid!" said Stonker, pumping first Suzy's dad's and then Suzy's mum's hand so vigorously that they became a blur. "You must be so very proud of your daughter."

"Er, well, yes," said Suzy's mum, reflexively.

"And I believe you already know Fletch?" He nodded to the fridge, where another troll had appeared. Fletch was older than Stonker, with skin as brown and creased as old tree bark. Tufts of wiry hair escaped from his ears and nostrils, and he wore his usual ensemble of dirty overalls and scuffed work boots. He directed a brief nod of recognition at Suzy's parents, tramped straight to the table, and helped himself to a seat.

"How's it goin'?" he said, picking a chicken wing off a nearby plate. He cast a critical eye over the mess of eggs and milk on the wall. "You've redecorated."

"Yes, we remember Fletch," said Suzy's mum curtly.

Suzy grimaced. Fletch was lovely once you got to know him well enough, but he didn't exactly make a good first impression. And three weeks ago, at this very table, she had revealed the truth to her parents by waking them from a sleeping spell and introducing them to him. Perhaps that hadn't been such a great idea.

Then her mum gave a strangled little squeak and retreated behind her dad.

"What's wrong?" Suzy asked.

Suzy's mum peered out from behind her dad and pointed with a quaking hand to the large, yellow bear that was squeezing out of the fridge. It reared up onto its hind legs, and the pink ribbon tied in a bow around its head scraped the ceiling. Its fur was brushed and gleaming, and even its blue denim overalls were clean and neatly pressed.

"Ursel!" said Suzy, running over and throwing her arms around the animal's waist. "You look great!"

"Rrrrorlf," Ursel replied, baring her huge fangs in a smile.

"Mum, Dad, this is Ursel. She's the Express's firewoman."

Ursel stuck out a paw, making Suzy's parents flinch. Suzy laughed. She had forgotten just how scared she herself had been upon first meeting Ursel all those months ago.

"It's very nice to meet you," her dad said, hesitantly taking the paw in both his hands and shaking it. He gave a nervous little laugh. "You're much bigger than I imagined!"

"Grrronf," said Ursel. "Hhhhrk rowlf."

"Pardon?" said Suzy's dad.

"Ursel says she'll take that as a compliment," said Stonker, with a smile. "But please think very carefully before you pay her any more."

Suzy's dad nodded hard enough to make his teeth rattle.

"She also wants to know if this is a traditional form of human dress, Mrs Smith," said Stonker, indicating her dressing gown. "Suzy was wearing one the first time we met her."

Suzy's mum blushed. "I was just going to get dressed," she said. "In fact, if you'll excuse me…"

"Wait, Mum," said Suzy. "This isn't everyone. Where's…?"

"Hello!" came a voice from the fridge. "Did I miss anything?"

Suzy broke into a huge grin as a young troll stepped into the kitchen. He had pale green skin and large eyes, and wore a red-and-gold Postie's uniform that was several sizes too big for him. He clutched a small gift-wrapped parcel, and looked around the kitchen with undisguised interest.

"Hello, Suzy!" he said. "So this is where you live! Wow!" He bustled over and gave Suzy a quick hug, then headed straight for her parents. "Hello there," he said. "I've really been looking forward to meeting you both. I'm Wilmot Grunt, Postmaster of the Express, but please just call me Wilmot." He laughed. "Suzy is the very best Postal Operative I've ever worked with."

"She's the only Postal Operative you've ever worked with," said Fletch.

Wilmot pressed his lips together in annoyance. "True," he said. "But she still does an exceptional job, and I count myself very lucky to have her on my staff."

Suzy glowed with pride. This was the sort of thing she had been hoping for. It seemed to be having the desired effect on her parents as well, as they visibly relaxed.

"That's very nice to hear," said her dad, managing a smile. "Thank you."

Suzy's mum stepped out from behind him and nodded at the parcel Wilmot was holding. "Is that a delivery?" she asked.

"Oh, this!" Wilmot looked at the parcel as if he'd forgotten he was carrying it. "No, this is for you." He stepped forward and presented it with a flourish.

"It's not often the whole crew gets invited to dinner, you see," said Stonker. "So by way of thanks, we got you a little something."

"Oh." Suzy's mum accepted the box and turned it over in her hands. "That's very kind of you."

"It's nothing, really," said Stonker, with a dismissive wave. "Just something to help out around the house, that's all."

"You can open it now, if you like," added Wilmot, eagerly.

Suzy's mum only hesitated for a moment before her curiosity finally won out and she tore open the paper to reveal a plain wooden box with a hinged lid. Suzy and her dad both huddled round her as she opened the lid and looked inside.

A puff of air escaped, brushing past Suzy with a faint smell of wood smoke. They looked into the box.

"It's empty," said Suzy's mum.

"Well it is now," said Fletch, as though this were the most obvious thing in the world. "You just let it out."

Suzy felt a nervous twinge. "Let what out?" she said.

"The boggart," said Stonker.

"The what?" asked Suzy's dad.

"Boggart," said Fletch, helping himself to a hotdog. "It's your basic household spirit. Roams around the place keepin' things neat and dusted. Turns up little odds and ends you might have lost – keys, loose change, that sort of thing. Pretty handy, really."

Suzy's mum gasped. "You mean we've got a ghost in the house?"

Stonker chuckled. "Dear me, no. We wouldn't lumber you

with a ghost. This is a spirit, and quite an unobtrusive one at that. Keep it fed and warm, and you'll hardly even know it's here."

Suzy's dad looked around the kitchen in alarm. "But where is it? I can't see it."

"'Course not," said Fletch. "Invisible, innit?"

Suzy was scanning the room as well. She didn't see anything, of course, but she caught a vague sense of movement from the corner of her eye, as though something had just darted under the table. When she turned to focus on it, there was nothing there.

"What does it eat?" she asked.

"Just leave a saucer of milk out at night, and it should be quite happy," said Stonker.

"I thought that was hedgehogs," said Fletch.

"Is it?" Stonker twirled the end of his moustache as he considered this. "I'm pretty sure it's boggarts. Anyway, just let it make a home in the fireplace and I expect it'll take care of itself."

"But we don't have a fireplace," said Suzy's mum.

"Really?" Stonker looked surprised. "How on earth do you keep the place warm?"

"With central heating," said Suzy. She got down on her knees and scanned the floor, looking for movement rather than detail. She let her eyes unfocus and, a few seconds later, she detected another little flurry on the far side of the room, zipping along the skirting board and hopping into a cabinet which stood ajar beneath the sink. "What happens if we can't feed and house it?"

Stonker's silence made her look up.

"Well," he said, shifting awkwardly, "I believe they can get a little obstreperous if neglected."

"A little what?" said Suzy's mum.

There was a crash from inside the cabinet. Suzy leaped to her feet as the door swung open and the contents were ejected one by one. Tins of shoe polish, a roll of bin bags, a sink plunger and a dustpan and brush all sailed through the air, forcing Suzy, her parents and the crew to take cover behind the table.

"A little rowdy," said Stonker, as a bottle of fabric softener whistled past his head. "Oh dear."

"What does it think it's doing?" said Suzy's mum.

"It can't be getting rowdy already," Suzy's dad replied. "It's only just arrived!"

"Hhhrunk," said Ursel, who was too big to hide behind anything, and simply swatted aside any projectiles that came too close.

"Me?" said Stonker. "No, of course I didn't feed it while it was in the box. I thought you had."

"Unf," said Ursel, shaking her head.

"Me neither," called Fletch.

"Nor me," said Wilmot, who was crouched beside Suzy. "Sorry. Was I supposed to?"

"For goodness' sake, make it stop!" cried Suzy's mum as another cabinet door sprung open, and the boggart disgorged an avalanche of pots and pans across the floor.

"We need milk," said Suzy. "Cover me!" She dashed across the room in a crouch while Ursel kept pace with her, shielding her with her body. Suzy found the carton of milk that had been hurled from the fridge – it was leaking badly, but there was just enough left inside to fill the small measuring cup that she retrieved from the floor. Then, being careful not to spill a drop, she approached the open cabinet. Ursel plucked a saucepan lid out of the air a second before it would have struck Suzy in the forehead, and raised it as a shield, her great forearms surrounding Suzy in a protective circle.

Suzy placed the cup on the floor in front of the open cabinet and the barrage of kitchenware stopped abruptly. Then she and Ursel beat a hasty retreat to the far side of the room, and watched.

There was still nothing to see, but Suzy thought she could hear a faint snuffling sound. Something dipped into the milk, causing ripples across its surface. The snuffling sound grew louder.

"See, Mum?" Suzy whispered. "There's nothing to worry about. Everything's under control."

The cup arced through the air and upended its contents all over her. The boggart gave a piggish snort and, blinking the milk from her eyes, Suzy thought she saw something leap off the floor into the sink. There was a splash, a gurgle, and then a groan of pipes that quickly spread out through the walls and the ceiling, until it sounded as if the whole house was coming apart.

No, no, no, no nooooo! thought Suzy, as she saw her parents clutch each other in fear. *This wasn't how it was supposed to go!*

As quickly as it had started, the noise died away, leaving just a comfortable ticking in the radiators.

"You know," said Stonker, "I'm beginning to think maybe it was hedgehogs."

"Unless our boggart's lactose intolerant," said Fletch. "Anyway, not much we can do now. It's got into the plumbin'."

"What on earth is it doing in there?" said Suzy's dad, looking fearfully around the room.

Suzy wiped the last of the milk from her face and stood up. "Perhaps it's trying to keep warm," she said. "We don't have a fireplace, but we do have a hot water boiler."

"You mean our central heating is haunted now?" he said.

"Sir," said Stonker. "You fail to understand. Ghosts haunt. House spirits inhabit. Your boggart is simply making a new home for itself, that's all. You'll probably find it calms down now."

Suzy didn't think he looked quite as confident as he sounded, but she also realized that her parents needed some reassurances, and quickly – her mother's lips were pressed into a thin line of disapproval, and her father still looked as though he expected monsters to emerge from the walls at a moment's notice. So far, this hadn't quite been the easy-going social event Suzy had hoped for.

"We'll get this mess cleaned up in no time," she said breezily. "And then we'll eat. I'm sure Mum and Dad have got lots of questions for everyone."

"Oh yes," confirmed Suzy's mother darkly. "Lots and lots of questions."

All aboard for the final
TRAIN TO IMPOSSIBLE PLACES
Adventure

Delivering OCTOBER 2020